C.J. BROWN'S DIAMONDS IN THE ROUGH

By Ron Nichols

Martin Sisters Publishing

www. martinsisterspublishing. com

All rights reserved. Published in the United States by
Martin Sisters Publishing, LLC, Kentucky.
ISBN: 978-1-937273-81-1
Editor: Brittani Wolanin
Literary
Printed in the United States of America
Martin Sisters Publishing, LLC

DEDICATION

To Mom and Dad. To my wife Betsy and my daughter Katie. To my sisters Bev Heppermann and Jan Cartmill. To my friends and associates who have supported and tolerated my creative endeavors through the years. I can never thank you enough. I love you.

ACKNOWLEGEMENTS

A special thanks to friend, musician, songwriter and novelist extraordinaire, Jon Chandler – who many years ago said to me, "You can do this." (Now look what you've done, Mr. Chandler!)

An imprint of Martin Sisters Publishing, LLC

Chapter One

From the moment her parents had broken the news that they received a grant to finish their studies on the forest people of Brazil, C.J. Brown had been so angry that she hadn't spoken to her mother or father (any more than she absolutely had to) for almost a week. After long, solemn hours of intense brooding and throat-numbing screams of anger into her pillow, C.J. finally realized that her actions would not alter or even delay the inevitable.

She could not go with her parents, and so C.J. would spend a ceaselessly boring summer, in an endlessly boring place, with what must certainly be an interminably boring, recently widowed, Great Aunt, whom she didn't even know and did not want to know.

Meanwhile, her university professor parents would be out in the middle of the jungle ensuring their place in the annals of anthropologic research history. Samuel and Sara Brown would be spending the summer of a lifetime, while daughter C.J. would contribute by having her summer sacrificed in the name of anthropology.

In just a few short days, she would pack some of her favorite books, most of her summer clothing, her bed and mattress. Her modest personal belongings would be crammed into a small moving van, and C.J. Brown would begin her long, boring summer of exile. She had been told, without the courtesy of being consulted, that she would be moving from her life in suburban St. Louis to some place in the hills of Arkansas to spend the summer with a distant relative. C.J. thought that she might as well have been a slave, an indentured servant or a prisoner for all the say she had in the decision. Despite her anger, C.J's opinion simply didn't matter. And that made her blood boil.

So she sat on the side of her bed with her chin resting in the palm of her left hand, mindlessly twisting a long strand of her blonde hair with the index finger of the other. She wanted to call her friends and rant about her plight. But C.J. knew a telephone call would only serve to intensify her growing resentment surrounding her predicament. Still, she had to do something – anything that would get her out of the bedroom which, for the moment, was serving as a temporary, self-imposed holding cell until she would be transported to her permanent summer prison. She brooded, flopped purposefully backwards on the bed, her arms outstretched. She stared at the ceiling and felt the anger rise again, her face flushing with rage. As her ire subsided, it was replaced with a suffocating cloak of melancholy that seemed determined to drown her in a dark, dank pool of dread.

C.J. decided she had to escape, at least temporarily, from her room and her worsening mood. She willed herself upright on the bed. As she sat, C.J. slid her feet to the edge of the mattress. She pushed both of her legs over the edge of the bed. As though they did not belong to her own body, she watched her feet dangle haphazardly six inches above the floor. Trying to dislodge her lingering dolefulness, she rose slowly, letting gravity pull her feet all the way to the floor; and then shuffled across the carpet-covered floor to a pair of yellow flip-flops that she had absently flicked off her feet the evening before. They were randomly splayed like two giant, deformed ears alongside her dresser. She squatted to arrange them side by side, and then slowly wiggled a foot into each. When she did, C.J. realized that her toenails desperately needed a new coat of nail polish. At almost the same instant she thought to herself, "Why bother? When I get to 'Sticksville,' the locals probably won't even wear shoes, let alone be concerned with basic fashion protocol like toenail polish."

Sticksville had been the name she had given to the town her parents had said would be her home for the summer. When C.J. had learned that the small Central Arkansas town had fewer than 200 residents, no shopping malls, no restaurants and no recreational venues, she concluded the pseudonym she had bestowed upon the rural settlement was appropriately accurate. It may have even been generous. It was a town only in name, she thought. It had nothing to offer a 13-year-old girl from the suburbs who had better things to do over a summer than waste her time there.

"Sticksville in the middle of the sticks," C.J. muttered to herself.

Though its actual name was Ricksville, C.J. had refused to call it anything other than Sticksville – except in the presence of her parents, who had initially tolerated her use of the defiant nom de plume, but who had grown weary of the increasing tone of sarcasm with each of C.J.'s utterances. Her parents had recently decided that C.J.'s use of the name was contributing to her generally foul mood, and had since forbidden its utterance.

Her parents couldn't stop her from using "Sticksville" in her mind, nor could they stop her from using the name among her friends, which she intended to do just as quickly as she could exit the house. On her way toward the hallway, she paused when she saw a familiar pouting face staring back at her in the dresser mirror. She wasn't impressed with what she saw and thought for a brief moment about making the effort to look more presentable, perhaps by applying a coat of lip gloss before leaving. Instead, she shrugged her shoulders, averted her gaze from the morose figure in the mirror and sauntered down the hallway, toward the back door of the house.

She had nearly reached her door to freedom when she heard a familiar voice echo down the corridor. "Where you off to, C.J?" her mother bellowed.

"Does she have video surveillance cameras in every room?" C.J. wondered. "How can she possibly know what I'm about to do?"

"I'm just going to Katie's," she replied in the general direction of the question.

"Be home by three," her mother added. "You need to start packing for the summer, you know."

"I know," C.J. replied with exasperation. "How could I forget?" she muttered under her breath. She quickly twisted the doorknob, drove her shoulder into the door and exploded out of the house and into her sun-drenched neighborhood.

*

"You're kidding, right?" Katie asked, completely shocked.

"Don't I wish," C.J. said, looking up from the comfort of her friend's purple beanbag. It was C.J.'s favorite place in Katie's poster-lined room. She had always sensed that the beanbag held her like a giant hand and C.J. had poured herself into it the moment she came through the doorway of her friend's room. From her reclined position on her bed, Katie rolled onto her side, propped her chin onto her palm and looked intently at her best friend.

C.J. didn't look back. She simply looked absently at the ceiling.

"Maybe your aunt can come live here with you," Katie said, trying to offer some hope to her despondent friend.

"And maybe Santa will bring me that diamond necklace I've always wanted," C.J. replied, quickly extinguishing the flicker of optimism Katie had attempted to spark. "Apparently Great Aunt Maggie," C.J. said, spitting out each word like it was a bitter seed, "cannot possibly leave her mansion in Sticksville." C.J. paused, took a deep breath and continued. "I've tried everything. It's no use. I'm banished to the sticks," she said dejectedly.

"You know that we can still talk on the phone," Katie said, again attempting to produce an acceptable offering of optimism. C.J. did not respond and an awkward, protracted silence filled the room. "Hey," Katie said, piercing the gloom that had enveloped them, "does Great Aunt what's-her-name have the Internet?"

"This is Sticksville, remember? I doubt if they even have electricity."

"You're kidding, right?" Katie asked, not knowing for certain that C.J. was being sarcastic.

C.J. exhaled deeply. "They'd better have electricity," she conceded, "but I doubt my old, decrepit great aunt has a computer." C.J. sank further into the beanbag – content to be swallowed up by both the fabric of the bag and by the murk of her depression."By the time this summer's over, I doubt you'll even remember what I look like," C.J. added, now fully committed to her self-induced misery. She had come to Katie's house to divert her thoughts away from the abyss of her despair, but instead she had thrown herself into the bottomless chasmin her best friend's room. C.J. consciously fought back her tears.

Another awkward moment passed in agonizing silence.

"That's crazy," Katie said finally. "And if you think I'm going to forget what you look like, think again sister!" In that instant, C.J. saw multi-colored spots appear before her eyes. She was blinded by the flash from Katie's digital camera. Katie was laughing, looking at the image of her shocked friend's face on the back camera display.

"Hey, what'd you do that for?" C.J. asked, rubbing her eyes, trying to wipe away the disorienting spots caused by the camera's bright flash.

"You can be such a loser sometimes," Katie said. "I can't believe you said that." She was still smiling broadly as she studied the image of her friend, still on the camera's display.

"You can't believe I said what?" C.J. said, feigning ignorance.

"That I'd ever forget what you looked like," Katie replied. "But that's not a problem now," she said smiling, looking at the photo. But you know, iff I didn't like you so much, you'd really piss me off."

"You'd better not let your mom hear you talk like that," C.J. said looking worrisomely at the door.

"See? There you go again. Always thinking the worst. I swear, you are the biggest pessimist I've ever known," Katie said. "Do you want to see how a silly pessimist looks?" Katie asked, holding the camera a few feet away from C.J.'s face.

Without responding, C.J. quickly lunged for the camera, but the instant she moved, Katie adroitly dodged her advance. The small, metallic blue device remained in her possession. "Not so fast super model," Katie said smiling. She held the camera behind her back. "Now tell me you'll never forget what I look like and then you can see how silly you look."

C.J. sank back down in the beanbag chair and waited.

"Tell me…" Katie prodded.

"Well all right," C.J. said. "I'll never…" she paused thoughtfully.

"Say it," Katie commanded as she smiled broadly, anticipating the concession. C.J. dropped her chin to her chest as though summoning the courage to comply with her friend's ultimatum.

"Say it," Katie repeated, attempting to coax her friend into acquiescence.

"Okay," C.J. said in apparent conciliation. "I'll never…" she rose slowly, holding her hands above her head as if to surrender. She paused.

"I'll NEVER let you keep that picture!" C.J. blurted as she simultaneously leapt across the bed for the camera in her friend's hand. Katie once again side-stepped her would-be assailant, leaving her pursuer sprawled, face-down and camera-less on the bed's comforter. C.J. instantly realized the value of Katie's experience in dodging attackers – namely her two younger brothers and sisters. Katie had had years of practice in playing keep-away, leaving her with cat-like reflexes and the ability to escape from almost any position in any room in the house. With no menacing younger or older siblings with whom to spar, C.J. was clearly out-matched in this game. It was, as far as C.J. could tell, one of the few drawbacks to being an only child.

"Oh no, no," Katie said, wagging her finger disapprovingly. She held the camera high with the other hand. "Say it, or you won't see it and I'll post it to Facebook and e-mail it to every boy in our class. You know I will." Katie waved the camera in the air, taunting her vanquished foe. "Go on. Say it," she repeated sternly.

C.J. could see the futility of her predicament. She let out a sigh. "Okay." C.J. held out her hand for the camera.

"Nope. You say it first. Then you get to see the picture," Katie said seriously – although her smile never faded. C.J. refused to capitulate and retreated to the comfort of the beanbag.

Katie was growing desperate to dislodge the depression from her friend. She suddenly remembered one of C.J.'s secrets.

"Say it, C.J. or I'll… I'll lock you in my closet!"

A look of terror suddenly enveloped C.J. and Katie immediately realized she had gone too far with the banter.

"That's not funny," C.J. said. She was so terrified of cramped spaces that the mere thought of being locked in a closet caused C.J. to begin trembling. As a child C.J. had inadvertently locked herself in a closet while playing hide-and-go-seek with Katie and two other friends. When she couldn't open the door, C.J. had panicked, hyperventilated, and then passed out. Several minutes later, when her mom and dad pried the door open to rescue their daughter, C.J. had regained consciousness, but she was trembling so uncontrollably that her parents had considered taking her to the emergency room.

"I'm sorry. I was just kidding," Katie said, apologizing as she leapt over to comfort her friend. Katie wrapped her arms around

C.J. and said, "I just don't want you to say things like that. You know it's not true."

"Okay. I'll never forget what you look like," C.J. said. She composed herself, looked into the eyes of the best friend she had ever known, then quickly added "...because you're such a butthead!" C.J. instantly covered her mouth, which was agape from the surprise of her spontaneous use of the near-expletive.

Both girls broke into uncontrollable laughter and then uncontrollable hugging. It was the first time C.J. had felt this good since she first heard the news of her summer plight.

As she reveled in the sweet rapture of her friend's embrace, C.J. wondered if she'd ever feel this good again, or if her best friend would still be any kind of friend at all when C.J.'s summer of exile was finally over. Now, suddenly, she was unable to control her tears. They flowed in streaming rivulets down C.J.'s cheeks and onto Katie's shoulders.

Chapter Two

"Hurry up, we've got to get on the road," her mother said as she passed by C.J.'s room. Her arms held a stack of boxes up to her chin as she waddled past the doorway to C.J.'s room. It was already late afternoon, and the trio had planned on putting a couple hundred miles behind them before stopping somewhere about midway between St. Louis and their final destination.

"I know, I know," C.J. said, more out of habit than as a sincere acknowledgement of the command.

With her bed gone and many of her books removed from their shelves, C.J.'s room seemed hollow. It was a symbolic emptiness that mirrored the emptiness in the pit of C.J.'s stomach and in her soul. She was dawdling purposefully – lifting each book from the shelf and placing it into the cardboard box with the precision of a jeweler setting a precious stone in its final golden fitting. It was the one thing, the only thing, she could control at the moment, and C.J. vowed to control it until the rented moving van with the "U-matic shift control" and "Hydromatic comfort ride," pulled away from its parking place in the front of her home. Reluctantly, she put the last book in the box and closed the lid. As she did, C.J. couldn't help but believe the happiest chapter in her life was also coming to a

17

close. She took a roll of cellophane packing tape and stretched a long piece across the two flaps of cardboard that served as the box's lid. With a black, broad tipped permanent marker she printed, "C.J.'s Books – Do NOT Open." She took a deep breath and exhaled, feeling as though she had sealed the coffin lid of a good friend before committing her body to the earth. However, in this case, C.J. knew it was her fate that was now inexorably sealed.

"Let's go, sweetheart," her father said, poking his head in the doorway. "Do you need a hand with that box?"

"No thanks, I've got it," C.J. said. She stood and then hoisted the box with both arms. It was heavier than she had anticipated. As she left the room, C.J. could not summon the will to look back into the great void that had harbored so many of her wonderful memories. She did not have the courage to consider all of the memories she might have made if a cruel, heartless fate had not intervened.

*

She awoke to the gentle prodding of her mother. As she stirred to consciousness, everything around her was bathed in an eerie, orange-tinged light – produced by a bank of parking lot lights suspended high in the muggy night sky.

"Come on, C.J., it's time to call it a night."

For a moment, she thought she was dreaming. She took a deep breath and focused her eyes beyond the red hood of the moving van and onto the neon glow of a sign that flickered the letters "VAC N Y." The second "A" and the second "C" had apparently burned out of the word and the proprietors felt no immediate need to have the sign repaired. Feeling a slight itch, C.J. involuntarily slapped at a mosquito that was in the process of siphoning some blood from her thigh. The sting from her self-inflicted swat, and the resulting spot of blood on her leg, left no doubt that she was not dreaming.

"Welcome to bug-infested Arkansas," she thought smugly.

Beyond the neon sign was a vast darkness that suggested the absence of all civilization – the absence of humanity – the absence of certainty. At that moment C.J. took comfort in knowing that her parents were close by. Also at that moment she realized her parents represented the only connection to her past and the only connection to her uncertain future. They would soon be off on an anthropologicical adventure of their own. This summer, C.J. realized suddenly, she would also be without her parents. She had spent the last couple of weeks brooding about missing her friends, but suddenly she realized that her very best friends – her parents – would not be in her life this summer either.

The ink-black night amplified the summer's ambiguity.

C.J. slid her bottom across the well-worn vinyl bench seat, and dropped several feet onto the gravel parking lot. As her shoes met the ground, they crunched against the gravel, making the sound of someone chomping corn flakes. Swarms of insects swirled haphazardly around the parking lot lights – like biologic electrons held mysteriously in orbit by some supernatural force. In the distance, C.J. could hear the melodic cacophony of crickets and frogs as their individual communiqués of courtship melted into a strange, hypnotic, pulsating, nocturnal song.

It was the last clear recollection of her first night in Arkansas. The three members of the Brown family lumbered down the long hallway of the motel, each dragging a wheeled travel bag behind as they made their way to their awaiting room.

Exhausted from the heat, which had arrived unseasonably early this year, the uncomfortable ride and her own emotional despair, C.J. mindlessly changed into her pajamas; brushed her teeth; rinsed her mouth; plodded to her bed; and then pulled the covers back from the mattress. She slipped herself between the crisp sheets that smelled of bleach and detergent. As the hotel room's air conditioner hummed, C.J. felt the cool air waft across her face. Just seconds after her head sank into the pillow, she was swept mercifully into a deep and consuming slumber that belied her consuming feelings of apprehension.

At that moment, she was simply too exhausted to care anymore.

Chapter Three

"We all understand that if we're ever going to get this project off the ground, we must locate and then acquire the proper source water," Hugh Gunther said to the two men and one woman seated around the oval walnut conference table. "And I think we've made it clear we're prepared to offer GeoTherm a significant incentive for finding that water – assuming you can do it," the overweight man said with a clear note of apprehension. He looked at the three GeoTherm representatives across from him and then continued with his monologue. "Honestly, I'm surprised a company of your size even won the contract, but I have to trust the judgment of Cornerstone's engineering team," he said. "Still, we have a heck of a lot riding on this, and I need your assurance that you're up to the task."

"You've hired the right firm, Mr. Gunther," a mustached, slightly balding man said, speaking for the team. Frank Rahe was president and lead geologist for GeoTherm – a firm of about 40 physical scientists and engineers. The company had been courting a client like Cornerstone for years. It was the kind of company whose ability to pay, matched its need for GeoTherm's services. It was a break-out client – one that could take GeoTherm to the next level of growth and profitability and no one knew that more than the man who was now speaking for the firm. Frank had launched the company 10 years before, and like many start-ups, the firm had faced cash flow problems on and off throughout its lifespan, which made the scientists and engineers it employed the victims of countless layoffs and constant employment uncertainty. As a result, recruiting and retaining experienced scientists and engineers had been a systemic problem for the firm.

But Frank knew if GeoTherm could deliver for Cornerstone, the struggling company would leapfrog over most of its competitors and would become the "go-to" firm for other major companies like Cornerstone. Success with this project would set GeoTherm up for long-term stability and would be a god-send to its principals and its employees.

"We may be a small firm, but we have the best experts in the field. We're small enough to be hungry, and nimble enough to get the job done," Frank said confidently. "Remember," he said, "it's not the size of the dog in the fight, but the size of the fight in the dog."

"Good," Gunther said forcefully, as he stood. He leaned his rotund figure over the table to look each of the three GeoTherm representatives in the eyes. The purpose of his meeting with GeoTherm was to put the fear of God in his consultants. Hugh Gunther was good at putting the fear of God into anyone, or anything he chose, and he wanted to make certain he achieved his objective today. He had a very large stake in GeoTherm's success, and he intended to motivate his trio to perform.

"Let me make sure you understand the scope of this matter," Gunther said in a way that suggested he was used to getting what he wanted. "No water. No processing facility. No processing facility, no profit." He paused. "And if there's no profit, the stock holders will not be happy. And if they're not happy," Gunther said letting his sentence trail off. He didn't need to finish the statement.

Everyone around the table knew the implications – and the resulting pressure for GeoTherm's success.

The man seated next to Frank Rahe was GeoTherm's founder and director of operations. He was one of the five principal partners in the firm. It would be his ultimate responsibility to accomplish the goal of finding the water source.

"GeoTherm happens to have one of the best – if not the very best," Trent Martin said, looking briefly at the woman seated to his left, "hydrogeologists in the nation."

Gunther, if he was impressed, did not show it in his demeanor. "Let's just make sure your confidence translates into results, gentlemen," Gunther said, obviously addressing the two principal partners of the firm and not the female geologist they had brought along to bolster Gunter's confidence in the firm's selection.

Christine Larson sat quietly. Her expressionless face belied the anger building inside her. Christine wanted to reach across the table and choke Gunther until he passed out. He, like so many other men she had known in the business world, appreciated and responded to only one thing – power. The development of her precise underground aquifer models – which she believed no one else in her field had mastered – would provide her with the key to the kingdom of knowledge. And with that knowledge came power. Christine promised herself that she would use that power ruthlessly when she finally possessed it. Maybe she would replace Gunther at Cornerstone one day, too. If she could single-handedly succeed in finding that water source, she believed Cornerstone would lure her away from GeoTherm, perhaps with the offer of a lucrative salary and as a partnerin that firm.

"Let me underscore the need to keep this search for, and the acquisition of the source water absolutely confidential," Gunther added vehemently. "It will come as no surprise to you that revealing our desire to acquire the source water may unnecessarily drive the property prices up. Additionally, we do not want our competitors to catch wind of our activities."

Throughout the briefing, Christine had purposefully avoided direct eye contact with Gunther – refusing to play the role of "groveling, would-be consultant" who would do anything to win favor of the all-powerful, cash-paying client. Christine saw herself as the quintessential, senior scientist and she would not stoop to that type of belittling behavior. But now, as the meeting was coming to a close, she decided to play her card.

"We're fully aware of the proprietary issues you mentioned, Mr. Gunther," Christine said with professional measure. "But I believe we should all be consistent in our explanation of GeoTherm's studies, especially when related to landowner inquiries."

"Consistent how?" he asked.

"My experience tells me, that neighbors talk. And no matter how clandestine our operations, some of those neighbors will eventually start asking questions when they see our trucks on the road," Christine said. She paused momentarily to purposefully raise the tension in the room.

"Let me put it this way. I believe we should be consistent in the story we 'feed them,'" Christine said as she used her index and middle fingers of both hands to simulate quotation marks around the words "feed them."

Frank and Trent wanted desperately to reduce the tension that was nearly palpable between Mr. Gunther and Christine, but neither could formulate a quick rhetorical solution. So they simply sat there quietly and hoped that Christine would not sink the company ship they had both spent nearly half their lives working to keep afloat.

Suddenly, Mr. Gunther broke into a smile. "I'm impressed," he said. "You're absolutely right. We do need a cover story." He looked at Trent. "I thought you said this was the best hydrogeologist in the world?" He didn't wait for a response. "You didn't say she was also the best strategist in your company."

Christine beamed on the inside, but sat poker faced at the table. Maybe Mr. Gunther did have a brain, she thought. Perhaps at least he was able to recognize genius – even if he didn't possess it, she thought smugly.

As the three GeoTherm representatives walked through Cornerstone's lobby on their way to the rental car parked near the glass building's front entrance, Christine smiled at the thought of her performance. She had trumped both of the firm's principals – and all they could do was watch as she stole the show.

Despite Gunther's last-second recognition of her brilliance, Christine was already formulating the words that would end his career when she finally ran Cornerstone.

RON NICHOLS

Chapter Four

Despite the advertised "comfortable, air-conditioned ride" promised in the eight-inch red letters on the side of the rented truck, the morning sun was merciless as it poured into the cab and slow roasted its trapped occupants. Hot air that smelled of mold and mildew, spewed through the dust-covered vents – "Mother Nature's bad breath," C.J. thought to herself. They had slept in, and got a late start on the final leg of their journey. While the extra sleep had been appreciated, by the time they loaded themselves into the truck just before noon, the heat and humidity were already oppressive.

Beads of sweat formed on her forehead then trickled down C.J.'s jaws before falling onto her thighs where those drops mingled with other beads of sweat before rolling off and disappearing somewhere between her legs and the truck's cracking vinyl seat.

The moisture gathered under her where it formed a sticky film that bonded her skin to the seat. To avoid the possibility of being permanently glued onto the padded bench seat, C.J. alternately lifted one leg, and then the other, just long enough to nearly evaporate the sweat upon which she sat. Every time she did so, it felt as though she was tearing a layer of skin off from the back of her thighs. She had taken a shower earlier that morning, but by now the smothering Arkansas heat, coupled with its oppressive humidity, had rendered that hygienic exercise completely futile. Her mother, her father and she were stewing slowly in their own sweat as they bounced along the two-lane, black-top highway. C.J. looked out through the windshield where white cirrus clouds stretched in wispy bands across the morning sky. They offered little hope of relief by way of rain or moderating temperatures and C.J. concluded that she and her parents would sweat like pigs, and bake like hams, until they arrived in Sticksville.

Yesterday, when they were only about 30 miles south of St. Louis, C.J. first complained about the absence of air-conditioning in the truck. Her parents, as they were too often prone to do, took the opportunity to remind her that regardless of how uncomfortable she might feel in the truck at the moment, they would be enduring intense tropical heat and humidity in Brazil for the entire summer. C.J. wisely chose not to remind them that their summer location had been picked by them, not for them, as had hers.

She said little as the truck made its way up and down the seemingly endless rolling hills of northern Arkansas. Out of sheer boredom she poked at the truck's radio buttons, pausing momentarily when the signal was strong enough to overcome the constant hiss of static. After a dozen trips up and down the FM and AM spectrum, C.J.'s efforts yielded little by way of reception except for a screaming preacher's oration on the wages of sin; a country station that apparently played music by performers who died years ago; and the whining babble of a some disturbed, conservative radio talk show host ranting about the liberal press. In frustration, she stabbed the power button with a forceful, punctuating poke of her finger. How fitting – C.J. thought as the noise from the radio was silenced – to be delivered back to the mid 20th century by a vehicle that dated nearly back that far. If only her parents would have allowed her to buy an iPad. At least then she could absorb herself in some decent music or video games. But her parents had always put academics ahead of pop culture and rarely embraced – or allowed C.J. to purchase – video games, and other entertainment distractions.

C.J. averted her eyes from the painted stripes on the highway to the seemingly endless barbed-wire fences enclosing meandering cows that passed by the window of the truck like animal figures on a carousel. Unless the scenery changed dramatically and quickly, C.J.'s worst expectations would not only be met, they would be exceeded. And exceeding her worse expectations was a tall order, because she had purposefully lowered any and all of them to avoid adding to her despair when she arrived in Sticksville and was forced to accept her fate.

*

A little before four that afternoon, C.J.'s father eased the truck off the main road and onto a broad shoulder that had been widened, apparently for the sole purpose of accommodating semi-tractor-trailer drivers who wanted to stop at the "Rainbow Cafe" for breakfast, lunch, dinner – or to acquire a half-gallon of caffeine-enriched coffee for the road.

"We might as well eat something, now," C.J.'s father said after the truck came to a halt. He rolled his head in a circle around his shoulders, apparently to stretch his neck muscles, rubbing the base of his neck with his left hand as he did so.

When he had concluded his self-massage, he turned to the two figures seated beside him and said, "I figure we're within 20 or so miles of Aunt Maggie's house,"C.J.'s father said, glancing at his watch.

"Good idea, Sam," her mother said. "I certainly don't want to be around either of you when you get hungry and cranky."

C.J. ignored her mother's attempt to add some levity to the situation – a situation that C.J. considered anything but amusing. The three poured themselves out of the truck and began trying to limber their stiff bodies before ascending the steep grade to the little store. A small, dark-skinned boy that C.J. judged to be about 10 or 11 years old, with big ears, round-rimmed glasses and closely cropped hair sped by on his bicycle. A loaf of Wonder Bread dangled and swayed, pendulum-like from his grip around the handle bar. He looked at the three strangers intently.

In a good-will gesture, C.J. produced a warm, genuine smile to send his way. In response, the boy stuck his tongue out at C.J. and pedaled off down the blacktop road.

"See, C.J.," her mother said, "you've already made a friend and you're not even in your new house yet." Her mother and father both laughed heartily. It was adult humor. But to C.J. it wasn't funny at all. Instead C.J. considered it a harbinger of things to come. She was stuck in a little town, with people who were too old and decrepit or too young and immature to converse with. And those were just the two citizens of Sticksville she knew about.

*

It was about an hour later when they turned left onto the dusty, gravel road that led to Ricksville. The dull-green highway sign with white, faded letters wasn't much bigger than a bumper sticker. Perched atop a rusting metal pole, the sign appeared weathered, worn and neglected – precisely the way C.J. felt as she sat affixed by her own sweat to the vinyl seat of the rental truck.

Had they not been instructed by the waitress at the Rainbow Cafe to "Keep an eye out for Otto's gas station, just after ya'll cross the second bridge you come to," they most certainly would have driven past it. C.J. wished they had.

The sound of the tires biting into the gravel road signaled a distinctive change in pavement, and it simultaneously signaled a change in direction for C.J. There would be no turning back now. She was headed to Sticksville. Soon she would be a temporary resident, but she vowed that as soon as she had the opportunity, she would be a "former temporary resident."

As they drove closer to their destination, C.J. could not help but fondly recall the memories of being with her friends back home –

the experience of waltzing comfortably through the Gateway Mall with her friends, inhaling the variety of blended aromas that permeated the massive corridors of the climate-controlled shopping Mecca. Lost in the memory, she took a deep breath, hoping in vain her olfactory memories would summon the scent of new clothes or freshly-baked pretzels. Regrettably, all she could smell was the body odor of her parents – and probably herself – mixed periodically with the ghastly, unmistakable odors from what had to be the manure of nearby cattle, horses and pigs. Everything – not just the odor – was so different here; it was as though she had been beamed to a different planet. It seemed as though she was the unwitting character in some ill-conceived science fiction novel.

The last store of any kind she could remember seeing from the cab of their truck had been "Otto's Service Station" at the turn-off on the corner of the highway. It was a two gas-pump station that doubled as a convenience store and bait shop. "Night Crawlers Sold Here" exclaimed the hand-printed poster in the lower corner of the weathered building's storefront window. A severely faded poster taped to the upper corner of the window read "Bread and Milk." It seemed to be hung as an afterthought, not as a bold marketing ploy to lure customers into the store. No other non-automotive related products were advertised anywhere with the exception of a rusting "RC Cola" thermometer that hung just outside the open glass door in the shade of the gas pump canopies. C.J. guessed that antiquity to be nearly as old as the building itself, perhaps 100 years or better.

About a mile up the road's gentle incline, C.J. noticed a grove of tall trees and the first mailbox she had seen since they'd exited the main road – a hint signaling the beginning of what she was told was her new "neighborhood." Within a few hundred yards, she noticed another mailbox, and then another. Each mailbox was a near-clone of the one they had just passed. Every rounded-top box sported a metal red flag along its side. The sole differentiating feature of any of the boxes was the name and address that identified the owner. Most of those names and addresses were crudely hand painted. A few were festooned with reflective, peel-and-stick block letters that were probably purchased at a hardware store in some distant town. Propped atop stilted posts, most of the mailboxes looked as poorly maintained as most of the larger, human-dwelling structures they fronted.

Her mother and father had told her to keep a sharp eye out for C.J.'s new summer home. Though C.J. knew "new" didn't mean "freshly built." It meant "different." C.J.'s only hope was that her "new" home looked better than most of the ill-kept dwellings they had passed as they entered the neighborhood.

"Oh, there's the mailbox," her father announced with no detectable enthusiasm in his voice. It was only at that moment, after weeks of self-reflection and self-pity that C.J. realized she wasn't the only person in her family who might have some reservations about going away for the summer. It had been a few weeks since she'd last heard the "It'll be a great new adventure speech" her parents had fabricated upon learning of their Newcastle Award for Anthropology. It was this award that funded their upcoming trip to the Brazil. C.J. hadn't been fooled by the promise of adventure in Arkansas. It was the sticks, afterall. There could be no adventure.

It hadn't, until this moment, occurred to C.J. that her parents might miss her, too. Parents have to put a brave face on all potential adversity. They have to do those sorts of things for the sake of their children, she surmised. And in a way, it made her proud to have parents who, despite their own misgivings and pain, would do whatever they could to avoid letting their own apprehensions and worry show. C.J concluded that parents had probably been doing these sorts of things since the first caveman announced to his wife and children that they'd have to be leaving their rapidly chilling cave to seek warmer confines to the south as the Ice Age began. "Oh come on kids, it'll be fun," the cave mom probably said. "Who knows, we might even get to bag a Sabertooth tiger along the way – unless it bags us first!" Hah, hah, everyone would laugh, and the family would trudge off into the great unknown. C.J. wondered if she would be as courageous if and when she became a parent.

The name on the mailbox, "M.J. Davidek," confirmed they were in the right place. "R.R. 14, Box 322, Ricksville, AR" was the address – C.J.'s new address.

"What does 'R.R.' mean?" C.J. asked.

"Rural Route, honey," her mother said. She was smiling. Still putting up a good front. C.J. felt obliged to smile back.

"No false advertising here," C.J. thought, "It doesn't get more 'rural' than this." But "Oh," was all she said in response to her mom's answer.

As they turned up the driveway, they were enveloped by the darkness created by the shade of towering oak and hickory trees that lined the narrow drive. In the darkness created by the dense canopy above, the heat released its grip on the occupants of the truck. C.J. took a deep breath, then exhaled in pained resignation. She noticed that her mother and father did likewise. She wondered if, in their case, it was a sigh of acceptance; a breath of courage; or emotional and physical exhaustion.

The house, while certainly no mansion, appeared to be in relatively good order – at least on the outside. The well-kept house was an exception to most of the dwellings they had passed. The one-story structure was small and C.J. wondered if there would be enough room on the inside to accommodate all of the books, clothes and bed they had brought with them in the rental truck. She had been promised a private bedroom and she would just die if she had to sleep every night on a rollaway in the living room.

Flower boxes nested purple impatiens under each of the three windows on the front side of the house. Because of the intense shade provided by the trees, impatiens were likely the only things with blooms that would flourish there. But C.J. noted that they helped give the place a sweeter, more welcoming ambiance. Black ornamental shutters trimmed either side of the three identical windows and helped give the white house a sense of completion and civility.

After her father brought the truck to a stop, her mother said, "C.J. and I will get to work unpacking and start getting her bedroom organized. Isn't that right, C.J.?" she asked just to see if C.J. was listening.

"Huh? Yeah. Sure. I guess," C.J. said absently, scanning her new environment.

"Aunt Maggie should be here in two days, so we'll just have ourselves a little country vacation until she arrives," C.J.'s mom said with a smile. But C.J. was too preoccupied taking in the sight of her new home to look her mother's way.

"It seems we're all still pretty tired," her father said. "Besides we have all day tomorrow to get everything unloaded and arranged. Help me find the blankets and sleeping bags and we can make us a spot to sleep on the floor tonight. By tomorrow we can get your bed and mattresses set up and you'll be able to sleep in your own bed again."

If the thought of sleeping in her 'own bed' was supposed to make her adjust more quickly to her new home, the attempt missed the mark. C.J. had already concluded that it would take longer than a summer for her to adjust to all of this.

"Once we get everything unloaded off the truck tomorrow, maybe we can pick up a few things in town," her mother said somewhat enthusiastically. "We need to get some food to stock the fridge."

"What town?" C.J. asked sarcastically. "Sticks…" she began to say before correcting herself, "I mean Ricksville doesn't have a grocery store."

"But, Hickory does, and it's just 15 miles from here. It even has a few specialty shops, I hear," her mom said.

C.J. wanted to say something smart like "It sounds like another Mall of America," but opted against it. There's funny, and then there's the kind of funny that comes with a price to pay. From past experience she knew that the former would get a laugh, the latter could get you grounded.

Though, from what she'd seen on the way into her new neighborhood, it seemed as though she was now grounded for the summer. What would it hurt to be grounded now? She was already grounded to a summer of isolation, surrounded by antiquity and consumed with perpetual boredom. Tomorrow, she promised herself, she would literally count the days to determine how many she'd have to endure before her parents returned from their great adventure so she could move back to the suburbs and be with her old friends. One day at a time, she thought. One lonely, sad, friendless day at a time.

RON NICHOLS

Chapter Five

Her father was already out pulling weeds and whacking at the tall grass around the house when C.J. managed to shuffle into the kitchen for breakfast. Her tangled hair and wrinkled pajamas mirrored her disposition and offered a tangible description of how she felt – unsettled.

Her mother had already unpacked some of C.J.'s things.

"Good morning, Sunshine."

"How does she do that?" C.J. wondered. "She can't possibly be as happy as she's pretending. She's stuck here in exile with me for the next couple of days, and then she's off to the jungles of Brazil. If there's ever an award category for 'Best Acting Mother Family Drama' she'd win hands-down," C.J. thought.

"Morning," C.J. replied with as much enthusiasm as she could muster. It wasn't much.

"Care for some toast and coffee?"

"Sure." C.J. tried to rub the sleep from her eyes, which were still adjusting to the daylight as it filtered through the trees and made its way, half-heartedly, into the kitchen. From every window all C.J. could see were the leaves and branches of trees. The prospect of living in a deep, dark forest made C.J. feel even more confined and alone. The contrast between the clean, well-manicured suburban subdivision where she wanted to be, and living amid the forest creatures where she was now living, served to further underscore C.J.'s feelings of isolation and regret. She had gone from being surrounded by cars and bikes and other houses to residing in a hillbilly jungle. "Why can't they just study the 'forest people of Sticksville? " C.J. wondered with some sense of bemusement.

Her mother poured C.J. a cup of coffee and placed it in front of her. When she smelled the coffee's aroma, C.J. imagined for a moment she was back in her old house – her real house, preparing for a day of adventure at the mall with her cadre of friends.

The sudden motion of a gray blur, and the bobbing of a tree limb outside the window caught C.J.'s attention, and she lowered her coffee cup from her lips. A moment later, there was another flurry of motion. Then she focused her eyes on a furry, bushy tailed rodent that moved with dizzying speed from one branch to the next and back again with remarkable precision and agility.

"It's a squirrel. Look," her mother said. "Breakfast right outside our window. It's like going to the drive up window at McDonalds, only the breakfast comes to you," her mother said, then chuckled.

"What are you talking about?" C.J. asked. She could tell her mom was trying to be funny again, but C.J. had no clue as to what she was talking about.

"They say squirrel meat is quite tasty."

"Ewww! Are you trying to be funny or do you just want me to hurl before I've even had breakfast?" C.J. asked.

Her mom laughed. "Some folks around here do eat squirrel. They say it's good fried and served with milk gravy."

"Tastes like chicken, I guess," C.J. said with a definite tone of sarcasm. Then added, "Well, I'm not eating one of those tree rats. I'll tell you that. I don't care if Aunt Maggie loves them – I'm telling you, I'm not eating them."

A moment later, the toaster abruptly spat two pieces of toasted bread upward before they settled back into their slots, temporarily interrupting the conversation. C.J. turned to see the toasted bread crusts sitting an inch or so higher than the top of the toaster. She scooted her chair away from the table, stood and padded across the linoleum floor in her terrycloth slippers. Before extracting the toasted bread from the narrow slots in the toaster, however, C.J. scanned the cupboards, and wondered which of the identical doors might harbor the plates. She opened the one nearest the toaster.

"Nope, not that one," C.J. thought. She took another stab in the dark. Glasses and stemware. "Strike two," she thought to herself. On her third try, the open cupboard revealed stacks of varying sized ceramic and plastic plates. Only a few appeared to match. She extracted a plastic plate from the shelf, and then sat it on the counter near the toaster before placing the still-warm toast atop it.

She ambled over to the refrigerator and pulled at the door. The dim yellow light inside revealed another stark reminder of C.J.'s new plight. The shelves were virtually empty with the exception of a half-gallon carton of milk; a half-stick of margarine; a near-empty jar of raspberry jam; a few pickles partially submerged in a glass jar; and a few other condiments that her mother had loaded into the cooler before they left their real home and headed to Sticksville. Great Aunt Maggie had apparently removed all of the perishables from her home before she left on what C.J.'s mother referred to as an "uncharacteristically impulsive trip" out of the state. She had insisted that she would be home sometime on Sunday, which would give C.J.'s parents plenty of time to drive back to St. Louis, and to prepare for their trip to Brazil.

C.J. seized the plastic tub of margarine from the inside of the door. She placed it alongside the plate, then realized she didn't have a knife, and had no idea where she might find one. It could be hidden somewhere within the dozen drawers around the kitchen. Having already grown tired of the "Can you locate the dish you need game," C.J. asked, "Do you know where the knives are?" "Second drawer on the left. Near the stove," her mom replied, from her position bending over the kitchen sink. She was rinsing the dishes she had just washed by hand.

"Thanks," C.J. said as she moved to and then opened the drawer. The house was older than their own, but C.J. was pleasantly surprised at how clean and orderly her great aunt had kept the place. She didn't know much about Great Aunt Maggie, but she appeared to be fastidious, at least when it came to house cleaning. "I just hope she doesn't smell like an old person," she thought again to herself. "And please don't let her wear old-ladies' rose perfume," she silently prayed to any divine entity listening. C.J. loathed rose-scented anything. She especially distained rose perfume.

By the time she had washed down a couple of pieces of toast with a cup and a half of hot coffee, C.J. had completely shaken her morning lethargy, and decided to get dressed. Her mother, who had always seemed to know what C.J. was thinking said, "Once you've brushed you teeth, and gotten dressed, you can help me carry in the rest of your boxes." Then, as though it was an incentive, "I'll help you get things set up in your room."

"Okay," C.J. replied. "There wasn't going to be anything to do around here anyway," she thought. Might as well use her ample free time to create, or rather re-create, her little piece of home, C.J. thought, "and spending a little mother-daughter time would be a good thing, too."

As she brushed her teeth and looked at her reflection in the bathroom mirror, C.J. wondered what it was about time that made it such a paradox: When you were having fun with your friends it passed at warp speed. When you had nothing to do, or hated what you were doing, it dragged so slow that you felt as though you were mired in some perverse space-time continuum. At the present, C.J. thought, she was undoubtedly in the latter.

As she thought about time and relativity, it dawned on her that today was June first. There were nearly three full months to go before school started. How ironic, that she, of all people, would now be counting the days till it did.

The first school day could not come soon enough as far as she was concerned. When school was in session, she would at least be back in civilization among the friends she was already missing so badly that it hurt. While not a big fan of the confines and disciplined routine of academia, she understood all too well that attending school was a small price to pay foremancipation from her current plight.

C.J. spat the white toothpaste foam from her mouth and rinsed with water before spitting again into the white porcelain basin. She wiped the moisture from around her mouth with a soft hand towel and looked at herself in the mirror again. As she gazed into the eyes of the figure looking back at her, C.J. realized that she had just come face-to-face with one of the saddest people she had ever seen.

By the time they took a break for lunch, her mother and she had moved every box from the truck into the house. Her father had taken a brief break from his self-imposed appointment as gardener and maintenance man to help C.J. and her mother bring in from the truck the box springs, mattress and the bed frame's head and foot board.

"I really appreciate your help, C.J.," her mother said after she swallowed her first bite of a peanut butter sandwich.

"No problem," C.J. said. It had been a lot of work, but the task had been a welcomed respite from C.J.'s obsession with boredom and self-loathing. She took a long drink of lemonade-flavored Kool Aid. The ice cubes clinked against the side of the glass.

"Why don't you take a little break after lunch and go for a bike ride around the neighborhood?" her mom both asked and suggested at the same time.

"What neighborhood?" C.J. asked in a way that implied she had not completely given up her sullen attitude.

Her mother ignored C.J.'s sarcasm.

"In fact, you can ride down to that little gas station we passed along the way," C.J.'s mom added. "Find out what kinds of things they sell there."

"You mean in addition to the night crawlers?" C.J. asked, facetiously.

"Ah, huh," her mom replied as she stood to walk her plate to the kitchen sink.

"Sure. Why not?," C.J. said unenthusiastically. She chugged the last bit of Kool-Aid from her glass, the exterior of which had become covered with small beads of water. By now, the heat had melted the four ice cubes into tiny, white slivers that floated atop the small portion of pink lemonade that remained in her glass. Before standing, C.J. simply swallowed the ice shards with a single, final gulp. She walked over to the sink where she placed her glass and plate alongside her mother's, before heading for the door.

Again, as if on cue, her mother shouted, "Be back by three at the latest."

"It won't take that long to ride down to the stupid gas station and back," she thought, but she simply responded, "Okay, I will."

As she exited the house, C.J. made no effort to dampen the impact of the screen door as it sprang back into the door frame, with a noticeable thwack – thwack!

"And don't slam the door," she heard, just as the slap of the wood-framed door reverberated throughout the house.

"Sorry," C.J. shouted back in the general direction of her mother's voice. "If they don't like the banging of a wooden screen door," C.J. wondered, "why doesn't someone put in a regular door instead?" It was just one more irritant in a long and growing list of things she disliked about her new environment. The list was getting longer with each passing moment. "Note to self," she mumbled to herself. "Start a list of things I most hate about being here." With so many "hates" already mentally noted, C.J. wondered if she could recite them all for her first written entry.

As she stepped outside, C.J. scanned her surroundings and found her bike leaning against the side of the house. It was one of the last things to go on the moving truck, and probably one of the first things her father had taken off. At least he had left it in a conspicuous place and she didn't have to hunt for it.

As she tossed her leg over the seat, C.J. was pleasantly surprised at how good it felt to get on her bicycle again. At least this was familiar, she thought, even though she was riding in unfamiliar territory, over unfamiliar ground. With the exception of an occasional shortcut across a neighbor's lawn, C.J. hadn't ridden on any surface other than hardened concrete or asphalt in her entire life. She was surprised at how smooth the tan powder of the dirt driveway felt as she pedaled over it. As C.J. coasted down the pathway, she turned to see that she was also kicking up a plume of dust that lingered momentarily in the air as she made her departure. For C.J., the dust trail was a bonus that implied she was going faster than she actually was. It was a nice visual effect that she thought added a bit of mystique to her journey into the unknown.

The smoother than expected coast down the driveway abruptly ended with a jarring, staccato shockwave as her front tire hit the gravel roadway intersecting the driveway. She had slowed to make the turn onto the roadway, but even at her slower speed, C.J. felt the jolt pass through her arms, her seat and her legs. The rumbling and jarring abated somewhat once she steered into one of the three semi-rock-free, concrete-hard channels in the roadway. These evenly spaced channels had been created as hundreds of car and truck tires pushed out from under their weight and spinning force, the once evenly distributed rocks from the roadway. The result, as C.J. found out, was that deep mounded rows of gravel formed on the sides of these rock-free channels. She also found out, within a few minutes of her maiden voyage, that those rows of gravel posed previously undetected steering hazards for bicycles and their riders, especially at higher speeds.

Pedaling along at a comfortable clip, C.J. noticed a white, drifting cloud just above the tree line. Above the noise of her own tires on the roadway, she could hear the roar of an approaching car. She instinctively veered her bike to the right, to put as much distance between herself and the approaching vehicle as possible. When she did, C.J. felt the bicycle slow from the drag of the deep gravel. Almost simultaneously, she lost control of her own steering. With much difficulty, C.J. wrested control of her bicycle back from whatever force was doing its best to upend her. Her tires had little traction in the deep gravel and she knew that if she did not regain control soon, she might find herself face-down in the roadway – just as the car hurtled toward her.

With great relief, C.J. was able to maintain control of her bike long enough to bring it to a safe stop well in advance of the approaching car. Had she tried to over steer in the gravel, C.J. concluded, the results could have been disastrous.

The car flew past a few moments later, spitting errant rocks and dusting everything, including C.J., with a white fog of roadway powder in its wake. She looked up in time to see the driver wave without really looking as he passed. When the dust dissipated, C.J. turned to see the car disappear over the hill, still spewing roadway dust in its wake. She walked her bike into one of the rock-less roadway channels, put her foot on the left pedal, pushed off with her right leg and mounted her bike all in one fluid motion. In an instant she was making good speed again. Unfortunately, C.J. could only assume, that her destination would be about as boring as everything else she had experienced so far. But at least it was a destination – in a place that offered few.

C.J. hadn't realized how jarring her bicycle ride had been until she bounced onto the firm blacktop roadway that fronted Otto's gas station. The noise from under her tires suddenly abated, and C.J. felt as though she were suddenly riding on air. Her arms and legs tingled from the absence of constant vibration and the smooth-as-silk sensation instinctively made her smile. The roadway sloped gently downhill, which meant that she could coast the rest of the way to the gas station. The wind in her hair felt refreshing and it served to evaporate the gathering beads of perspiration on her forehead. As the bicycle picked up speed, C.J. sat up straight on her seat, relaxed, and felt herself smile while taking full advantage of this downhill, gravitational gift.

C.J. noticed that there were no cars parked in the shade of the metal overhang where the two gas pumps stood in tandem on a raised concrete island. From the rust on the pumps and the peeling paint on the posts that supported the corrugated metal overhang, C.J. could see that the gas station was in the same general state of disrepair as most of the homes she had seen in the area. She rolled into the shade and over a black rubber hose. When she did, a bell on the side of the building ding-dinged and, too late, C.J. realized she should have steered around the innocuous hazard that was obviously there to signal the proprietor of arriving customers. She was relieved that no one came out of the building in response to the alarm.

She found a place near an antiquated pop machine to park her bike and used her right foot to lower the kickstand. She walked tentatively toward the open glass door that was held open by a small wooden wedge under the door's metal frame.

The smell of oil and grease engulfed C.J. the instant she walked into the building. Strangely, she was also immediately consumed with an overpowering feeling that she was being observed – by someone or something. She looked toward an open door to her right that led to two, large garage bays. In one of the bays, she could see a car suspended on a hydraulic lift. The other bay appeared to be empty. C.J. pivoted back to her left, and looked past a few metal grocery shelves that were stocked minimally with bread, hamburger and hot dog buns, powdered doughnuts, a few bags of candy, mayonnaise, catsup and assorted canned goods.

Still feeling uneasy, C.J. felt a compulsion to look down and to her left. A strange feeling enveloped her but her trepidation was eclipsed by a need to comply with some strange, silent command. As she turned C.J. met the gaze of two unflinching, liquid-brown eyes. She was instantly paralyzed by fear. Sitting before her, staring directly into her eyes was one of the biggest dogs she had ever seen in her life. Unable to discern if it was a gentle giant, or a beast bent on ripping her to shreds, C.J.'s heart pounded in her chest and her face flushed from the rush of adrenalin that was now involuntarily coursing through her veins.

Her head was swirling. First she considered screaming, but feared the noise might instigate an attack. Her legs began to tremble – seemingly begging her to let them run.

About the time she decided to bolt out the door and take her chances outrunning the beast, C.J. noticed a large swishing motion behind the gigantic animal. She consciously told herself to breathe and finally was able to do so in shallow, tentative breaths. It was then she realized that that the swishing she had seen was the giant yellow dog's proportionately giant tail. The dog panted contentedly, the corners of its mouth turning upward, resembling what C.J. thought looked like a friendly smile. She felt herself somewhat relax. The huge animal struggled to rise, and after a tentative moment, managed to do so. With its head lowered, but tail still wagging, the animal lumbered slowly toward C.J. She knew now, for certain, the dog meant her no harm. Even if it suddenly went into a psychotic rage, C.J. felt certain she could easily outrun the geriatric canine.

But she didn't need to.

The dog hobbled up to C.J., looked up for a moment, and then plopped himself on her foot. C.J. almost buckled under the burden of the dog's weight as it leaned against her leg. She steadied herself and patted the dog's enormous head to assure the massive animal that she was delighted with his choice of seating arrangements. If she moved, C.J. feared the dog would fall helplessly to the concrete floor. Against her leg, she could feel the rhythm of the dog's panting. Watching droplets of slobber from the dog's tongue fall one after the other to the concrete floor, C.J. felt immense sympathy for her new friend. Feeling the heat from the dog's body against her leg, she suddenly realized how much more intense the early summer heat must be for a creature that had no sweat glands, and that was shrouded with fur. She looked compassionately into the creature's big eyes and was deeply moved by a feeling she had never experienced before. A spirit flowed within her; a spirit that both frightened and amazed her; a spirit that both worried her and consoled her.

The experience was strange and alluring.

Again, C.J. looked down into the empathetic eyes of the perpetually panting dog. The furry creature fixed his eyes on her in a way that made C.J. feel at one with the creature. She did not know how long their eyes were transfixed when a voice suddenly shattered the silence, and broke the semi-hypnotic state she was in.

"I see you've met Duke." The voice said "Duke" in a soft and gentle, southern way that accentuated – even prolonged the "u" so that it sounded more like "Duuke."

She turned to see a thin man of average height in grease-stained, blue overalls. The figure walked decisively toward her while wiping his hands on a similarly stained brick-red rag. As soon as he had closed the short distance between them, the man enthusiastically plunged his hand in C.J.'s direction. The abrupt motion startled her a bit.

"I'm Otto," the man said as he offered his hand in friendship.

C.J. tentatively returned the gesture. Otto's hand was as hard as a concrete, and his fingers were knurled like the roots of an oak tree. When she looked down, C.J. realized that the olive-skinned man shaking her hand was missing two fingers, and at least one of the remaining fingers was "less than whole." It certainly didn't affect Otto's vice-like grip, however. And despite the warmth and sincerity of the handshake, C.J. was relieved when Otto finally released her hand from his.The man apparently wasn't aware that his gesture of hospitality could be painful to someone on its receiving end.

"I'm C.J.," she said. "C.J. Brown." She looked up and smiled, averting her eyes from the man's grotesquely formed appendage.

"Good to meet ya, C.J.," the man said.

"Duke," Otto said abruptly, glancing down at the immense dog. "It's just plain rude to just park yourself on somebody like that. Get off her." He motioned with a toss of his head for the dog to move.

The dog looked at Otto, then up at C.J. The creature seemed to be looking for C.J. to intercede on its behalf.

"Oh, it's okay," C.J. said in the dog's defense. She looked down and continued to pat the dog's enormous head. "I like it." Duke looked up, still panting. It appeared to C.J. as though the dog was actually smiling the way dogs do sometimes. Then the dog suddenly laid down, sprawling across C.J.'s feet. It was as though the big dog had decided that he wanted to keep her right there – and that he would use the entire weight of his body to do so. C.J. realized that if she had wanted to move, she absolutely could not.

Otto rubbed the half-day's growth of his salt and pepper whiskers quizzically with his left hand. "Humm. I've only seen him do that with one other person," he said, apparently genuinely bewildered by the dog's behavior. Otto continued to scratch at his whiskers – as if by doing so he could summon an explanation.

"Duke. Move. Go lay down on your blanket," Otto said more forcefully. This time the dog complied. "You must be special, young lady." Another moment of contemplation passed, then a smile suddenly formed on Otto's face as his eyes brightened. "Oh, now I remember who he's taken to like that before."

"Who?" C.J. asked.

"Maggie," Otto said, smiling, looking at C.J.

C.J.'s ears perked up. "Maggie?"

"Yeah. Maggie Davidek. You know her?"

"Kind of," C.J. said. "She's my great aunt. Well, I haven't actually met her, but I'm staying with her this summer." C.J.

pointed out the window and in the general direction of her neighborhood.

Otto seemed to look even more deeply and intently into C.J.'s eyes. She felt as though the man was looking into her soul, searching for something – something tangible.

"Oh, so you're the summer visitor," Otto finally said after a long moment. "Maggie mentioned that you'd be movin' in."

"Uh huh," C.J. said, diverting her eyes away from Otto's, and back down at the dog, who was now resting on his crumpled blanket. It was weird, but every time she looked into the dog's eyes, C.J. felt a sense of peace and calm resonate though her entire body. Duke looked in her direction, then put his chin between his front paws and closed his eyes.

"Well," Otto said, "welcome to the neighborhood, C.J." He wiped his hands absently with the grease rag as he walked around the counter. "I sure wish there were more kids around, but I'm afraid you and Dusty are about it."

"Who's Dusty?" she asked with more enthusiasm than she anticipated.

"Haven't met him, huh?" Otto asked in reply. "Little kid," he said and held his hand about to his ribs to approximate the subject's height. "About eight years old, I'd guess – though I can't say I really know for sure. Skinny. Wears round, thick glasses." Otto chuckled to himself and shook his head. "Real piece of work he is."

Otto had just described the little boy who had stuck out his tongue at C.J. when she and her parents had stopped for lunch at the café outside of town. "I think I may have seen him at the Rainbow Cafe yesterday," C.J. said. "He was riding a bike." If he lives anywhere near here, that was a long way to ride on a bicycle, C.J. thought to herself. "And he was carrying a loaf of bread," she added.

"Yep. He lives on that bike. Probably had to ride all the way there, since I'm closed on Sundays," Otto said. "I suspect you'll meet him anytime now. He's..." Otto searched for the right words but apparently came up short. He stopped and repeated his earlier characterization, "...he's a piece of work." Otto gently shook his head from side to side, smiled and chuckled again.

"Hey, I need to get back to work, so let me know when you've finished up your shopping. I don't have much to speak of, but I try to carry what I can. I do it mostly for the few folks who live around here, so they don't have to drive into Hickory all the time."

"Thank you," C.J. said. "My mom just wanted me to see if you had bread and milk and stuff."

"That I do have," Otto said.

"It was nice to meet you," she said, realizing that she should probably go. C.J. looked at the sleeping dog. "And Duke, too."

"See ya around," Otto said, then quickly disappeared around the open doorway, which separated the auto bays from the consumer goods section of the station.

"Thank you," C.J. said to the man who was no longer around to hear it.

She stood for a moment in the silence and looked one more time at the shelves and then down at the dog.

"Bye, Duke," she said. The big dog opened his eyes momentarily as C.J. walked out the open door. She passed the faded green brontosaurus "Sinclair" decal in the corner of the window and then walked parallel to the painted cinder-block building as she set her sights on retrieving her bicycle.

"Bye, C.J."

"Bye, Otto," she said without looking. When C.J. turned, she could see Otto busily working in the grease pit of the car bay a dozen yards away. She looked around for someone to associate with the voice, but all she could see was Duke sitting, panting in the open doorway. Still looking like he was smiling.

"Oh well," she thought, "I must be hearing things."

She walked over to her bike and then walked it around the bell hose this time, being careful not to roll her tires over the hose and trip the "ding-ding" bell.

C.J. mounted her bike and began picking up as much speed as she could, knowing that she'd have to pay gravity back for what she had borrowed from it when she coasted the last quarter-mile of her ingress to the station. She was only on the asphalt for a few moments before her tires rolled into the gravel of the unpaved roadway – a roadway, which led back to her so-called neighborhood. Feeling somewhat reassured that she had at least met one nice person and one nice dog, C.J. felt her mood improving slightly. And the more she thought about that big, beautiful dog, the more she wondered what had really happened back there. At some level she felt – really felt – as though she had actually communicated with that dog. That, of course, was absurd. It was pure nonsense. But no matter what her logical brain told her, she just couldn't shake the feeling that something weird – something wonderful – had happened when she looked into that dog's eyes.

And as she continued to pedal up the grade, C.J. wondered if it would ever happen again.

RON NICHOLS

Chapter Six

"It can't be, Charlie. It simply can't be," Maggie Davidek insisted.

"I'm afraid it is, Maggie," the man in the three-piece suit said to her as he fingered through the papers in the manila folder before him.

"You mean, we...," Maggie corrected herself, "you mean I don't have anything – anything at all?" Maggie asked, still unable to comprehend the magnitude of her impending financial predicament.

When Maggie got in her car to drive to Springfield yesterday, she believed with all of her heart that she would return to Ricksville with the knowledge that she would live the remainder of her retirement years in relative financial comfort. But Charlie Gibbs, her accountant and friend of more than 40 years, had wasted no time in telling Maggie the ugly, naked fiscal truth. He was an accountant – practical and methodical – he could think of no "soft" way to tell her. Even after seeing, in black-and-white, the proof of his blunt assessment, Charlie wished he had crafted a more diplomatic way to break the news to her. Maggie looked straight ahead – shock and disbelief possessed her.

"But... it... can't be," Maggie pleaded. "Henry... Henry had made all of the investments," she said.

Charlie took a deep breath and exhaled as though he were exorcising some unspeakable demon from within. "I'm sorry, Maggie. I've looked at everything. I've tried to find every potential asset Henry may have stocked away. But his investments just didn't pan out the way I know he wanted them to..." He stopped. Saw the tears well in Maggie's eyes. God, he hated this part of his job – revealing the cruel, harsh, fiscal facts to his clients. Having to do so to a friend was all the more painful. They certainly hadn't mentioned that aspect of his profession when he was studying for his CPA at the University of Arkansas in Pine Bluff.

Maggie knew about the "investments," and how her husband, the eternal optimist, had insisted that those investments were the key to their happy and prosperous retirement. At this moment, Maggie was feeling neither happy nor prosperous.

"But I'll be able to keep the house and the property, won't I, Charlie?" Maggie asked in a tone that was more like a wish than a professional inquiry.

"For a while, Maggie. Another year, probably." Charlie took a deep breath and willed the courage to summon what he knew had to be said. "Without any source of outside income, you probably won't be able to make the county taxes for very long – and, frankly..." He paused.

"What is it Charlie?" the 70-something, gray-haired woman asked from across the desk.

"Maggie." The man leaned forward to take her hands. "You'll still need to come up with living expenses. I mean, you still have pay off the rest of the mortgage on the place, and you'll need to eat and pay for utilities and all of that. A Social Security check will only go so far. You're in good health now, but what if you get sick? You know what health care costs are these days. Then there are always upkeep expenses on the house and your car." His points were practical and honest, but at the moment not very welcomed.

He went on nonetheless. "Look, Maggie, what I'm saying is you might as well liquidate now. Try to get what you can out of the place. I can help you if you want me to. I've got a good friend in the real estate business. He owes me a favor or two, and I'll get him to waive his commission for you. Then, maybe you could move into a smaller apartment or perhaps you could move in with some relatives. If you're lucky, maybe you can get enough out of the old place to invest and..." Charlie stopped. He realized too late that it was an "investment" that her husband had made – the one in that diamond mine in South Africa – that now left Maggie, for all practical purposes, destitute.

Sitting in the leather chair of the tastefully decorated office, Maggie heard the echo of Henry's voice, telling her how certain he was of this "investment." But now the only certain thing in Maggie's world was that she had nothing – except a small house and a few acres of near-worthless, Central Arkansas countryside. And, based on the scenario Charlie had just outlined to her, she wouldn't have it for very long.

"I'm profoundly sorry," he said as Maggie lowered her head into her weathered hands and began to sob. Charlie felt helpless, sitting in his executive chair. He agonized in painful silence, not knowing what words to offer that would alter, or even mitigate, Maggie's unfortunate fiscal situation. After several interminably-long and awkward moments, Charlie could bare it no longer. He rose from his chair and walked slowly around the desk, knelt down alongside Maggie's chair and reached for her hands. As he took them, he could see Maggie's tears as they rolled down her wrinkled cheeks, pooling briefly in one of her face's furrows before cascading down into the next. It was the saddest thing Charlie had ever seen. Even though he knew he was not responsible for the sadness, he could not help but feel guilty by reason of simple proximity.

Maggie looked back into the accountant's pale blue eyes and saw a sadness that betrayed his stoic, professional persona. She saw his agony and realized that she was the source of it.

"Thank you, Charlie" Maggie said sincerely, patting the thick hands that tenderly held hers. "I appreciate your advice. But that old place is all Henry and I..." her words trailed off. "All I have now," she said.

Maggie, making a brave effort to compose herself, sat erect in the chair. "I almost forgot, Charlie. What do I owe you?" she asked. Then quickly added, "And don't say 'nothing.' I know better than that."

"Nothing. You owe me zero dollars. Henry paid me in advance."

Maggie knew that was a lie, but at the moment – feeling completely drained – she didn't have the strength to feign the pride necessary to mount an objection. "Thank you, Charlie. I know Henry would be thankful for all of your help."

Maggie rose from the chair. Charlie steadied her, holding her arm as she stood erect. He wanted to hug her – to hold her – to do something that would make her feel better, but he simply leaned on his desk as she turned and walked toward the inner doorway.

"Maggie," Charlie said as she reached for the brass doorknob that accentuated the dark mahogany door. "I wish things had turned out better. I really do."

Without looking back, Maggie muttered more to herself than to her friend, "So do I, Charlie. So do I."

He watched in silence as his friend ambled across the polished wood floors of the outer office and opened the lobby's main door. She was wearing a simple black dress and black leather pumps that thudded with each tentative step across the hardwood floor. From afar, Charlie could read the body language of a woman who was still mourning the loss of her husband. Now, regrettably, he had the added to Maggie's burdens by adding that she was an impoverished widow to boot.

When he heard the door close, Charlie thought the door's echo punctuated the end of a chapter in Maggie Davidek's life. He thought about how cruel life could sometimes be, said a silent prayer that there would be happier chapters ahead for his friend, then walked back around the desk. After he sat down, he slid open the lower drawer on the right-hand side of the hand-crafted desk. He peered at the bottle of Wild Turkey bourbon lying amid an unkempt drawer full of notepads, and pens and junk he hadn't had the inclination or discipline to throw away. That drawer, ironically, was the one – the only – unorganized part of his life. Then he glanced with one eye at the ticking antique clock across the room. It was only three o'clock in the afternoon. A disciplined man, he never had a drink before five. But after what he had just experienced, he made a once-in-a-lifetime exception to his self-imposed rule.

The bar was now open.

Charlie extracted the half-full bottle of dark amber liquid from the drawer and then turned in his swivel chair to remove an almost-clean glass from the computer table behind him. He poured the liquid into the glass – about two fingers' width high. Then added another finger's worth. He took a generous sip. He felt the burn from the whiskey in the back of his throat. The warmth from the liquid washed over him like a gentle current.

"You damned old fool," Charlie said to the ghost of Henry Davidek. He took another sip of the potent fluid and held it briefly in his mouth before swallowing. "You damned, old, diamond-chasing fool."

Chapter Seven

C.J. stopped at the top of the hill to catch her breath. She was grateful that the grove of trees provided a shady respite from the merciless fever of the sun. She noticed a mailbox on the other side of the road. Directly across from it, she saw a driveway, which cut through the trees and seemingly vanished into the darkness. C.J. could only assume there was a house somewhere within the abyss created by the leafy canopy. There was a stillness that amplified the darkness and intensified the earthen smell of rotting logs, flowering vines and decaying leaves in the undergrowth. It was a curious emanation of both life and death.

C.J.'s better judgment beckoned her to move on – to mount her bicycle and pedal beyond this place. C.J. did not.

She walked alongside her bicycle through the soft, powdery dust of the driveway. She stopped momentarily to examine the single, snake-like trail of bicycle tires in the brown powder dirt. She could also see countless tennis shoe impressions that paralleled the serpentine ones created by the bicycle tires. She traced both sets of impressions to the point where she stood. She looked further into the darkness and contemplated reversing course – following her own set of prints back to the road. She had never been a thrill seeker throughout her entire 13-year life. C.J. could not understand why suddenly, in this strange new place, she was overcome with a need to push further and further into the unknown darkness like some brave, new-world explorer. Perhaps, she thought, it was caused by pure boredom.

C.J. looked ahead and looked behind her again. She took a deep breath as if to summon her courage.

"Oh my gosh," C.J. whispered to herself, suddenly aware of her mother's deadline. "The time." She glanced at her watch. It was 10 minutes till three. C.J. knew she'd have to turn around quickly or she'd be late making her three o'clock deadline.

In the instant she turned, she saw him. And C.J. almost jumped out of her skin.

"What you doin' here?" the younger boy said somewhat defensively. His elbows rested on his bicycle's handbars.

"My God," C.J. said. "You almost scared me to death. Where'd you come from."

The little boy peered at C.J. through round, Coke-bottle-think, wire-framed glasses. "I asked you first."

"I was just taking a ride," C.J. said, her heart still pounding from the rush of adrenalin that was still coursing through her veins.

"I need to get home," C.J. said, more aware than ever that her deadline for returning home was fast approaching.

"I'll ride with you," the little boy said without asking for an invitation to accompany his new acquaintance.

C.J. mounted her bike and began to pedal in the direction of the road. The little boy rode quietly beside her.

"You must be Dusty," C.J. said once they neared the main road.

"Yep. Otto told you, didn't he?" he asked.

"How'd you know I was talking with Otto?"

"I know'd lots of things," he said matter-of-factly.

"Did you follow me?"

"Nope, but I found you," he said. "I seen you the first day you came here, too," he said.

"Outside the cafe," C.J. finished for him.

"Yep."

"I saw you too. By the way, why'd you stick your tongue out at me?" C.J. asked.

"Cause you made a face at me," Dusty replied.

"No I didn't."

"Yes you did," he countered.

"No," C.J. said indignantly. "I DID NOT."

Dusty turned and purposefully studied her face for a long moment. "No. I guess you're right. You must look like that all the time." Dusty laughed at his clever pejorative.

"Oh you're really funny." C.J. paused. "Funny looking that is."

Dusty appeared stung by C.J.'s retort. A quick wit and tongue often landed her in "Guiltville," even when trading barbs with her peers. C.J. realized that the poor little boy couldn't have known that he was dueling with a master. She had sliced him as adroitly as a butcher cuts through a carcass.

"Hey," she said, trying to limit the damage from the wound she'd just inflicted. "That's a joke."

"I knew that," Dusty said, though something in his eyes told C.J. he did not.

He changed the subject. "Want to see my rock collection?"

Under normal circumstances, C.J. would have passed. But she was easily prone to remorse, and decided that looking at Dusty's stupid rock collection might be just the penance necessary to alleviate her guilt. "I can't now, I have to get back home," she said sincerely.

The disappointment on Dusty's face was apparent.

"How 'bout first thing tomorrow?" C.J. asked.

He smiled brightly. "Okay!"

In an instant, Dusty was flying down the road, and disappeared around a bend waving good-bye as he did. He had vanished almost as quickly as he had appeared. C.J. wondered where he could have disappeared to. It was as though he had blended into the dust –

evaporated into thin air. But as she rounded the curve she saw a dilapidated mailbox with the name "Gowins" painted in box letters along the side. Down that road somewhere, C.J. presumed, is where he lived. She hadn't asked, and Dusty apparently thought everyone knew where he lived. Since there simply weren't that many houses around, C.J. concluded, that was probably the place. She'd find out in the morning.

*

To stock up on some groceries for Aunt Maggie, the Browns had decided to take that trip into Hickory when C.J. returned from Otto's. Though embarrassed to be seen driving around in the rental truck, C.J. was relieved to be going somewhere beyond Ricksville. And besides, C.J. had concluded, they'd never see anyone they knew anyway, so what difference would it make if someone gawked at them in their rental truck.

"So tell me why I've never met this 'Aunt Maggie?'" C.J. asked from the passenger seat in the rental truck. In the passenger-side mirror, C.J. could see the plume of dust behind them as the truck rocked along the gravel road.

"Maggie and Henry spent a good portion of their lives living abroad," C.J.'s mom said. "And, I guess the truth is we've all lived rather busy lives."

"Okay, so tell me again why I need to stay with her, in her house, for the entire summer?" C.J. asked with a noticeable tone of incredulity. The question had been fermenting in her mind since she had first been told of her summer "arrangement."

"Well," her mother said, "As your father and I tried to explain to you before, we wanted you to stay with family while we're doing our research..."

"Family? I don't even know her," C.J. said impatiently.

"You just haven't seen her since you were a toddler," her mother replied. "Aunt Maggie – she's my aunt – your great aunt is about our only living relative. When your Uncle Henry died last year, we all agreed that spending time together would be good for both of you."

Silence filledd the truck as C.J. pondered spending a whole summer in the company of some old lady – some old widowed lady – she didn't even know. It was a rare instance indeed, when C.J. and her mother weren't talking when they were together. But only the hum of the engine and the road noise from the truck tires could be heard as she turned her head away from her mother and looked mindlessly at the pastures and cropland they passed. Each section was hemmed in by three strands of sagging barbed wire that were held aloft by rotting wooden poles. She fought the urge to cry.

She was going to lose no matter how much she complained, reasoned, begged, or cried. Still she would not go down without firing one more verbal volley. Finally C.J. blurted, "But why do I have to stay with her, here?"

"Because she needs you, C.J., and, frankly I think it's time you stopped just thinking about yourself," her mother said, exasperated. "Besides," she added, "this isn't a prison, and three months isn't forever."

Tears welled up in C.J.'s eyes and she turned her head to avert making eye contact with her mom. She had never felt more alone, helpless and frustrated in her life.

It wasn't just leaving her friends and her comfortable suburban neighborhood that she resented. It wasn't just being cast into an environment that offered virtually no entertainment or social prospects for a 13-year-old girl. And it wasn't just that she was being forced to stay with someone – some old lady – she didn't even know.

No. The truth was, C.J. was going to miss her mom and dad. And worse, she had a terrible feeling deep in her stomach that they would never come home again – that something would go wrong for them in the forests of Brazil. As the tears rolled down her cheeks, C.J. wished she could just close her eyes and wake up tomorrow – three months into the future – her mom and dad picking her up, and taking her back home, waving good-bye to her old, great aunt. With her face still turned toward the monotonous landscape, C.J. quickly wiped the tears away with the back of her hand. She was going to have to face reality. She was stuck here in Ricksville. And all the fantasizing in the world was not going to change a single thing. As she dabbed the last bit of moisture from her face, C.J. resolved to endure and to prevail – despite what fate had dealt her. She took a deep breath to regain her composure and said a silent prayer for her parents' safe return.

Chapter Eight

C.J. ate breakfast, got dressed, and was on her way out the door before 8 a.m.

"Be sure to be home by noon," her mom said as C.J. dashed past her. "Your Aunt Maggie will be here soon, and I'll need your help to tidy up a bit before she returns," she shouted to the fleeing figure.

"I will," C.J. said, and then exploded out the door. This time, however, she retreated quickly enough to snag the screen door with her left hand before it thwacked rudely against the door frame. Though still early in the day, the heat was palpable, especially in the areas absent of shade. Because it was still early in the day, long shadows from the immense trees offered few pockets of direct sunlight as C.J. pedaled toward her destination.

When C.J. finally arrived at Dusty's house, she could not believe her eyes. Did he – did anyone – actually live here? Before she saw it, she heard a dog barking incessantly as she approached the house. The pacing beast was tethered to a post near some ill-maintained out building that looked as though it would fall over in the slightest breeze or collapse from the weight of its own decay. The dog strained menacingly against its shackle, eyeing C.J. with something between suspicion and malice. C.J. prayed – literally prayed – that the chain was strong enough to hold it.

As the beast tramped back and forth, tugging unsuccessfully at its restraint, it kicked up puffs of taupe colored dust from a near-perfect circle of well-worn ground. The circumference of the perimeter was delineated by the maximum length of the dog's tether. Any vegetation that had once grown within the circle had been snuffed out, succumbing to the continual grinding of the animal's paws and claws.

Beyond the earth-beaten circle, knee-high weeds elbowed each other for space and soil. C.J. summoned the courage to walk her bicycle toward the house, along the path that snaked its way amid the pens and the other out buildings that comprised the unkempt compound.

She had walked less than 20 yards when she first heard the malicious voice.

"What do you want?" The voice commanded. C.J. held her breath – frozen by the chilling tone. Her heart was pounding so hard C.J. could feel the blood pulsing in her ears. "Oh my God," she thought, "I'm going to die." And with that thought, she realized almost comically – that she was experiencing the fight or flight syndrome she had read about in her biology class – her SAFE and secure biology class back in civilization. Ironically, in her case she thought the phenomenon should be more accurately described as "flight or fight or freeze." And it was "freeze" that was definitely winning at the moment. It seemed as though she was in one of those terrible dreams where the boogieman was upon her, but yet she could not move a muscle. Only this time, C.J. knew, this wasn't a dream.

Finally, she turned her head slowly in the direction of the voice. And as she swiveled her head, she saw it – just off the pathway – not 10 yards away. It was the same brown menacing dog that she had seen near the out building, just moments before. The creature peered through the weeds and kept its penetrating eyes fixed upon C.J.

The animal crept slowly toward her. C.J. held onto the handlebars of her bicycle and managed to walk slowly backwards as the beast approached.

"What do you want?" C.J. heard the question again. Where was it coming from? It couldn't be the dog. That would be preposterous, she thought.

"Nooth... nothing," C.J. heard herself say. She tried to swallow, but the lump in her throat would let nothing go down – even if she had managed to produce enough saliva to swallow.

"What do you want?"

"I... I... just wanted to see Dusty," C.J. finally said.

To her utter amazement, the animal stopped, raised its ears inquisitively and tilted its head slightly to one side. Then, inexplicably, it turned and vanished back into the weeds. As quickly as the animal had appeared, it was gone. Just like that – it was gone.

C.J.'s heart continued to pound and she suddenly felt very weak – relieved, but weak. She continued to scan surrounding foliage for any signs of the animal.

"Cleotis is gone," another voice said. "You needn't worry."

C.J. turned to see an elderly lady wearing a colorful sun dress just a few feet away from her.

"I... I... just came to see Dusty," C.J. repeated – clearly frightened.

"He's around here somewhere, honey. Why don't you walk with me up to the house. You look like you could use some lemonade," the lady said.

"Ah..." C.J. hesitated.

"Now don't you worry," the frail, slightly slumped-over woman said, "Ole Cleotis won't hurt you – he just wanted to know if you meant any harm. You come on with me and we'll rustle up Dusty."

C.J. wanted to cry – wanted to run, but when the old lady touched her elbow, C.J. felt the sudden sensation of being completely safe. Without consciously deciding to do so, C.J. found herself walking alongside the woman up the dusty pathway that led to the house. She looked up at the shed where she had seen the tethered dog – the same dog that had challenged and approached her only moments before. Unbelievably, it appeared to be bound to the post in the ground, just as she had seen it before. And it was still tugging tirelessly at its shackles.

"You just set your bike down here, sweetie, and come on in. I think a glass of lemonade will do you a world of good," the lady said as they came within a few feet of the back of the house.

"I wish I'd knowed I was gonna have company – I woulda cleaned the place up a bit," she said. "We don't get many visitors around here." A bright, almost glowing smile appeared on her face and C.J. felt genuinely welcomed.

"You just sit right here and let me get us something to drink," the woman said as she pulled one of the simple wooden chairs away from a well-worn square wooden table in the kitchen. C.J. absently moved to the chair and sat down.

As the woman busied herself with the preparation of the refreshments, C.J. scanned her immediate surroundings – the way folks do when they come into a completely unfamiliar environment. She tried to be discrete – shifting her eyes only briefly, from one open doorway to the next. The house, though modest in its furnishings, appeared to be absolutely spotless.

"Where you from little lady," the woman asked, her back still turned to the business at hand.

"Ah, St. Louis. Well, I mean, now I'm living with Aunt Maggie down the road, but I'm from St. Louis," C.J. said.

"Lawd Almighty. You come to live with Maggie did you?" the lady said as she brought the two tall glasses of lemonade to the table. The ice tinkled against the sides of the glasses when she sat them down.

"Yes, ma'am," C.J. said.

Looking C.J. squarely in the eyes, the little lady said, "I hope Cleotis didn't scare you too much. Honest, he wouldn't of hurt you for nothin'. He's all bark and no bite that one is. But he's good to have around – I'll tell you that. You know, with just me and Dusty here by ourselves."

C.J. was not as confident about the dog's benign intentions. Somehow, C.J. still believed that, if given the chance, the dog may have shredded her to pieces. But she still didn't know how the dog got untied, then apparently re-tied in such a short period of time, unless of course, someone had helped.

"It's okay," C.J. said, not too convincingly.

"I'm glad you're staying with Maggie, bless her soul. Losing Henry so suddenly. It's something you never get over – I knowed that for sure – Lawd don't I know," the woman said more to herself than to C.J. "Yep, you'll be a real blessing to her. Yes you will."

The little woman talked so much and with such velocity, C.J. could only listen. The little lady's energy belied her frail frame.

"So you already know Dusty, do ya?" the woman asked. Before C.J. could answer the woman went on: "He's a piece of work, that one is," the woman said shaking her head, chuckling to herself.

"That's what I hear," C.J. said quietly.

"Here's to new friends and new adventures," the woman said enthusiastically raising her glass.

C.J. raised her glass and the woman reached her bony arm out and clanked her glass into her host's. C.J. took a tentative sip. The lemonade was exquisite. It was absolutely the most refreshing drink she had ever had.

"Oh my gawd," the woman said so suddenly that C.J. nearly dropped her glass, "Where are my manners?"

The woman thrust her dirt brown hand in the direction of C.J. so abruptly that it caught her by surprise.

"I'm MeMaw," the woman said. "At least that's what folks call me. Been called that for so long, I've almost forgot my Christian name. I like this one better though. It fits me. Do you know what I mean?"

C.J. nodded absently.

"Sorry for not introducing myself." The old woman reached her hand out toward C.J. and it seemed, for an instant, to dangle in space and time, just a few inches above the table's wood grain.

C.J. fixed her eyes upon it, then cautiously extended her hand in kind. The woman clasped C.J.'s hand and held it. When she did, C.J. felt a strange, almost unearthly power that was both comforting and unsettling. C.J.'s first reaction was to retract her hand, but she could not. C.J. looked into the clouding brown eyes of her hostess and said without thinking, "I'm C.J. C.J. Brown."

"It's good to know you C.J. Brown," MeMaw said. But instead of releasing her hand, the old woman held it with both of hers and looked deeply into C.J.'s eyes – studying her in a profound and soulful manner.

C.J. didn't know what to do but look back into her hostess' eyes. For an instant, C.J. felt consumed by the intensity of the woman's silent inquisition. After a long, intense moment, MeMaw smiled her bright smile and whispered, "You have the gift, don't you girl?"

C.J. didn't understand the question. "Ah, I don't think so," C.J. stammered. "Ah, what gift?"

"Oh I think you knowed," MeMaw said, now wearing her precocious smile. "They talk to you, don't they? That's what really spooked you about Cleotis wasn't it?"

"Who talks to me?" C.J. asked as though she had no idea about what the woman was talking about.

"They talk to you, I can tell. I can tell you're just like Maggie – I've felt it before – in her hands – you've got the gift just like Maggie, I knowed it," the woman said with growing certainty.

"I... I... don't know what you're talking about," C.J. said.

"Ain't nothin' wrong with it, honey. People have all sorts of different gifts in this world. You just happen to have that one,"

MeMaw said as she released C.J's hand and then took another long drink from her sweating glass.

"I'd better go, ma'am. My mom will be wondering where I am," C.J. said. But before she could stand, the back door exploded and a small, energetic figure bounded into the kitchen. The two seated figures turned their heads to see Dusty standing before them.

"Look who came to see you, Dusty. It's your new friend," MeMaw said.

He looked at the two glasses of now half-filled lemonade sitting in front of C.J. and MeMaw. "And how come she gets lemonade so early?"

"Dusty Gowins, you mind your manners, you hear me? This young lady is a guest in our house, and I will not have that kind of talk coming from you." MeMaw said with an intensity that took C.J. by surprise.

It was clear from Dusty's immediate change in attitude that he respected that intensity, too. "Yes ma'am," Dusty responded sincerely. "I didn't mean nothin' by it."

"Good," the woman said confidently, "You tell this young lady that you're sorry you forgot your manners."

Dusty looked a C.J. She could tell from the look in his eyes he didn't want to say anything to her at all, let alone apologize to her.

"It's okay, ma'am, he doesn't need to apologize," C.J. said abruptly, hoping to avert any additional embarrassment for Dusty.

"It may be okay with you," MeMaw said forcefully, "but it ain't okay with me. I didn't raise that boy to end up like them other hellions."

Silence engulfed the room. C.J. felt less comfortable now than she had when being challenged by the snarling dog earlier.

Dusty didn't wait long to comply with his grandmother's command.

"I'm sorry I forgot my manners," he said less than enthusiastically. He began to head off out of the kitchen, but the voice of MeMaw snapped him back as though he had reached the end of some invisible rope.

"Dusty," she said slowly. The boy stopped. "C.J. here, will need you to ride back with her to her house," the woman said – surprising C.J.

"Ah that won't be necessary, ma'am," C.J. said standing up.

But without looking toward her guest, MeMaw said, "Dusty won't mind, will you?" She did not wait for, nor expect, a reply. "Besides, it's the neighborly thing to do. Isn't that right, Dusty?"

"Yes ma'am," Dusty said without hesitation. "I'll ride with you home," he said in the general direction of C.J.

"Great," C.J. thought. By no fault of her own, she had managed to further alienate the one person in her immediate world who was even close to her age.

MeMaw turned to C.J. That warm, engrossing smile returned. "You come by again and bring that Maggie with you when you do. We three ladies will sit on the porch, have some iced tea, and just gab," the woman said. "By the way, when is Maggie coming back?"

"She should be home today or tomorrow – my folks have to leave tomorrow, so I guess she'll have to be back then," C.J. said.

"I'm glad to hear it, I sure am. I guess the only good thing about losing Henry is that she'll be able to settle down to a more normal life instead of tromping off all over the world doing whatever those two did," MeMaw said with a look that suggested she had no idea what Maggie and Henry did for a living. "It was good to meet you my dear," she said, then leaned down and whispered. "Dusty's a good boy, don't you worry. Before this summer's over, you two'll be the best of friends," MeMaw added.

C.J. seriously doubted it. She looked over in time to see Dusty walking toward the back door. "Thank you for the lemonade, ma'am," C.J. said.

"You're very welcome dear. And please call me MeMaw."

"Thank you," C.J. forced the words from her mouth, "MeMaw," she said unnaturally. She followed behind Dusty just in time to see the door abruptly whack in front of her. She grabbed the rusting metal handle on the weathered wooden doorframe, opened the door and turned – holding the handle to dampen its impact once she had stepped outside.

Just as the door closed behind her, C.J. heard MeMaw say, "That Maggie's going to be so surprised that you have the gift, too. She's gonna be really surprised."

With Dusty a full 20 yards ahead of her on his bike, C.J. quickened her pace. She retrieved her bicycle from where she and MeMaw had left it, put her left foot on the pedal and began to push off. As she mounted the bike, the last sounds C.J. heard coming from the house was MeMaw laughing, repeating to herself, "She's gonna be really, REALLY surprised."

Ahead of her, C.J. could see that Dusty suddenly skidded his bicycle to a halt, kicking rocks and dust to the side of the path as his back tire pivoted to the side. C.J. closed the distance between them, then brought her bike to a more civilized stop.

"I almost forgot to show you my rock collection," Dusty said, still breathing quickly from the exertion of pedaling.

"Oh yeah. Sure." C.J. said, feigning interest. "Let's see it."

The two made their way toward an outbuilding, about a hundred feet to the west of the house. It was like the other ill-kept buildings in the area. Faded and peeling paint curls clung tentatively to the rotting and splitting vertical plank boards. Dusty lifted the handle on the door. With some exertion he pushed the door forward and it scraped along the concrete floor. He lifted up on the handle and walked the door further ajar to accommodate C.J.'s entrance.

"Come on in," Dusty said with a smile. C.J. entered the dark confines with some trepidation.

As he did every day, Dusty walked over to a bench where an electric motor hummed. A quart-sized cylinder rotated continually, making a constant grinding noise as it did. Without touching the cylinder, Dusty looked intently under the unit.

"I have to make sure it hasn't lost any water," Dusty said to C.J., assuming she wanted to know what he was doing. The tumbler had been a gift MeMaw had given him two years ago and since that time, all that Dusty had ever requested for Christmas or his birthday were refill "grit kits" for it. Dusty loved collecting rocks, and the tumbler turned out to be the perfect complement to that hobby.

The original kit came with a bag of rough "semi-precious gemstones," a couple of packets of grit, and a bag of polish powder. After seeing the smooth, polished, multi-colored rocks that were the result of his first production batch, Dusty was hooked. His biggest problem was getting his hands on enough of the grinding grit to satisfy his tumbling lust. While it was possible to order a variety of different stones from the manufacturer, stones were never in short supply in the hills and creeks that surrounded Dusty's home. Plus, being a "rock hound" was a perfect complement to his other passion – fishing. When the fish weren't biting, rocks could always be acquired. "This is where I polish the stones," Dusty told C.J. as he pointed at the tumbler. He retrieved a small coffee can from under the shelf and removed the plastic lid, then unceremoniously emptied the contents on the wooden workbench alongside the tumbler.

"Here are some of my rocks," he said proudly.

To C.J.'s surprise the polished, smooth, multi-colored stones glistened brilliantly in the light that poured in through the single window over the workbench. She picked one up and held it.

"Wow," she said, "these are beautiful. Where'd you find them?"

"All over," Dusty replied matter-of-factly.

Dusty explained to C.J. that the hard part for him was deciding which of his favorite finds would be among the select handful that were chosen to be smoothed and polished in the tumbler. Space was limited, and he had learned that he couldn't always judge a rock by its outside appearance.

On the bottom shelf of the wooden workbench where the tumbler whirled, was another small pail of evidence that verified this geologic truth. Dusty reached under the bench and fetched the pail.

"See these? I found them in this spring cave I used to go to all the time. Before MeMaw told me I couldn't go there anymore." He shook a few of the translucent stones from the pail into his hand. Though fairly small, the stones shimmered in the sparse light of the shed.

Dusty loved the small cave where he had found these and several other multi-colored stones. Cool air blew constantly from its rocky mouth where chilly water bubbled to the surface and formed its own small creek. The small opening allowed just enough room for Dusty to duck-walk through. Dusty explained to C.J. that he had splashed in the water as he ventured deeper into the opening, but he didn't have to crawl, so he was able to keep his clothes dry. He only ventured in as far as the light from the outside would allow him to see. "I was going to take a flashlight with me the next time," he said somewhat excitedly, then said with palpable disappointment, "But MeMaw says I can't go in the cave anymore."

Reliving his great cave exploring adventure, Dusty went on to explain that on his way out, light from the cave's opening revealed several, small glimmering stones. He had scooped them up, using his un-tucked T-shirt as a collection pocket as he duck-walked his way back out into the sunlight.

"They looked real pretty in the light," he said. "I thought they'd tumble good."

Dusty went on to explain that he had had to wait several days for his previous batch of stones to complete their polishing before he could begin the process of transforming the ones he had just acquired into what he had hoped would be smooth, translucent beauties.

When he finally began the process of tumbling these stones, Dusty told C.J. that he had to resist the temptation to open the tumbler every day to check on the stones' progress toward perfection. He had learned the hard way, that opening the cylinder to check the stones only invited persistent leaks – leaks that could eventually ruin the grinding or polishing process. So with the discipline of a professional gemologist, Dusty waited six full days before opening the tumbler for the first time. Normally, four days of tumbling in the course grit would have been enough to render the stones sufficiently smooth enough to proceed to the medium grit, but Dusty wanted these stones to be absolutely smooth before moving on to the next phase.

"But you know what?" he said. "It didn't work on those rocks," he said.

Upon opening the cylinder, and much to his surprise, the stones had looked as though they hadn't been tumbled at all. They almost seemed impervious to the grit's erosive properties.

In the end, Dusty explained, he had wasted even more of his precious course grit and more than a month of tumbling time in a futile effort to smooth and polish the stubborn rocks from the spring. Irritated, he said he had thought about tossing them into the hog pen, but having wasted so much time and money on them, he simply couldn't muster the courage to do it – despite his anger. Plus, he reasoned, they were his only specimens from a cave he'd likely never be able to explore again.

So they had sat there in the rusting metal pail for more than a year. In fact, Dusty hadn't bothered to look at them again until this moment. He returned the few that he had spilled into his hand to show C.J. back into the pail and turned his attention to the successfully polished stones.

"I didn't think some of these would turn out very pretty, but I went ahead and put them in anyway," he said as he poked at a few of his favorites. "As it turned out, some of the roughest ones turned out to be the best."

C.J. thought philosophically for a moment. "Maybe the same can be said of people," she said.

"Yeah, I guess," Dusty said, without commenting on what C.J. thought was a clever and apt analogy. Dusty unplugged the motor unit and lifted the cylindrical barrel from its crib, then shook the barrel gently and listened for the sound of water splashing over the rocks. Based on his few years of experience, the barrel sounded like it still had the right amount of water in it. He returned it to its cradle and plugged the unit back into the electrical outlet that was nailed to a two-by-four that formed one of the wall studs. The unit instantly hummed to life and soon the drone of muffled grinding permeated the little outbuilding again.

"Guess we'd better go," C.J. said. "Thanks for showing me your rock collection. They're really nice."

"Thanks," Dusty said without further comment, and headed out the door.

RON NICHOLS

Chapter Nine

She knew her niece and her husband would be waiting for her when she arrived. Maggie had had the foresight to send them a key to her place so they could help get their daughter – her grandniece – settled into the house for the summer.

At first Maggie was filled with joy at the prospect of spending some time with C.J. She hadn't seen her since she was just a toddler. The idea of having a young and energetic presence around the house seemed like a good way to fill the void that Henry's death had created, at least temporarily.

But after her initial excitement Maggie was filled with apprehension. It could very well be that that cute little toddler might have grown into one of those body-pierced, whacked out, non-conforming, ill-mannered, generation-something kids she had seen from time-to-time when she and Henry had ventured into a large city. But then she dismissed those notions, realizing that Sam would raise her daughter better than that. Whatever C.J. had grown up to look like (piercings or not), Maggie was confident she'd be a good person.

But now that she was driving back to Ricksville, Maggie was consumed by an anxiety so pervasive, that it took all of her energy to stave off the near-constant impulse to weep. Had it not been for the fact that she needed to concentrate on keeping her 2005 Toyota on the road, Maggie realized that she could just as easily succumb to her absolute grief. And although she could have driven the extra 30 miles or so this afternoon, returning a day earlier than the Browns expected her, Maggie knew she had to take the evening to "get herself together," before she had to don the faux persona of a great aunt who, despite her recent loss, still had it together. She couldn't let the Browns leave the country with the impression that they had left their only child in the possession of some old, hysterical nut case.

Maggie nudged the turn indicator with her left hand, to signal her intent to veer off onto the exit ramp that would take her to the town of Lowton, about 30 miles from her home. She'd have to drive another four miles to get to "downtown Lowton," since the new highway had bypassed the business district when it was constructed some 30 years prior. A wave of nostalgia rushed over her as she eased onto the "Old Little Rock Highway." That was the name that the locals had given Route 33 many years before when it was the main traffic artery for anyone heading south to the big city. Now, of course, it was mostly just a feeder route to the business district – or what was left of that business district.

She remembered how she and Henry had driven through the little town almost every time they went to Little Rock to catch a flight to another location – in search of precious stones or metals. She could not count the number of geologic firms that had hired Henry through the years. He was good at his profession and he stayed very busy. Henry could have left Maggie behind on these "jaunts of geology" as he called them. After all, most of Henry's colleagues refused to take their spouses along, citing the danger, cost and desolation as primary reasons. On those rare occasions when he believed his destination was too unsafe, even Henry reluctantly left Maggie behind. But throughout their 50-plus-year marriage, it was a rare instance when Henry and Maggie did not travel together. It was the one thing Henry had always insisted upon: They would spend as much time together as they possibly could – even when Henry was working. In light of today's revelations, Maggie thought, it would have been more prudent for her to stay behind and start her own career and to stock the travel money away for more practical applications. If she had, maybe he'd have some sort of pension or nest egg to carry her through her "golden years."

Maggie had studied to be a teacher at Southwest Missouri State University in Springfield. She had met Henry, who was studying geology and mining engineering at the University of Missouri in Rolla – at an off-campus dance outside of Springfield. The Rolla engineering students – most of whom were boys – always enjoyed venturing down to sow the fertile fields of co-eds at SMSU. Many of the girls there embraced the prospect of meeting new boys – especially boys who would likely have lucrative careers as engineers upon graduation.

She smiled unconsciously as she remembered the first time she laid her eyes upon Henry Ray Davidek. It was as though the moment had occurred only yesterday. Maggie had been talking with her friend Becky, who was actively scanning the room for prospective dance partners. On the far side of the floor, she saw him – talking enthusiastically to another co-ed. To this day, Maggie could not tell you why she locked her gaze upon this particular boy – there must have been 100 or more in the hall – but the instant he looked up, their eyes were transfixed on each other. His penetrating blue eyes seemed to glow in the purposefully-inadequate light of the cavernous room. Maggie was mesmerized as Henry strode over to her – confidently making his way past the featureless pairs of figures that embraced and shuffled amid the other couples on the floor.

As she drove on into the town, she remembered Henry's coal black, wavy hair and his muscle-covered frame as he approached her that evening. She was probably the only girl, she recalled later with great fondness, who wasn't looking for romance that night. Her best friend had dragged her there because she didn't want to go to the dance alone.

"God, he is handsome," Maggie thought when he stood before her that night. If there was such a thing as "love at first sight," Maggie, realized, she was bearing witness to the phenomena.

A day after his own graduation, Henry drove his '48 Ford the 90 or so miles from Rolla to see his fiancé graduate with honors from SMSU. The very next day, amid the white flowering dogwood and crimson-hued redbud trees that splashed the greening hillsides, the two were married in a small chapel in northern Arkansas.

As though awakened from a trance, she quickly glanced at her watch. It was only 6 p.m., but the news and anxiety of the day had taken its toll on her. If the only hotel in town had a vacancy, Maggie concluded, she would stop for the night – get her thoughts together, regain her composure, and head home first thing tomorrow. Now that she had so little income, she knew that the extra expense of renting a hotel room so close to home was a luxury she could not really afford. Yet, the $65 she would spend on the room seemed a small price to pay for the appearance of composure. Once she checked in, she would drive through McDonald's, get a burger and a Coke – at a senior's discount – and enjoy her meal while she sat on her bed watching some lame television show on T.V. With any luck, she would drift off to sleep, and dream about the good times she and Henry had had together as they traveled the world looking – always looking – for the Kimberlite diamond pipe that they never found.

Had they found that diamond mine, Henry promised her, she would get the biggest and most brilliant diamond from it. But she didn't really care about the diamonds. The best gift he had ever given her was a lifetime of love and companionship, and, of course, the time she and Henry had spent together. Those memories grew more precious with each lonely, Henry-less day.

Maggie pulled into the parking lot of the modest, but well-kept motel and turned the ignition switch off. Out of years of habit, she reached between the seats and pulled the parking break handle until it refused to be lifted further. Then she grabbed for her purse sitting on the passenger seat. She sat the purse on her lap as she opened it with a quick tug of the zipper, reached in and snagged her wallet. As she fingered through the green bills, Maggie estimated she had about $300 in cash. She snapped the wallet closed and replaced it back in the purse before she unlocked and opened the car door. The late afternoon air was warm on her face as she walked up the sidewalk to the hotel lobby.

As Maggie opened the lobby door, a cowbell, hung on the hydraulic door return, clanked to alert the clerk of the presence of a customer. As the bell shattered the silence, Maggie was confronted with the brutal reality that she could not – would not – be able to live on memories alone. She would have to make some difficult decisions soon. As she drifted off to sleep later that night, Maggie Davidek resolved that she would put off that decision as long as possible – at least through the end of the summer, when the Browns returned to take C.J. home.

RON NICHOLS

Chapter Ten

Christine Larson gripped the steering wheel with her left hand and hoisted her portly frame onto the padded seat of the company's Ford Diesel, four-door pick-up. It was one of the half-dozen or so GeoTherm vehicles that were parked behind a series of construction trailers on a large, gravel parking area. The interior of the pickup was dusty and Christine noticed shards of spent sunflower seeds on the floor mats. "Men are such pigs," she said to herself as she punched the key into the ignition. When she started the truck the fuel gauge needle rose steadily to the "Full" mark on the dashboard indicator. "Well at least the swine re-fueled it before bringing it back," she said aloud. The courtesy only moderately mitigated her festering anger.

An undercurrent of anger seemed to always course through her veins. Christine wore a chip on her shoulder the size of Arkansas, but it hadn't appeared there overnight. Like the slow buildup of minerals that form stalactites and stalagmites within the caverns of some dark cave, Christine's chip had become the most prominent feature of her personality. As a result, few of her colleagues at GeoTherm chose to socialize with her outside of the workplace. She was so consistently unpleasant to those around her that the majority of her colleagues only conversed with her when it was absolutely necessary to conduct business. And even then it was with great reluctance.

The chip on Christine's shoulder began to grow almost as soon as she entered grade school, when her above-average size and above-sized aggressive behavior, had alienated her from her fellow classmates. Had she been a boy, it was likely she would have been considered a leader among her boy peers. As a male, her teachers would most likely have considered her aggressiveness and competitiveness – especially when coupled with her keen mathematical and scientific mind – character attributes that would serve her well later in the business world. But girls, Christine would learn all too soon, were judged by an entirely different set of standards. Girls are supposed to play nice.

Christine did not play nice.

Throughout her life, each time she was touched by one of these double standards, Christine became more determined to persevere in spite of them and to make anyone who got in her way pay for the injustice she had experienced.

She had worked hard, studied endlessly, and had been accepted into one of the most prestigious universities in the country. Her entrance exam scores were among the highest ever recorded. Yet, because she was a woman, Christine did not receive an academic scholarship. Despite her superior grades and college aptitude test scores, Christine watched as her male counterparts withlower scores landed scholarships.

She studied hydrogeology at a time when few women pursued scientific careers – let alone those scientific careers that would take them – often alone – into the field for weeks or months at a time. As an undergraduate, her professors had tried to guide Christine into what they considered to be a more "gender-appropriate" career path. Nursing and teaching were the two most often recommended. Despite the pressure, Christine held her ground. She would not be bound by some archaic stereotype imposed upon her by people possessing smaller minds.

Christine never attempted to repress her anger, nor moderate her supremely confident manner. As a result, her graduate professors and fellow graduate students did their best to avoid her. And while Christine's confidence in her studies was immense, her self-confidence in all things outside academics, was woefully lacking. Christine realized early in life that she was not considered pretty or even cute. "Plain" was about the nicest characterization of her appearance Christine had heard – or would ever hear – and she had accepted – and then embraced – her inevitable lot. And she made no attempt to ever "give nature a hand," as a fellow graduate student had once suggested.

"Men don't participate in such nonsense," she had once replied to a fellow female's suggestion to "make herself more presentable in public," and Christine vowed she would never lower herself to take part in such superficiality. To compensate, she had avoided nearly all possible social contact. Fun, if she could find any, was not something that would help her career and therefore it was not something she would squander her discretionary time pursuing.

After graduating with honors, Christine found that her exemplary grades added little to her marketability. It was still an "all-boys" club in the rough and tumble world of engineering, geology and mineral development and extraction. For years she labored in glorified secretarial roles, working for men twice her age, but possessing only half her intellect. Through the years, and with the slow, but certain melting of society's glacier of gender-bias, Christine elbowed and clawed and worked her way into positions more commensurate with her talents and education. And although the gender-bias she had experienced as a student, had all but released its grip on women in America in the decades that followed, Christine had never eased her grip on the resentment she harbored for having experienced it.

Six months ago, when she landed the lead scientist position at GeoTherm, she vowed that she would make her mark on the company, on the hydrogeologic world, and on her bank account. She would one day own this company, Christine had envisioned, and then she would call the shots – exacting revenge on the system. And where possible, making the people, who had stunted her career and her life, pay in the process.

As she pulled out of the parking lot, and onto the main road, another nearly identical GeoTherm truck was turning into the lot. The occupant of the vehicle waved as he passed. It was a perfunctory salutation, but Christine did not return the gesture of goodwill. She was focused. She was on a mission. And she would literally run over anyone who got in her way.

Chapter Eleven

"Hey, slow down," C.J. yelled ahead, trying in vain to close the sizable gap Dusty had created in the few short moments of his head start.

Dusty continued at his current pace, unhampered by C.J.'s pleading.

"Hey, slow down will ya? I thought you were going to ride home with me?"

Dusty appeared to be unaware of, or impervious to C.J.'s request.

Then suddenly and deliberately, he skidded his bike to a halt. His back tire spewed a cloud dust across the road as he did. Apparently, he was trying to make a point. The dust hung in the air for several moments before settling in, on and around the weeds that were already coated with an ample layer of road grime.

C.J. continued to pedal feverishly, steering her bicycle to stay in one of the two dust-covered ruts that formed the driveway. When she got to within a few yards of Dusty, she sat on the seat and coasted, trying to catch her breath before at last stopping alongside Dusty.

"Why are you staying at Miss Davidek's ?" Dusty asked out of the blue.

"I don't have a choice," C.J. said. "My folks are going to spend the summer in the rain forest of Brazil."

"Where?" Dusty asked.

"Brazil. It's somewhere in South America," C.J. replied.

"Why don't you get to go?"

"My parents are working. They're anthropologists," C.J. said.

"They study ants?" Dusty asked.

C.J. fought the urge to laugh. "No, they study the cultures of people – they're anthropologists. In this case mom and dad will observe and then write about the social make-up and core values of a group called the forest people who live there."

"They get paid to do that?"

"Kind of. They teach at a university. Research is part of their job."

"Seems kind of silly to me," Dusty said.

"Why do you say that? Aren't you curious about other people and how they live?" C.J. countered.

"Sure. But I wouldn't give up my summer to learn about anyone, let alone people in South America," he said matter-of-factly. "I guess that's why you get to stay with Miss Davidek."

"And that would be why exactly?"

"If you had to go with your folks, you'd have to give up your summer," Dusty said with a tone of exasperation. "Now, you can have fun here."

C.J. could not bring herself to respond to that absurd concept. So she quickly changed the subject. "You know, you don't need to come with me. I'm a big girl. Why don't you just head back to your house?" C.J. proposed.

"Look. If I get back home and tell MeMaw I didn't ride back with you home, she'll skin my hide," Dusty said.

"Then don't tell her. I promise I won't tell her," C.J. added.

Dusty shot a "you must be insane" look in C.J.'s direction. "She'll know," he said with certainty. "Come on, let's just go." Dusty mounted his bicycle and headed up the slightly sloping road. "I'll just wait for you there, so you might as well come on," he shouted over his shoulder.

Exasperated, C.J. mounted her bicycle and pedaled to catch up and ride alongside Dusty in the second of three rock-less paths that formed the road.

"She really wouldn't know if you didn't ride with me all the way home you know," C.J. said, pedaling comfortably alongside.

"Yes she would. She knows things. She knows lots of things that other people don't. It's a gift," he said confidently.

"A gift?"

"Yep. She knows things before they happen and she knows when people aren't telling the truth and sometimes she sees things that other people don't," Dusty said without looking at C.J.

"Lots of parents are that way," C.J. said, thinking of her own mother's uncanny ability to anticipate her thoughts and moves.

"MeMaw's different," he said. "She knows a lot of things – and not just about me."

"Are you saying MeMaw is psychic?"

Based on Dusty's blank expression, C.J. quickly added. "You mean you think she can read people's minds?"

"No. I wouldn't say that," he said. "She just knows things. Most of the old people round here just say she's got 'the gift.' But it ain't much fun for me. I can tell you that." Dusty said.

"What do you mean?" C.J. asked.

"Most kids can sneak a thing or two past grown-ups if they have to – you know – tell a little white lie," he said. "But not me. MeMaw knows before I even start talking if I'm about to try to pull one over on her. She's always known. I haven't been able to get away with squat since I could talk. And it's all because of her darned 'gift.'"

"Well most parents – ah, or grandparents – know when their kids are telling a lie," C.J. repeated as they made their way under a grove of hickory trees that provided a cool tunnel of shade for the two cyclists.

"I'm telling you MeMaw knows EVERYTHING – sometimes before it happens," Dusty said again.

C.J. didn't say anything, but remembered MeMaw's deep, penetrating look and her warm, enveloping touch that seemed to flow through her soul like a warm, gentle summer breeze. C.J. remembered vividly MeMaw's face and eyes as she held her hand and said to C.J., "You have the gift, don't you?" In retrospect, she realized it wasn't a question. The old lady knew – or at least believed she knew that C.J. had some kind of gift. What kind of gift, C.J. had no idea. The whole incident was beginning to creep her out a little so she decided to change the subject. "How long have you lived here," C.J. asked, smiling her warm and contagious smile as she did.

"As long as I can remember," Dusty said, glancing at C.J. He seemed to be warming to his new neighbor.

"Can I ask you something," C.J. interjected.

"I guess," Dusty said. He figured she'd asked whatever she wanted to anyway.

"Is MeMaw your mother?"

"MeMaw? No. MeMaw means grandmother. She's my grandmother," Dusty said chuckling.

"So what happened to your real parents?"

Without warning, a speeding truck suddenly veered around the curve – hurling rocks and careening nearly out of control just a few dozen yards in front of them.

"Look out!" Dusty screamed, as he made an abrupt right turn into the weedy ditch to evade the impending collision.

C.J. who had been riding her bicycle in the middle pathway of the road, executed a sharp turn to the left, but the front wheel of her bicycle skidded in the deep row of rocks between the furrows.

She was quickly losing control of her bike. Just as she was about to fall, her front tire plowed through the mound of rocks and bounced onto the third rut. C.J. looked up in time to see a menacing metallic grill bear down upon her like the jaws of a giant mechanical beast.

Dusty managed to stay upright on his bicycle, but was now over his head in the forest of weeds that lined the roadway. The comet-like trail of dust and rocks smothered him like a choking blanket from which he could not extricate himself. He could not see the truck as it passed, but he heard the roar of the engine and the grinding clatter of its wheels as the ghost-like truck consumed the rocky roadway in front of it.

As suddenly as it appeared, the truck and its sounds were gone, but the fog of dust lingered in the air as the silence consumed him. Dusty squinted to peer through the dusty fog. He could not see any more than a few feet in any direction around him. Dusty voluntarily coughed to clear his throat, which had been rendered parched by the explosion of dust and adrenaline that was now coursing through his veins.

Moments passed as the dust slowly settled back to the earth from which it came, and the roadway and surrounding view slowly reappeared. Regaining his senses, but with his heart still racing wildly, Dusty tossed his bike aside and scanned the scene for his riding companion. A wave of panic overwhelmedd him. C.J. should be somewhere close by, but he could not see, nor could he hear any signs of life. "Could it be that she was struck by the truck and flung yards away?" he wondered. Dusty listened intently for any sound, and ruefully anticipated hearing the muffled sounds of moaning or crying. He remained absolutely still, but heard nothing other than the pounding of his own heart.

He was about to call her name, but then realized he didn't even know it. She was just some girl and he hadn't even thought to ask her name.

"Hey. Where are you? Hey!" is all Dusty could think to shout into his immediate surroundings. He walked back down the road in the direction of his house, hoping to find the girl – smiling that bright smile he had just seen a few moments before. But as the scene cleared and brightened, he saw nothing but a deserted road in front and behind him. Never had he felt so alone – so frightened.

He yelled again. "Hey! Are you okay?"

A thousand thoughts tumbled through Dusty's head as he considered his next course of action. While he did worry about his riding companion's condition, he also feared for his own since he had been tasked to "take this young lady home." If the girl got hurt, MeMaw would likely conclude that Dusty had been derelict in his duty.

A slight movement in the weeds on the other side of the road caught his attention, and he moved cautiously in that direction. The vision of a bloodied, appendage-severed body suddenly filled his mind. What if she were near death, or worse needed mouth to mouth resuscitation like in the movies? Dusty had the sudden impulse to run, but then saw his riding companion rise.

His relief was instantaneous.

"Hey, are you okay?" he asked.

"Yeah, are you?" C.J. responded. She attempted to dust herself off.

"Sure. But I thought you were... ah... you were..."

"Well, we're both lucky we weren't killed. Did you see how fast that idiot was going? Damn," C.J. said without thinking.

"We'd better get you home," Dusty said, now more concerned about his riding companion than he had ever been before. "And ride on this side with me," he added pointing to the road rut on the right side.

"Yeah. Okay," C.J. said. "Man, she didn't even slow down," she said, still thinking about her near-death experience.

"She?" Dusty asked. "How do you know it was a she? It happened so fast."

"It was the last thing I thought I was ever going to see – I'll never forget her face," C.J. said seriously.

They rode along quietly for several minutes.

"By the way," Dusty finally said. "What's your name? You never said."

"It's C.J. C.J. Brown," she said, then added, "I don't think you ever asked."

Dusty looked – really looked at C.J. for the first time since he had been around her. Then he saw C.J.'s warm smile again.

This time he couldn't maintain his false aloofness, and realized too late that he was smiling back at her. As they neared the entrance to Maggie Davidek's driveway, Dusty stopped. C.J. turned to go down the driveway, and stopped as well.

"Do you want something to drink?" she asked.

"No thanks. I'd better get home."

"Thanks for riding with me," C.J. said – really meaning it.

"Next time try not to get killed," Dusty said.

For a moment C.J. thought he was mocking her then she saw Dusty's precocious smile as he turned back to wave good-bye.

RON NICHOLS

Chapter Twelve

C.J.'s heart was finally beating at a near-normal rate as she coasted down, then back up the dirt driveway that led to her aunt's home. When she looked up, she saw the dark blue Toyota parked behind the rental truck and concluded that Great Aunt Maggie had finally arrived. She also concluded that her summer sentence of exile was about to begin. With each turn of her bicycle wheels, the stark reality of her parents leaving was growing closer and all-the-more real.

She wished to herself again that there could be some other way for her to spend her summer. But C.J. was forced to concede, as her mother had said so many times before, that it was time to "buck up and get on with it."

C.J. tossed her bike aside and entered the back of the house through the screened porch with trepidation.

"Mom, Dad. I'm home," she announced more tentatively than normal.

"We're in here, honey. Come on in and meet your Great Aunt Maggie," she heard her mother say from the living room. The words somehow found their way down the hall and through the kitchen.

C.J. walked quietly through the kitchen, looking down at her dusty jeans in time to hastily whack some of the most obvious earthen powder off of them. She hadn't thought about how she might look after her fall into the weeds until just this moment. She tried to preen as best she could – dusting her shirt and tucking in her shirt tail. With her parents about to leave for three months, C.J. had no intention of explaining that she had nearly been killed by a passing motorist. Besides, she didn't want her aunt to dote and worry needlessly about her every time she left the premises – which C.J. hoped would be often.

Like an actor about to make her entrance onto the stage, C.J. put on her best smile as she rounded the corner into the room.

"Hi sweetheart," C.J.'s mom said from her position on the sofa. She was seated next to the woman C.J. assumed was her Great Aunt.

C.J. had been told her aunt was nearly 70 years old. In her mind C.J. had pictured a plump, wrinkled, hunchbacked woman scooting a walker across the floor and muttering incomprehensible utterances to no one in particular. But the bright, only slightly graying woman seated next to her mom appeared to be in much better shape than C.J. had imagined.

The woman sprang to her feet with an ease and grace that surprised C.J. Before she could react, C.J. felt herself trapped in the bear hug clutch of her Great Aunt Maggie. At five foot six, and slender, the two were nearly identical in height and weight.

"Oh my goodness," the woman said. "You are every bit as beautiful as I thought you'd be."

C.J. blushed slightly, but then realized she could have looked like the Elephant Man and her aunt would have been compelled to say the same thing.

"Thank you," C.J. said perfunctorily.

"C.J., do you remember Aunt Maggie?" her dad asked.

"Well." C.J. hesitated. "Not really. Sorry."

"Well that's okay, sweetheart," Maggie said. "I wouldn't have thought you would since you were only two or three the last time I saw you. But don't worry, we'll have lots of time to get caught up this summer."

Lots of time, C.J. thought. Too much time was a more accurate assessment.

"So have you met anyone in the neighborhood yet?" Maggie asked.

"A couple of people," C.J. said, without much emotion.

"I think you'll have a great time here – and I'm delighted to have some company," Maggie said. "Oh my gosh," she added, "I just realized I have nothing thawed to fix us for lunch. I didn't want anything to go to waste in the refrigerator, so I..."

"That's okay, Maggie," C.J.'s dad interjected. "We picked up a few things right after we arrived. Sara and I will make some sandwiches for all of us."

C.J. realized that this would be the last meal she would share with her parents for a long, long time. Often, when her parents had insisted that they eat dinner together, C.J. resented the imposition of having to sit down and talk about her day at school. But with the realization that she wouldn't be able to break bread with her parents again for a long time, she became consumed with melancholy.

C.J. fought to suppress a lump in her throat. That lump was always the precursor to a more demonstrative expression of her emotions. If she could preempt the lump from forming, she might not cry.

She thought she had pulled it off, but when the Missouri license plate on the rental truck disappeared around the corner of the driveway, C.J. could not stop the tears. It wasn't a sudden, uncontrollable loss of emotion, just the quiet release of feelings that had been building for more than a month. In just a few moments, C.J.'s emotions eased out of her the way air from a plastic bottle of Coke escapes when the plastic cap is gently twisted.

Before they left, C.J. had hugged – really hugged both her mom and her dad. She kissed them both, too. Hugging her parents was something she had done automatically most of her life, but this time she did not want to let go. She couldn't stop thinking that it might be the last time she would be able to show them how much she loved them. Simply saying "I love you," was an expression that seemed woefully inadequate this time.

With the truck gone, and after a few quiet moments, Maggie put her arm around C.J.'s shoulders. C.J. used the sleeve from her own shirt to hastily wipe the tears away.

"Don't you worry about those tears," Maggie said sweetly. "It's a woman's right. That's why we're the more stable sex," she said with a sly smile.

"Hey. You mind going with me to the grocery store?" Maggie asked. It was a diversionary tactic, C.J. knew. Still, the diversion was welcomed. "The freezer's full," Maggie continued, "but we'll need a few things – like chocolate ice cream – to keep us two growing girls energized." She looked at C.J. with a smile.

"Sure," C.J. said without much enthusiasm. "Mind if I clean up a bit before we do?"

"I noticed you were a bit... ah dusty," Maggie said. "You get all that from just riding your bike?"

"I know, it's so dusty out there," C.J. said.

"That's for sure," Maggie said. "Hopefully, we'll get a good thunderstorm to break this dry spell."

After a moment, C.J. took a deep breath, and the two headed back to the house. As she reached for the wood-frame screen door on the back porch, Maggie said, "They'll be okay, C.J." It was as though her great aunt was reading C.J.'s most personal thought. "Everything's going to be just fine," Maggie added with a sweet and sincere smile and patted her great niece gently on the back.

As C.J. cleaned up in the bathroom, Maggie walked out on the porch and scanned the familiar hills that seemed to vanish slowly into the hazy horizon. As she stood on the porch that represented her only major financial possession, Maggie felt the tears well in her own eyes. Even though Charlie had suggested she consider moving in with family, Maggie knew she would never purposefully impose herself on anyone – especially her "family." The truth was, even if they had asked her, Maggie was too proud and too independent to do such a thing to the only family she had left. She looked up at the sky and then again to that point on the horizon where the hills and the sky blended into togetherness. Maggie said a silent prayer for strength. She prayed that God would grant her that strength for at least for the next couple of months while C.J. was here. Hopefully, Divinity would grant her that one simple request. For in her entire lifetime, she hadn't asked God for much and she didn't think three months of strength was too much to ask for. She did not want her only niece – grandniece – to remember her as a helpless, and weeping, old woman.

She heard C.J. coming down the hallway toward the porch. Maggie lifted her arm to her face and used her cotton shirt sleeve to blot the tears of uncertainty from her own cheeks.

———

"So tell me about your school," Maggie said as C.J. handed her two cans of pork and beans from the brown paper grocery bag.

"Like what?" C.J. asked, not knowing where to start.

"Well, what's it like? What's your favorite class? Who's your best friend? Are the boys cute?"

C.J. was surprised by the last question. The astonishment was apparently evident on her face.

"What," Maggie asked, "you think I'm too old to remember cute boys?"

"No. No. Of course not," C.J. replied. "Yes. There are a couple of cute boys there."

There was a long moment of silence as C.J. continued to hand can after can of various provisions to Maggie. Finally Maggie set down one of the cans on the counter, turned and said, "I'm sorry I'm making you miss your summer. I know it can't be very fun for you to spend a full summer with me here away from your friends."

"It's okay," C.J. said unconvincingly. She agreed completely, of course, but courtesy prohibited her from saying so.

"You know I love having you here, but your mom and dad called to ask me if you could stay," Maggie said honestly.

"Yeah, I figured."

"Of course, I'm sure they thought it would be good for me, too. Having you here with me after Henry's death."

"I'm sorry about that," C.J. said, finally realizing she wasn't the only one who was missing out on something. Then she added, "You don't have to take care of me."

"I know. And you don't have to take care of me," Maggie said with a smile. "I may be old, but I'm not infirm."

"I don't think you're that old," C.J. said assuredly.

"Why thank you, C.J," Maggie said, then added after a pause, "I think." Maggie chuckled, then folded the paper grocery bag and forced it into a metal clip that held a few others on the inside of one of the lower kitchen counters.

"How 'bout we agree to this," Maggie said after a moment of contemplation. C.J. was both impressed and relieved by Maggie's candor. C.J. could tell that Maggie was a woman who possessed a good deal of confidence. "You're free to do whatever you want – come and go as you please – just let me know where you're going and when you'll be back," she said. "Just be very careful out on the road," Maggie cautioned. "Those people drive like idiots."

"Yeah, I know," C.J. said, wishing she hadn't said so – so quickly.

"I know there's not a lot to do around here, but I see you brought a stack of books to read – I have a bunch I've wanted to get to, too. Should you want to pass on our local religious television programming – which I'm sure you will find difficult – you can call your friends whenever you want," Maggie said. Maggie's smile was broad and contagious and C.J. was amused by the woman's wry sense of humor.

"You don't need to ask – just do it. I bought one of those phone cards for you at Wal-Mart," Maggie added. "You've got 700 minutes you can use anytime you want. I put it on your dresser."

In just a few hours, C.J. had begun feeling less like an indentured servant and more like a roommate. She instinctively wanted to return Maggie's kindness.

"I want to do my share of the cooking and housework and whatever else you need me to do," C.J. said. She meant it.

"Fair enough," Maggie said. Then she switched topics. "How 'bout I grill us a hamburger for dinner?"

"I'll slice the veggies and warm up the pork and beans," C.J. added.

After dinner as the two cleaned their plates and Maggie loaded the dishwasher, a refreshingly cool breeze blew in through the windows, causing the laced curtains to swing haphazardly from the metal rods, which held them above the windows.

Maggie looked outside with a discerning eye. "Maybe we'll get a little rain after all," she said. "It's been almost two months since we've had a good soaker."

"It does seem rather dusty," C.J. said.

"Speaking of Dusty, have you met him?" Maggie asked. He might be about your age – maybe a little younger."

"Younger," C.J. said definitively. "After Otto, he's was the next person I met."

"You met Otto already?"

"Uh huh. And Duke. He asked about you, by the way," C.J. said then quickly added, "Otto that is."

"He's a good man. He has always been so good to Henry and me. And I love that Duke. Isn't he a little sweetie?" Maggie said.

"I wouldn't say 'little,'" C.J. interjected, handing Maggie the last dirty plate to be placed in the dishwasher.

Laughing, Maggie said, "You've got a good point there. He's a big 'en, you're right about that!" She closed the dishwasher door and pushed the "start" button. The appliance began to hum.

After several moments of quiet contemplation, Maggie said, "You know, I think I'll start on one of those books right away." "You're welcome to join me on the porch... but you don't have to," Maggie added.

"I think I'll start one, too," C.J. said. "Meet you out there."

For C.J., the screened porch offered an outdoor experience without the inconvenience of the outdoors. The fresh early evening breeze wafted across her face as she rocked gently in one of the two wooden rockers that sat adjacent to a wicker table, and a wicker love seat. In the distance, periodic white-purple flashes illuminated portions of the ink night.

"Most likely heat lightening," Maggie said, averting her eyes from her book momentarily.

Flying insects, attempting to draw near the reading lamps, were held at bay thanks to the metal screens that enclosed the wood-framed porch. The silence of the country night seemed surreal to C.J. Its pervasiveness was interrupted only occasionally by the barking of a distant dog, or the hooting echo of a nocturnal owl. It was so different from the noise and activity of the world from which she came. C.J. was both fascinated by the silence, and simultaneously frightened by it. Unfortunately, the combination of the silence and desolation had C.J. considering the perfect Hollywood horror film scenario: Two women, all alone, in the middle of nowhere – hunted and haunted by a deranged serial killer. The very thought of such a scene made C.J.'s heart race. She looked up from her book to see Maggie already engrossed in her own.

"Why don't you have a dog?" C.J. asked abruptly. Rather than actually reading her book, C.J. had been thinking how much safer she would feel if she had one like Duke – nearby right now.

"Huh?" Maggie said, returning from the fantasy world of her book. "Oh. Ah, I suppose mostly because Henry and I traveled all of the time," she said, using the break to take a sip of some red wine she had poured for herself about a half-hour before. "We figured it just wouldn't be fair to have a dog you weren't around to care for."

"You'll be around now, won't you?" C.J. asked.

Maggie hadn't planned on telling anyone about how her financial situation might force her to sell her home and property, so she dodged the question by asking one. "I suppose. Why the interest in dogs?"

"I just thought with you being all alone, and since you and Duke are such friends..."

"Otto say that?"

"Yes. Actually, he said something like 'I haven't seen Duke take to anyone like you – other than Maggie."

"So how did Duke take to you?" Maggie asked with increasing interest.

"I think he liked me. He came right over and sat on my foot. Then he looked up at me and seemed to..." C.J. couldn't bring herself to say what she wanted to say.

"Seemed to...?" Maggie asked.

"Well. This is a little weird, but he seemed to understand exactly what I was saying and I seemed to know..." C.J. couldn't finish the patently absurd statement.

"Seemed to know what he was thinking," Maggie said, finishing C.J.'s sentence.

Without thinking how strange this exchange had been C.J. simply answered honestly. "Yes," she said slowly. Then added, "But that's crazy."

"Maybe," Maggie said. She looked back at her book for several moments, "But maybe not." C.J. couldn't tell if Maggie was serious or not.

"Are you saying that dogs can communicate – with US?"

Maggie smiled. "They do it all the time, sweetheart." She took another sip of wine and set her book on the wicker coffee table. "Did one ever wag its tail at you, put its ears back and come over to you?" Maggie asked.

"Sure."

"And you knew from those signals that the dog wanted to be petted right?

C.J. nodded.

"Well, you did what it wanted you to do, didn't you?

C.J. smiled.

"I'd say that's being a pretty good communicator, don't you?" Maggie asked.

"That's not the kind of communication I'm talking about, though," C.J. said.

"Nor am I necessarily," Maggie said. "I'm simply saying that a dog's ability to communicate is only as good as the human with whom they're trying to communicate."

"Meaning?" C.J. asked.

"Meaning, I think some people are better listeners than others," Maggie said assuredly. "Don't you agree?"

"Well, I guess," C.J. said. Maggie's message was beginning to sink in. "I agree that some people are more sensitive than others – to certain things. But the notion that a dog can talk – ah communicate – is a little too extreme for me."

"Why do you say that?"

"Because it's impossible," C.J. said.

"Is it impossible for you to smell the scent of, say a raccoon that walked through the woods a few hours ago, or the scent of a quail that has landed in a field?" Maggie asked.

"Yes. But," she quickly added realizing that Maggie was going to make a point about a dog's unique ability to find scents, "I don't have the sensitive nose that dogs have."

"Right. Not even all dogs can do what I just described," Maggie said. "Some breeds are endowed with certain traits that give them the ability to do what seems impossible for us. Among those breeds some of those dogs are even better – or more 'sensitive' – than others."

C.J. let the words sink in.

"So you believe dogs can talk to people?"

"I believe that some dogs can talk to some people," Maggie said.

C.J. wanted badly to ask if Maggie thought she was one of those people. However, posing the question just seemed too bizarre. But then again, she thought, this whole conversation had been a bit bizarre.

"Aunt Maggie?" C.J. asked sincerely – realizing it was the first time she had addressed her 'Aunt Maggie' – "Are you one of those people?"

——-

Maggie was already dressed and busy re-cleaning her already clean house when C.J. ambled out of her room, yawning.

"Morning C.J.," she said as she placed one of the several small marble art statues back down on the table she had just dusted.

"That's cool," C.J. said. "What is it?"

"Oh, it's just one of the many souvenirs that Henry and I picked up in our travels," Maggie said. She looked at it fondly, obviously remembering Henry buying it for her in the open air market near Johannesburg.

"Does it mean anything?"

Maggie's expression suggested she didn't understand the question, so C.J. modified her question. "Does it have any cultural significance?" she asked in a way that sounded just like her two anthropological speaking parents.

"I don't know, to be honest with you," Maggie said. "I just like it."

"Me, too," C.J. said, studying the smooth soap stone sculpture. It had a soothing, feminine gracefulness about it. C.J. wondered if the artisan was a man or a woman.

"Breakfast?" Maggie asked, breaking the temporary spell the statuette had on C.J.

"Oh, I'll just eat some cereal. Thanks. I can get it." C.J. replied, turning her attention to walking to the kitchen.

C.J. ate in silence. For a lack of other reading material, C.J. read the back of the cereal box three or four times before scooping the last floating corn flake from the pool of milk.

Maggie walked into the kitchen about the time C.J. was walking her cereal bowl to the sink.

"So what do you have planned today, C.J.?" Maggie asked

"Nothing, really," C.J. replied.

"I'm sorry I don't have a computer," Maggie said.

"That's, okay," C.J. said, wishing her aunt had an Internet connection. At least that way she could Facebook or e-mail some of her friends back in St. Louis.

"Later this week I'll drive us to the library in Murphysboro and you can e-mail your friends from there," Maggie said, as though she had read C.J.'s mind.

"That'll be great," C.J. said. "Could I check out a book or two?" C.J. asked.

"Of course. We'll check them out on my card. Any particular subject you're interested in?" Maggie asked.

"I was thinking I might do a little research on dogs," C.J. answered.

"Speaking of dogs, I almost forgot," Maggie said. "After you get dressed, would you mind riding your bike down to Otto's and getting us some bread? For the life of me, I don't know what's happened to my mind. We were just at the store yesterday, and I'll be darned if I didn't forget to pick up a loaf."

"No problem," C.J. said. Then she remembered the envelope her parents had left for her to give to Maggie after their departure. It had something to do with groceries, and the bread request apparently was enough to jog C.J.'s memory. "I forgot to give you something," she said abruptly vacating the kitchen. C.J. returned a moment later with the envelope. "Mom and dad asked me to give you this after they left."

Maggie looked at the envelope for a moment and then opened it. Inside was a note folded around a check made out to "Margaret Davidek" for the sum of $4,000. Maggie unfolded the note and read it.

Dear Aunt Maggie, Sam and I knew you'd make a big fuss about not taking any money, so we decided to have C.J. give it to you after we left – pretty clever of us, huh? This is for C.J.'s share of the groceries and for a little spending money for the two of you. Thank you so much for taking care of C.J. while we're away. I hope the two of you have a wonderful, fun-filled summer together. Love, Sam and Sara.

Under normal circumstances, Maggie would have torn the check up into tiny pieces without giving it a second thought. Since last Saturday, Maggie realized she was no longer living under "normal circumstances." Instead, she put the check back into the envelope and placed it on top of the refrigerator.

"I'll just give this back to them when they return," Maggie said, sounding surer than she actually was.

"Mom and dad made me promise that I would make sure you cashed that check," C.J. said.

"Oh they did, did they?" Maggie asked with a sly grin.

"Yes, ma'am, they did," C.J. said.

"Well you've presented me with the check. There'll be plenty of time to cash it later. There's no need to talk about this anymore," Maggie said decisively. She hoped the few thousand dollars she had in her personal savings account would last through the summer. That way, at least, she wouldn't have to cash the Brown's check.

"Here's some money for the bread," Maggie said, placing three, one dollar bills in C.J.'s hand. "Get yourself a soda if you have enough left over."

C.J. looked at the money that had been forced into her hands.

"Okay. I'll head down to Otto's in a few minutes," she said.

"Just keep an eye out for those idiot drivers, sweetheart," Maggie said.

"I will, Aunt Maggie," C.J. said. "I will."

"Oh. And please tell Otto and Duke I said, 'hello,' and that I'll stop by and see them both soon."

Chapter Thirteen

For Dusty, fishing was pure joy. As a plus, MeMaw didn't mind when he took off on an all-day fishing expedition. As long as he brought home a few bluegill, catfish, or crappie, MeMaw didn't ask many questions about his quest. His friend Otto always appreciated receiving a stringer of fresh fish on those occasions when Dusty had been an especially lucky angler. He liked the thought that a periodic delivery of fish seemed a fair exchange for the extra night crawlers that Otto always provided free-of-charge when Dusty was short on cash. Dusty was always short on cash.

He had fished so often during the summer that he was intimately familiar with all of the productive holes along Simmons Creek. More importantly, he enjoyed the unfettered freedom that fishing offered. MeMaw, as much as he loved her, had a way of cramping Dusty's free-spirited style – he liked being his own boss whenever he could. Between chopping wood, feeding the animals, helping with the cooking, and his schoolwork, Dusty didn't find much time to be his own boss. Summer offered a reprieve from the schoolwork, but he still had his domestic responsibilities. Still, he had more time to fish, and he took advantage of every opportunity the summer months afforded.

Despite her obvious age, MeMaw was a strong and healthy woman. As the years went by, Dusty realized he had been required to take on more and more responsibilities around the farm. By MeMaw's design, or otherwise, he didn't have time to get into the kinds of mischief that other kids seemed to find themselves in. Even if he had the time, Dusty didn't think himself foolish enough to try to find that mischief. The prospect of dealing with an angry MeMaw was not a pleasant one.

MeMaw taught him to fish about the same time she had taught him to swim, which was about the same time she taught him how to look for the most likely places where poisonous copperhead snakes would likely be hiding in the woods or around the outbuildings. As best Dusty could remember, he learned all three of those important skills before he learned to walk. Two of those skills could save your life. The one that wasn't potentially life-saving – fishing – was, according to his teacher, essential for the health of the soul.

Outside of academics, MeMaw taught him just about everything he knew. At 11, Dusty was more self-reliant than most adults. What he didn't know, is that the knowledge and self-respect MeMaw had instilled in him was all part of her grand plan.

MeMaw had seen with her own eyes, what can happen to children with too much idle time on their hands. Her own daughter, Dusty's mom, had left Ricksville 12 years ago to pursue what she told her mom would be a "better life" in Kansas City. That better life, it turned out, manifested itself as drug addiction, alcohol addiction, and physical and emotional abuse at the hands of Dusty's father – who had left his mother several months before Dusty's birth. Dusty, MeMaw had always said to no one but herself, was the one good thing that came from his mom's bad choices. She had realized all too late that she had made the mistake of demanding too little from her daughter. She would not make that mistake again with her grandson.

A few months after Dusty was born, his mom called asking for money to "help with the baby." MeMaw sent her $250. A week later, she called again. But this time it was from the county jail.

MeMaw wasted no time in driving her 1982 Chevrolet pickup more than 300 miles to convince her daughter to let her have the baby "just for awhile." "When you're back on your feet," MeMaw had said, "I'll bring the baby back to you. All you have to do is call." But the call never came. MeMaw had not seen nor heard from her daughter since the day she had first held Dusty in her arms. Part of MeMaw wanted desperately to know what had become of her daughter. The other part of MeMaw did not. She certainly didn't want Dusty to be back with a mother who was unable or unwilling to care and provide for him. In the country, she had assumed, there would be fewer detractions that might lead a boy into mischief. Here, Dusty could learn responsibility, respect and self-reliance, MeMaw had concluded. So far, her plan was working.

Despite his independent lifestyle and remote fishing forays, Dusty had had no major brushes with real danger. He had come upon dozens of copperheads and even a few timber rattlers during his time in the woods, but his keen senses – and MeMaw's thorough instructions – had always combined to keep him out of harm's way.

Fishing had a way of providing a pleasant diversion from anything that bothered him. That's why Dusty had decided to go on this particular morning. As he traversed the slope leading down to the creek, Dusty kept seeing a picture of the ghost-white truck hurdling toward him and C.J. Like a bad dream, Dusty kept replaying the scene over and over in his mind. He still was unable to determine how C.J. escaped yesterday's incident without so much as a scratch. About half-way through his journey, Dusty concluded that C.J. was either lucky or blessed with a guardian angel.

As he always did when he walked through the bushes –
especially near the water – Dusty looked and listened for any
movement that might signal the presence of a snake. As he neared
the water, he'd have to add cottonmouths to the list of venomous
ones that could strike without warning. He had been told by
MeMaw and others who had grown up in the area, that one 15-
year-old boy had been wading about knee-deep in a shallow pool
on Simmons Creek years ago, when he bumped into what he
thought was an innocent mass of floating leaves. But it wasn't a
mass of leaves. It was a cottonmouth nest, teaming with dozens –
if not hundreds – of tiny cottonmouth snakes. The boy was found
dead the next day, floating face down in the water. The sheriff had
said he was bitten at least one hundred times and had been injected
with enough venom to kill 50 or 60 men. He was dead, they said,
in a matter of seconds.

There were lots of stories that circulated throughout the hills of
Arkansas about critters that killed their unsuspecting or careless
victims. Dusty suspected that some stories were folklore; others
exaggerations; and still others outright fabrications. But some,
whether completely grounded in fact or not, could make your skin
crawl. They could also leave such an impression, that even careless
boys in constant pursuit of adventure, would think twice before
splashing into a pool of standing water in these parts. The story of
the cottonmouth nest was one such story.

Dusty walked along the sandy creek bank – made wider by the
unusually dry weather – until he found an outcropping of rocks
that marked his favorite bluegill fishing spot. Other parts of the
creek were better for catfish, but Dusty had learned that this was
the place to catch the biggest, and best bluegill – assuming the fish
would cooperate.

He liked this spot, too, because of the cool, spring-fed brook
that emptied into the creek at this point. Unlike the main channel
water of Simmons Creek, which was generally saturated with
suspended soil sediment from farmland erosion upstream, this little

brook was crystal clear and seemed to always flow – regardless of the time of year or how little it had rained. Dusty had once followed the little brook to its source a couple of miles to the north. It's how he came to find what he now called Spring Cave. To reach this gem-rich, subterranean cave, Dusty had to climb over a barbed-wire fence about halfway up a steep slope. When he finally snaked his way into the cave, it was as though he had found the treasure of a lifetime. He had been so excited by the few stones he had found during his brief foray that he promised himself that he'd go back and explore as much as he could.

The spring cave's rocky face was largely obscured by dense undergrowth. At the source where the water spewed out into the light, the opening appeared to be a large, gaping mouth, about five feet wide. The crystal clear water flowed from the right side of the mouth and tumbled down a chin-like bunting of black rock four or five feet high.

Dusty climbed upon that rock-chin outcropping and squatted to peer into the mouth's opening. He could hear the hollow echoing of water as it cascaded somewhere deep within the cavern. The light penetrated very little into the cave, and he could see only a few feet into the chasm so he duck-walked and slithered a few yards into the darkness. He wanted to go further, but good judgment apparently got the best of him, and he opted to retrace his steps back to the cave's entrance. It was there, during his egress, that he found the handful of translucent stones he had been unable to tumble successfully.

When he returned home, fishless, MeMaw had admonished Dusty "not to go where you went today." It was another case of MeMaw's most inconvenient gift.

"You don't trespass on other people's property. Do you understand," she had said after extracting a confession from her grandson. "We've got our own land, and you can fish and hunt on it until the cows come home. But don't you go traipsing around on other people's places unless they invite you there." To this day, he had complied with MeMaw's stern prohibition.

Dusty sat down on the largest of the five smooth rocks that jutted out into the water. The grouping of rounded gray rocks looked to Dusty like the knuckles of a giant stone fist. He often wondered, as he sat, sun-drenched on those rocks, if he were actually sitting on the hand of God.

After climbing upon the fist, he sat his tackle box and worm cup – the one with some of the free night crawlers donated to him by Otto – on the face of the rock. He laid his four-foot fishing pole across his lap. After threading a portion of a large worm on a hook, Dusty flung the line, the hook, and the red-and-white bobber into a dark pool of gently swirling water. The bait and bobber splashed and he watched the bobber slowly drift and swirl in the water below.

After a few minutes of waiting in vain for the bait to be taken, Dusty knew he'd have to slide the bobber up or down the line. Bluegill congregate at different depths at different times of the year, MeMaw had taught him. "If you're fishin' where they ain't," MeMaw had professed like a great angler-prophet, "then you ain't gonna catch 'em."

If, however, he could find the right depth, Dusty knew he'd be able to catch enough fish for MeMaw and himself, and have a few extra for Otto.

———

Christine Larson had discovered what appeared to be a perennial stream source on one of the Farm Service Agency's farmland aerial maps a few days ago. She had carefully studied the on-line image from the agency's web site. The stream was unquestionably spring-fed, and could very well be the source water GeoTherm had been tasked to find for its most important client. If she could test the water, and get a precise measurement of what she believed would be the stream's more than adequate flow, she'd be in a great position to "deliver the goods" to her client. The final part of the puzzle would be actually acquiring that source for the client. That, Christine suspected, could be done without much effort – by making the owner very rich with her sales proposal.

Everything looked good on the map, but only a visit to the site – and a sampling of the water, would confirm if the water quality and mineral parameters would be met. If they were – as Christine predicted – then GeoTherm could acquire the prize for their client and complete the transaction. By doing so Christine would be the winning quarterback in the Super Bowl of geohydrology. More importantly, she would have no peer within the company. In fact, Christine would have no peer within her field. By landing this deal, she would be responsible for GeoTherm's success with their biggest and wealthiest client.

The president of GeoTherm was one of those "team" coaches, insisting that the GeoTherm team would win "as a team" or "lose as a team." But, she had loathed the prospect of having to involve a team of half-wits in her discovery. That's the principal reason she had undertaken most of the research on her own time. It was also a way of keeping her discoveries beyond the intrusive eyes of her so-called colleagues. Her so-called "team" of male colleagues would only serve to dilute her individual accomplishments. Christine vowed that she, and she alone, would bring the prize catch home.

The day before, Christine had driven like a mad woman from her office to a spot where she determined she could pull off and park the GeoTherm truck without much notice. She had drawn a line from the spot to the spring, and had concluded it would take her about an hour to reach by foot. She had been looking at the map when she nearly spun out of control around a corner. Why these country bumpkins had not paved their dangerous roads she wondered, was a mystery to her. Worse, the local children apparently didn't have the sense to stay the heck out of the roadway. She nearly hit one of them, but hearing no thud or feeling no impact, knew she had not. Maybe the close encounter with her truck would serve as an instructive lesson to those little bumpkins, Christine thought.

After about 15 minutes of searching, she found the tree covered access road that ran perpendicular to the main gravel road she was on. The access road, which was only wide enough for a single vehicle, led straight to a barbed-wire access gate. Christine looked at the gate and decided to turn the truck's ignition off. When she did, silence closed in around her. She sat for a moment, contemplating her options.

Under different circumstances, protocol would require her to gain consent of the property owner first, but anything that slowed process could endanger Christine from winning the "triple crown" (finding the water source, confirming the water quality, and acquiring the water source). She would have to break a few of the company's rules to be successful. But so what, she thought. Without risk, there would be no reward.

She turned the ignition switch on, and with that, Christine Larson decided she would drive back to this location tomorrow before she headed into work. She would pull her truck far enough off the roadway and into the brush, so it could not be easily discovered. Then she would traverse the fence, and get her samples. No one on the "team" would have to know. And no one on the team would ever know – until it was "money in the bank."

*

The eastern sky had just begun shedding its evening darkness when Christine took the last full gulp of tepid coffee from the plastic-lined, stainless steel cup that also served as the Thermos bottle's lid. The metal cylinder was dented and tarnished, but it was still a heck of a good coffee vessel, she thought. Christine had purchased it with her first paycheck from her first job right out of graduate school. Having her own supply of coffee close at hand meant she wouldn't have to spend any billable time running to the break room to fetch her caffeine. More importantly, having her own coffee supply meant she wouldn't have to spend any time in the break room at all, running into people she didn't like – which was just about everyone who didn't acknowledge her academic and professional credentials on a regular basis.

She twisted the lid back on, and a trickle of the brown liquid rolled down the side of the Thermos before she tossed it, unceremoniously, onto the passenger seat of the truck. Christine pulled the company's Global Positioning Unit from the left breast pocket of her field jacket and saw the positional indicator pointing in the direction of her pre-programmed trek. Before she left her apartment this morning, Christine had entered the approximate latitude and longitude settings into the GPS unit from a detailed county map she had taken the liberty to borrow from GeoTherm's plot and map case.

According to that unit, the spring source was less than a kilometer away – 983 meters to be precise. That was, however, 983 meters "as the crow flies," and Christine would not be traveling by air. If she was lucky, she figured her ingress would take her about an hour to complete, the egress, slightly less since, by then the sun would be up and she would have the benefit of walking back to her truck in full daylight. If all went well, she would be back at the truck, with the water samples in hand before most of the county's residents had had breakfast. She knew she would have no time to waste in order to find the spring, take the samples, and get to work on time. As a back-up plan, Christine had packed her cell phone, and would use it to phone in some lame excuse for being late if the situation warranted.

She picked up the foot-long, black flashlight that would serve to light her way until the sun rose above the horizon. With a quick glance at the sky, Christine could see that dawn was approaching. It would be sometime, however, before the sun's light would penetrate the thick canopy of oak, hickory and walnut trees around her so the flashlight she had brought along would be essential for her mission.

This morning she parked the truck in the location she had spotted yesterday afternoon – sufficiently off the road, concealed by the thick brush. She folded her map and tucked it into one of the many pockets in her field jacket. She snagged the well-worn leather strap of her canteen, and slung it over her shoulder. Finally, she patted her field jacket pockets to ensure that the six plastic bottles she had tucked in there before she left her apartment, were still in their proper place. With one more pat, she confirmed they were.

She slid off the vinyl seat and felt her boots hit the ground. Christine quickly closed the door to douse the cabin's dome light. With only the single beam from her flashlight to guide her, Christine – with branches and twigs and leaves crunching under the weight of each step – began her journey toward what she hoped would be the hydro-geologic equivalent of the Mother Lode.

Chapter Fourteen

The sun had been up about an hour when the red-and-white bobber darted on the surface of the water and then disappeared. Awakening from his lethargy, Dusty bolted upright. With a practiced twitch of the wrist, he set the hook then lifted his first catch of the day from the creek and onto his rocky perch. When he did, the big bluegill flailed about, fluttering from the end of the monofilament line, its lip pierced with a barbed hook that still sported a portion of the unconsumed night crawler. The deep blue scales along the side of the fish's body complemented the bluegill's mustard yellow belly. It was a beautiful fish, Dusty thought. But it was an even better tasting fish.

Dusty clamped the fish with his left hand. With well-practice precision, he expertly twisted the hook from the fish's mouth. He smiled. This one was a keeper, he knew. It was twice the size of his hand and weighed, he guessed, nearly a pound. If he could catch another three or four like this one, he'd have all he needed for dinner with MeMaw this evening. She'd be in a good mood when he brought a few more like these home. Add a few more on top of that, he thought, and he'd have enough to share with Otto, too. It was still early, he realized, but it was shaping up to be a good day.

Dusty reached into his tackle box and found a yellow, nylon rope stringer. He pushed the metal point through the fish's gill and it came out through its gaping mouth. He then threaded the stringer point through the metal O-ring and he walked his catch down to the edge of the stream and plunged the point into the mud alongside the stream. With the excess rope from the stringer, he then placed his catch into the water near where the water from the cool brook flowed. Dusty knew the cool water from the brook would help keep any fish he caught alive and well and fresh for a very long time. The strong bluegill tried to swim off into deeper waters, but could go only as far as the rope would allow it to venture.

He had re-threaded the remaining section of night crawler onto the hook when a motion in the bushes caught his attention. Instinctively, Dusty crouched down to avoid detection. He laid his rod and reel carefully on the rock and stayed motionless for several moments. It might be a big white-tail buck, Dusty thought. The bucks tended to be more noisy and less timid than their female counterparts. It wasn't often he'd been able to see a big stag with an impressive rack moving through the brush. The thought of viewing one this morning was exciting and Dusty felt his heart quicken its pace.

After watching the motion in the underbrush for a few minutes, Dusty realized the movement was unlike anything he had seen associated with a wild animal. This realization caused him to be even more cautious and vigilant than he normally would have been. Still crouched, Dusty raised his head slowly to try to glimpse a view of the visitor – whatever it was. Finally he heard the heavy breathing, then grunts of exertion, then awkward footsteps. From his position, he could still not see the visitor, but now he knew for sure that it was not a buck – unless that buck was convulsing and dying.

The rustling continued and then abated when the visitor reached the outer bank of Simmons's Creek. His first glimpse of the visitor came as it made its way up the pathway in the direction of the road. Dusty stayed near the bank, keeping a low profile even though the visitor was moving hastily away from him. As best he could tell from his limited view, it was a woman. The shoulder-length, straight hair was his first clue, but the most pronounced feature of the visitor was a wide, ample backside, jostling to and fro as she hiked up the slight incline of the trail.

Suddenly, the woman stumbled and fell, apparently on one of the many rocks that jutted up from the pathway. Dusty fought the urge to laugh. He knew from experience that this was the most treacherous part of the pathway, especially for someone who was unaware of the semi-concealed obstacles. Even the sure-footed Dusty had taken a fall along the trail on two different occasions. When the woman righted herself from the fall, Dusty noticed her hands were free. It seemed curious to Dusty that she was not carrying a fishing pole or a shotgun.

He was perplexed as to why any woman – especially one that wasn't hunting or fishing – would be out here alone so early in the morning. It was a mystery, indeed, but it was not enough of a mystery to preempt Dusty from trying to catch a few more fish like the one he had just landed. Presently, he got back to business and threaded the remaining bit of worm back onto the hook. Then he flung the line, the hook and red-and-white bobber back in the deep pool and went about the business of waiting for his next fish to bite.

*

By the time the sun was a quarter of the way into the bright summer sky, Dusty had caught 14 fish, but kept only seven. He had landed five really nice ones, and two more that he deemed large enough to keep. The others he tossed back into the creek – giving them a chance to live and grow for another day. The seven "keepers" that were on his stringer represented a very productive day.

Dusty glanced at the sun, and guessed it to be about 10 o'clock. The morning had gone quickly. Time, he thought to himself, certainly didn't go this fast when he was sitting at his desk in school.

The frenzied activity that kept him so busy earlier, slowed down to a crawl. What few bites he was getting now, were from the little pesky fish that were too small to eat, but that were plenty big to eat every one of his worms if he'd let them. This, he concluded, was nature's way of saying it was time to close shop.

With that realization, Dusty packed his fishing gear, and pulled the stringer from the creek. With his stringer of fish in one hand, and his fishing pole and worm container in the other, Dusty began walking home. His trek took him along the very pathway that the unknown visitor had taken just a few hours before. As he reached the incline of the upper stream bank, Dusty looked down to avoid tripping on the jetted rocks that poked from the ground. The rocks had always looked to Dusty like a crooked set of teeth that protruded from the gums of the earth.

As he carefully navigated his way through the rocky course, he noticed something out of the ordinary lying under the green, umbrella-like canopy of a may apple plant, just off the path. At first he thought it was just another empty beer can that some careless fisherman had tossed aside walking to or from his favorite spot along the creek. But as he looked more carefully, Dusty could see that this was no empty beer can. It was a small translucent plastic bottle, not much bigger than one of the prescription bottles his grandmother had on her kitchen table.

After he picked the bottle up and examined it carefully, he wondered if the container was somehow connected to the visitor he had seen earlier that morning. The bottle could not have been there for very long, for with the exception of a little smudge of dirt on a white label affixed to it, the bottle had no outward appearances of weathering. It must have been dropped by the woman visitor this morning, because it was near this very spot that he had seen her trip and fall, Dusty thought.

He held it up to the bright sky and peered through the clear liquid within it. The colorless fluid looked to Dusty like plain old water. But the bottle wasn't big enough to be much of a vessel for drinking. He rotated it and noticed a set of hand-printed numbers on the label. He wondered if the numbers held any significance, but the mystery wasn't compelling enough to let seven, beautiful bluegill, spoil in the increasing (or rising) heat of the day. He could always examine the bottle more carefully later, so Dusty slid it in his front shirt pocket and continued homeward.

He smiled. The day had been full of surprises. And now he was about to surprise MeMaw, and later Otto, by bringing home dinner.

Chapter Fifteen

If she hadn't stumbled on those blasted rocks, Christine might have been able to head straight to work. But when she fell, she had ground dirt stains into her khaki pants, so she'd have to implement her plan to call into the office with an excuse for being late. This time, she'd blame it on some stomach problems. Christine had announced to her office mates that she was suffering from ulcers, so having a stomach-related problem would be consistent with her well-known medical background. Christine would tell the office receptionist – in a voice that was wrought with discomfort and exhaustion – that she would try to be in just as soon as she could. The all-too perky receptionist would then tell her boss about Christine's shaky physical status. The 20-something receptionist with the perfect little size-one body and sprightly personality, would likely add her own opinion that Christine probably should stay home. Christine would insist on coming into work later. Her insistence on coming into work despite her malady would be one more indication of her dedication.

After she made the call to the receptionist at GeoTherm, Christine headed straight for her apartment. The fall had put a slight dent in her otherwise perfect plan, but given the sweat she had worked up hiking to and from the water source, she was well advised to take a shower and change her clothes anyway. Having not physically exerted herself for years, she had forgotten how quickly the combination of Arkansas humidity, sun and exercise could make one look and feel as though they had just been baptized – in a river.

With her Audi's air conditioning on full blast, Christine continued to plot out her next steps in her calculating mind. She would have to be careful, she reminded herself. She'd have to keep the details of her clandestine mission a secret from her co-workers at whatever the cost.

Christine had already decided that she would label the water samples she had collected in such a way so the invoice from the lab would appear as though the mineral analysis was for one of her half-dozen food processing clients. Vegetable processing facilities had water analysis work done routinely, so the cost for the analysis wouldn't set off any alarm bells when another line item appeared on the lab's monthly billing statement.

Plus, by avoiding a connection with the real client, Christine wouldn't run the risk of someone from "the team" gaining access to what she considered to be her proprietary information.

For the sake of the team, Christine would continue to run her groundwater models as a way of stalling until she had the prize in her hand. Then she would deliver it to the president of GeoTherm in person. The team wouldn't know, until it was too late, that Christine had not only held all of the cards, she had also stacked the deck. And since she would be the only person with complete, comprehensive knowledge of the source water, Frank Rahe would have no choice but to let her deliver it to Hugh Gunther. What neither Mr. Rahe nor Mr. Gunther could anticipate knowing is that she would have the inside track on acquiring that source water, too. Christine Larson will be a one-person solution for Cornerstone. In the end, she concluded, Cornerstone would be foolish to let Christine get away without making her a permanent and significant employment offer. And that offer, she knew, would be her first step on her journey to corporate success and professional vindication.

After she closed and locked her apartment door, Christine slid her field vest off her shoulders and slung it over the back of one of her kitchen chairs. She fished in the two front waist pockets to retrieve the six plastic bottles that held the spring water samples she had taken at the spring source and at several points along the creek. The left pocket yielded three of the sample bottles, but the right pocket only yielded two. It was likely, Christine thought that one of the bottles slipped from her vest and was resting in the seat of her Audi or on the floorboard. It wasn't a big deal, she assured herself, if she never found the bottle. After all, five good samples would be more than adequate to assess the quality of the water and its trace mineral content. Now all she had to do was put the bottles in her briefcase, and make sure she invoiced an unsuspecting client for the lab work. She had already done the hard part – all she had to do was wait for the results from the lab.

RON NICHOLS

Chapter Sixteen

C.J. was looking forward to seeing Otto and Duke again – especially Duke. After her discussion with Aunt Maggie the past evening, C.J. was eager to put some of the odd notions of canine communication to the test. Besides, she had bonded with that old dog and couldn't wait to see him again.

Fortunately, C.J.'s ride to Otto's gas station was completely uneventful, encountering no lunatic drivers on this leg of her excursion.

After circumnavigating her way around the bell hoses, C.J. put the kickstand down on her bicycle and parked in the shade cast by the building, near a humming Coke machine. C.J. walked confidently inside, where once again she was greeted by Duke.

"Hey there, big guy," C.J. said warmly to the immense yellow dog. He was already walking toward her, tail wagging.

"How you been?" she asked as she cradled his big head in her hands. C.J. patted the dog's shoulder then hugged his thick neck.

"That's good to hear," C.J. said without thinking. Then she stood up suddenly, her heart racing. She looked down at the dog with a look of panic.

"What's wrong? Why stop petting? Duke like it."

C.J. turned to run out the door, but the instant she started to go, she stepped immediately into Otto who was walking in from the auto bays.

"Whoa, there, C.J.," Otto said trying to avoid the collision. "Where 'ya off to so fast?"

"I... I... I need to pick up a loaf of bread," she said.

At that moment, Otto and C.J. both turned their attention to something that moved past the window and then bounded through the doorway.

"I brought you some fish, Otto," Dusty announced loudly, holding aloft three good sized bluegills from his stringer. You want me to clean 'em for you?" he asked, his smile beaming.

"Wow. Those are nice ones. That'd be great if you could clean them. You need a knife?" Otto asked.

"Nope. I have one," Dusty said. You have some newspapers for the guts and scales?"

"You can use today's," Otto said snatching the latest edition of "The Bugle" from where it was spread out on the counter. "Not much by way of news in it today anyway," he added.

C.J. simply stood there listening to the strange conversation.

"Oh, hi C.J.," Dusty said, nonchalantly.

"When you're done, come get me out of the shop and I'll get those into the milk cooler," Otto said, pointing to the fish.

"This is great," Otto said enthusiastically to C.J. and Dusty. "Duke and I were just gonna have biscuits and gravy this evening. But now we'll dine like kings."

Dusty had been proud to deliver his gift, but Otto's animated reaction to his offering made Dusty feel like he was walking on air.

Dusty took the newspaper and the fish and headed out the door.

"What's he going to do with those fish," C.J. asked with trepidation.

"He's going to clean them. That's nice of him, don't you think?" Otto asked.

"What do you mean clean them?"

"You know," Otto said – thinking she really did know – "scale them, gut them and cut their heads off. Get them ready to fry up."

"I think I'm going to hurl," C.J. said without thinking.

"Well you can't eat them without cleaning them," Otto said.

"I think I'll pass," C.J. said.

"You're kidding, right?" Otto asked. "I can't think of better eating fish than bluegill. You and Maggie should come by sometime when I fry up a bunch." Then Otto turned and went back to work in the auto bay of his shop.

Only C.J. and Duke remained in the lobby. Dusty's entrance and the resulting conversation had the fortunate effect of temporarily diverting C.J.'s attention from her odd encounter with Duke. Had she been unrestricted in her exit, C.J. would have been halfway home by now, wondering if she should check herself into one of those mental institutions.

But now she stood there in the silence, looking down at the dog – who sat there panting – looking back at her.

"Otto'll give me fish tonight."

"You are not talking," C.J. whispered directly to the dog. "This is crazy,"

"You nice."

C.J. stared at the dog.

Duke came over, sat on C.J.'s foot and leaned up against her. He looked up, still wearing what looked to C.J. like a grin.

"How do you do that?" C.J. whispered again.

"Do what?"

"That!" C.J. said pointing down at him.

"Same as you."

Oh great, C.J. thought, I'm not only going crazy, I'm going crazy with a dog that's my intellectual equal.

"What mean?"

"What?" C.J. whispered again to the dog, then looked around to make certain they were alone.

"What intel-lect-ual?"

C.J. thought for a moment.

"I didn't say intellectual," C.J. said softly.

"Yes."

"Intellectual," C.J. said the word silently to herself.

"That word."

"Wait, I didn't say anything," C.J. thought to herself, purposefully conducting an on-the-spot experiment.

Suddenly Duke turned his head in the direction of the door, his ears perked. "Dusty come. Dusty nice."

C.J. didn't hear or see a thing, but within a few seconds, Dusty came bounding through the door, the fish apparently cleaned and wrapped in some of the newspaper sheets that weren't used to dispose of the unwanted parts of the fish.

"Hey, Otto," he yelled. "The fish are clean," he yelled again in the general direction of the maintenance bays.

Otto reappeared in the walkway, entering the retail section of the store a few moments later. He was wiping grease from his hands with a well-worn rag.

"Thanks, Dusty," Otto said as he took the fish and walked toward the back of the store where he opened an aluminum door, with a polished chrome handle. It was the service door for the milk cooler. Otto emerged a moment later.

"How you doin' on night crawlers?" Otto asked Dusty.

"Good. Still have quite a few from the last time," he said.

"Let me know when you need some more. If you want those big ones, you got to bait 'em with a full hook," Otto said. "Don't be stingy with those worms," Otto directed.

Smiling, Dusty said. "I'm not stingy, just careful not to let those buggers pick me clean."

C.J. listened to Dusty and Otto's conversation like a stranger in a strange land. She understood the words, but not the meaning of them. And she wasn't going to ask. The last time she had, C.J. had learned more about bluegill cleaning than she had ever hoped to know.

"I'd better get home then," Dusty said.

"Me, too," C.J. said.

"What about the bread," Otto asked.

"Oh, I almost forgot," C.J. said. "Yes." She ran and picked up a loaf off the middle metal shelf.

"It's two dollars even," Otto said. "Just set it under the Dr. Pepper bottle there," he said pointing to an empty bottle on the counter near the cash register.

"What about tax?" C.J. asked.

"Included," Otto said, already walking back into the shop. Then he turned and said, "Thanks again for the fish, Dusty. Tell that MeMaw of yours not to be such a stranger."

"I will," Dusty yelled, as he walked out the door.

C.J. followed.

"Bye, C.J."

"Bye," she said. Expecting to see Otto's smiling face, C.J. turned and instead saw the big yellow dog sitting in the middle of the doorway. Panting and smiling as usual.

RON NICHOLS

Chapter Seventeen

Dusty and C.J. were climbing on their bikes when they saw a white truck drive by the gas station. It appeared to be identical to the truck they had encountered a couple of days before.

The vehicle slowed as it passed the gas station. The driver, apparently, considered stopping. This time C.J. and Dusty were both able to clearly see the driver as she surveyed the station.

When she saw the rounded scowling face, framed by a mop of graying hair, C.J. had no doubt that it was the same driver she viewed in that terrifying instant before she and her bike plunged into the ditch.

"That's her," C.J. said.

"That's what I was thinking, too," Dusty said.

"I thought you said you didn't see her before," C.J. said.

"No. That's the woman I saw when I was fishing this morning." Dusty realized he still had the plastic bottle of water in his shirt pocket. "She dropped this," he said holding the bottle by its cap."

"What is it?" C.J. asked.

"I don't know," Dusty said. He handed the bottle to C.J. "You tell me."

"It looks like water," C.J. said, holding the bottle toward the bright sky so she could see the contents.

"I could have told you that," Dusty said. "I think I know what those numbers are, too," he said, placing his finger on the label.

"Yeah, those look like GPS coordinates," C.J. said. "My mom and dad write stuff like this in their field notes all of the time."

"No it's not. Those are latitude and longitude numbers," Dusty said decisively.

"It's the same thing."

"You said GPS something."

"GPS coordinates are latitude and longitude numbers. It's how you can tell exactly where something is," C.J. said.

"I know," Dusty said. "We studied that last year. I wonder where this is," Dusty asked, pointing to the numbers on the label.

"I don't know. But bet I can find out tomorrow when I get on the Internet at the library in Murphysboro," she said. "You have something to write with?" C.J. asked.

"No. But Otto does," Dusty said tilting his head in the direction of the open door of the gas station.

"I'll hold your bike," C.J. said to Dusty. "Go borrow a piece of paper and write these numbers down just as they're listed. It might be sort of fun to find out where this came from."

She handed the bottle back to Dusty. "And whatever you do, don't taste what's in there," she said as an afterthought.

"Do you think I'm stupid?" Dusty said somewhat defensively.

"No," C.J., said apologetically. "You may be a piece of work," she said, "but you're definitely not stupid."

Dusty smiled, and then sprinted – bottle in hand – to transcribe the GPS coordinates onto a piece of paper.

*

C.J. and Maggie had loaded the dishwasher after dinner and then retired to the back porch to read their selected books. The drone of the dishwasher in the kitchen could not be heard over the incessant symphony of cricket and cicada chirping that started every evening at this very time. It was like clockwork. Maggie, as she had done for years, poured up a glass of red wine and sat it on the table. It helped her sleep, she had told C.J. – even though C.J. hadn't asked about her nightly habit. One glass a night, Maggie's doctor had said, would help with her iron levels, too. Iron levels or not, Maggie, enjoyed her one vice – her one daily glass of fermented grapes after dinner.

C.J. tried to get into her book, but she had only managed to get through the first two chapters. The book's characters had not yet developed to a point where C.J. cared about them, and the plot was developing about as fast paint dries. To be fair, C.J. thought, even if she had a compelling read, she could not shake the experience she had had earlier in the day with Duke. As she looked at the words on the pages in front of her, C.J. wondered if she should broach the subject again with Maggie. The whole experience was just too unreal. Maggie apparently believed that dogs could communicate. But there's a heck of a difference between "communicating with" and "have a conversation with" a dog, C.J. thought. The difference was, as Mark Twain had written about a totally unrelated subject, like "the difference between a lightning bug and lightning."

The minutes dragged on. C.J. waited for an appropriate time to begin the conservation. But every time she looked up to see if Maggie was giving her eyes a break, C.J. was disappointed. Maggie had not even taken one sip from her glass of wine. Regrettably, her aunt was clearly engrossed in her book.

"If I tell you something, do you promise not to send me to the loony bin?" C.J. blurted, unable to wait for a polite break in her aunt's reading time.

"What, sweetie?" Maggie asked, looking up. The trance-like grip of concentration had been broken.

"If I tell you something," C.J. repeated, "do you promise not to think I'm crazy?"

"What could you possibly tell me that would make me think you're crazy?" Maggie asked as she reached for her glass of wine.

"I talked with a dog."

Maggie froze briefly, keeping the wine glass from touching her lips. She averted her eyes from C.J. and then took a sip from the tall stemmed glass. A moment passed in silence as Maggie considered her response. She sat the glass down on the table slowly, without uttering a word.

"Well? Do you think I'm crazy?" C.J. asked impatiently.

"When exactly did you talk with this dog?" Maggie asked evenly.

"Today. It was Duke. But now that I think about it, he talked to me before, I just didn't know it."

"I see," Maggie said, in a cool, professional tone.

C.J. had heard that tone in movies – it was a tone used by psychologists who had already concluded that their patients really were crazy.

"I didn't believe it either," C.J. said defensively. "I mean, it's too crazy. I didn't want to believe it." C.J. was running out of energy. She looked for sympathy or for understanding from the woman seated on the wicker love seat across from her. She saw nothing but a distant stare in her aunt's eyes.

"You think I'm crazy don't you?" C.J. said dejectedly.

Several awkward moments passed. C.J. was just about to burst into tears and run to her room, when Maggie finally said, "You're not crazy, C.J. You have 'the gift.'"

Maggie sat her book on the table beside her glass of wine. She smiled at C.J. and said, "Honey, I have it, too."

Chapter Eighteen

C.J. awoke the next morning feeling like she had awakened from a weird dream. She also felt strangely vindicated. She had to remind herself that she had not been dreaming. Without question, it had been the most bizarre conversation she had ever had, but it had been real. As she lay in bed, the tree-filtered light now streaming into her room, she felt a strange peace as she replayed the conversation in her mind.

"With 'the gift,'" her aunt had told her, "came a burden." As Aunt Maggie revealed her experiences with "the gift," she had learned at a very young age, that there were few people who would or could believe in things they did not, nor could not personally experience. Consequently, Maggie had kept her gift secret.

Even Maggie's husband, Henry, did not know about her gift. She had revealed her secret to only one other person since the first time she had tried – and failed – to convince her parents that she had the gift. That person was MeMaw. As it turned out, Maggie didn't reveal her secret as much as MeMaw had extracted it from her.

During their remarkable evening conversation, C.J. described to Maggie, her own encounter with MeMaw, and how she seemed to know about the gift before C.J.

Maggie nodded and smiled. MeMaw, it seemed, had a very special gift of her own.

In the end, Maggie explained that she was able to actually communicate with only a small percentage of dogs throughout her life. Maggie explained that her experience had taught her a dog's size, breed, temperament or age, was directly correlated to its ability to communicate. Maggie had suggested to C.J. that she believed it was more a result of her own limitations, rather than the dog's. Maggie admitted that she had a unique gift, but it too, had its limitations. Still, the insight she had received from the beautiful perceptions of the dogs she could converse with, made Maggie believe that her gift was a marvelous one.

C.J. tossed her bed sheet aside and slipped her feet into a pair of slippers. She hadn't given them much thought until she looked down and saw that the front of each slipper had two brown eyes, and a black, round, fluffy nose. When she looked down at her puppy slippers, C.J. realized with some amusement that she would never be able to look nonchalantly at another dog for the rest of her life.

"I'll need to stop at Otto's for some gas," Maggie said as they neared the gas station. "It'll be good to see Duke again," she said and then added almost as an afterthought, "and Otto, too, of course."

Maggie pulled her Toyota to the right side of the island, just a couple of feet from one of the two rusty pumps. As the tires rolled over the small black hose that stretched across both sides of the island, C.J. heard the now-familiar clank-clank of the bell on the outside of the building. An instant later, Otto came strolling toward the car, wiping his hands of grease with his ever-present grease rag.

Maggie got out of the car.

"Hi, Otto," she said. "How are you?"

Otto was grinning.

"I'm doing good, Maggie. I'd give you a hug..." he said arms spread – showing the preponderance of fresh oil and grease stains on his overalls – "but I don't want to add to your laundry."

Maggie laughed. "I hear you've already met C.J.," she said as C.J. opened the passenger door and stood.

"Sure have," he said. "A very nice young lady you have there. Duke is certainly struck with her, too," Otto added.

"Speaking of Duke," Maggie said, "I'd better go say 'hi' to that fellow."

"I'm sure he'll be glad to see ya," Otto said. "I presume you want her topped off?" Otto asked as the two began walking toward the building.

"That'd be great. Thanks!" Maggie said.

Duke was already standing at the door, his tail swinging wildly. It was the one part of his physique that still moved with rapidity.

"Hi there, Duke," Maggie said with a smile that could not be contained. "It's good to see you, Duke," wrapping her arms around the dog's massive neck.

"I'm fine, Duke," Maggie whispered just loud enough for the dog to hear.

"Worried."

"Don't you worry, big fella, everything's okay," Maggie added.

C.J. felt as though she were eavesdropping on a conversation between two friends. She felt somewhat self-conscious about her inadvertent intrusion.

Duke walked over to C.J.

"She nice. Duke happy."

"I'm glad," C.J. said. "You like my Aunt Maggie, don't you?"

"Aunt?"

"It's family. She's part of my family."

"Nice."

"It sure is, Duke. It sure is." Maggie patted his big head. He looked up smiling. She looked down smiling.

"Otto come."

On cue, Otto came in through the open door. He went to the cash register. "It came to $22, Maggie. You want me to put it on your account?"

"No, Otto. I'll pay cash." Maggie handed him a twenty and two one dollar bills from her billfold.

"Thanks, Maggie," he said as he took the money and placed the bills in the appropriate slots. With a check of his hip, the register drawer slammed shut.

"Maggie," Otto's voice and demeanor softened discernibly, "I'm sure sorry about Henry."

"Thank you, Otto," Maggie said. She had said that phrase so many times in the last month – to so many people who expressed sympathy about Henry's death. Still, it was good to hear and it was good to know that people cared. That always mattered.

"You need anything – anything at all," he said, "you let me know."

C.J. looked down and saw that Duke was lying on his blanket on the concrete floor – his chin on his paws – jowls draped over them. He lifted his eyebrows to expose his big brown eyes.

"Maggie sad."

"Thanks, Otto. I'll..." Maggie paused. Then she looked at C.J. and continued, "We'll be fine."

"You two be careful," Otto said with a more brightened tone. "Heading out to shop at Murphysboro?"

"We might stop and shop a bit," Maggie said, "but our primary objective is the library."

"Have fun," he said.

"See you two later," Maggie said to Otto and Duke right before she slid into the driver's seat.

The car pulled away and Otto headed back to replace a water pump on a fairly new Dodge pickup. Only had 40,000 miles on it, and already it needed a new water pump. "Junk," he thought. "Absolute junk."

Duke moved his head so that it rested on the crumpled blanket under him, and then closed his eyes. It didn't take long for the big dog to drift into slumber. In his dreams he saw Maggie laughing. She was patting him and then threw a fuzzy yellow ball for him to chase. He was running fast and jumping around like a puppy. He was very happy – but more importantly so was Maggie.

It was a good dream.

*

Christine looked at her computer screen with apprehension. She was looking at the "report card" on the water samples she had submitted to the lab. She opened the e-mail attachment from the lab the instant she saw the subject line: "Sample 0411." She scrolled down past all of the disclaimer text and definitions, and stopped her curser on the good stuff. Then systematically, she scrolled down, one line of data at a time – scanning each line as though each contained the answer to the mystery of life itself.

Calcium: Less than 5 parts per million; Magnesium: Less than 8 parts per million; Sulfate: Less than 10 parts per million. Sodium, potassium and phosphorus were below 10 parts per million. All of the trace minerals were well within the water quality perimeters Cornerstone was looking for.

Christine's heart was racing. When she arrowed her cursor down the screen to the nitrate data line, she finally allowed herself to smile. Her hydrogeologic models were right – again. Only a few minor elements were even detected – boron and molybdenum. Those too were so insignificant, that they were simply noted as "trace." Only barium was detected in significant quantities – and this was not an exclusionary element in the water quality parameters defined by Cornerstone.

No matter how you sliced the data, Christine thought confidently to herself, she had a winner! She had found, within the search area parameters, the perfect water source. Now all she needed to do was delay the GeoTherm team for a few more days – and do a little after-hours real estate negotiating. The hard part was over. She knew what she had to do next, and best of all, Christine knew that she would be successful.

*

The library was bigger and much more modern than C.J. had envisioned. Based on the antiquity she had experienced in Ricksville, C.J. had imagined a library about the size and vintage of the schoolhouse in the re-run episodes of "Little House on the Prairie." Instead, the library was something of an architectural gem – combining an earthen stucco frame, with almost seamless panes of green tinted windows. The building, which sat atop a hill in the downtown section of Murphysboro, shone like a giant emerald mounted in a stone setting.

"What time do you want to meet?" C.J. asked Maggie.

"How 'bout 11:30? That way we can beat the crowd when we break for lunch. We can always come back if we're still not finished," Maggie said.

"Sounds great. I'll be in the computer section if you need me," C.J. said as the two walked past the stone granite water fountain that graced the library's front courtyard.

"Going to e-mail your friends?" Maggie asked.

"Probably," C.J. said, "but I also need to do a little research on the Internet."

"I'll be in the fiction section on the second floor," Maggie said. They entered the beautifully decorated lobby. "Let's be sure to check out a couple of chick flick videos before we head home," Maggie said with a sly smile.

She might be 70, but her Aunt Maggie, C.J. had concluded, was a pretty cool woman.

"Meet you back here," Maggie said. With that, C.J. scanned the area to find the computer section of the library.

Internet searches can be very instructional, but they can also be very frustrating, C.J. knew. She was familiar with the major search engines that scanned millions of websites for certain words. You could hit the jackpot right off the bat, or you could spend hours going down one rat hole after the other in a frustrating spiral of futility.

C.J. found an unoccupied computer monitor, sat down, and fished out of her pocket the piece of paper upon which Dusty had transcribed the numbers from the small bottle he had found. She began with the obvious search engines. She used quotation marks to type "how to find GPS coordinates," and then hit the return key. In a few seconds a list of sites filled the screen. Like a professional sleuth, C.J. scrolled down the list, looking for the site description that best fit her query.

After checking out a few empty leads, C.J. found the precise web site she was looking for: It was called terraserver.com.

After just a few short minutes of clicking and scrolling, C.J. landed on the page that held the answer to her specific question. On this particular page, she could input the GPS coordinates that were written on the bottle and then view an aerial photo of the precise location. It was almost too easy.

When she input the numbers, a gray, fuzzy photo appeared on the screen. It could have been any place in the world, as far as C.J. could tell. A window on the left navigation bar of the web page allowed her to "zoom out." She clicked the mouse a few times and the picture broadened. It took her a moment, but she made the connection between what she had seen on the ground, and what that view might look like from the air.

It was her general "neighborhood."

She decided to pay the 25 cents required to print the page. After a "control-P" she hit "return" on the keyboard and the little ink-jet printer sitting next to the computer's tower hummed to life, and in less than a minute spat out the image she had seen on the screen. C.J. clicked the mouse to zoom in on the photo and then hit "Control-P" again. Like before, the printer produced the image. Her work was done. Now she'd have to hope Dusty could make out the map's geographic features well enough to locate the precise location indicated on the bottle.

C.J. sat back in the padded, chair and exhaled deeply. Not bad, she thought, not bad. After reveling for a few moments in her research success, C.J. realized it was time to logon to her e-mail account and send Katie a quick update. It wouldn't take her long to convey what a miserable summer she was having in "Sticksville." She would tell Katie about most of her experiences during her first few days away from St. Louis. After a moment of quiet contemplation, she decided she'd pass on trying to explain to Katie her new-found "gift."

Chapter Nineteen

"Why can't you get us there?" C.J. asked with a tone of frustration. She now had an investment in the outcome of the mystery and was not about to give up so easily. Not after all of her Internet sleuthing.

"MeMaw," Dusty said with a tone of dejection.

"What about, MeMaw?"

"She'd know if I was to go there," Dusty said. "She found out the first time. I know she'll know."

"You've been here before?" C.J. asked pointing to the location on the map.

"Yep. Once. That's where the cave is. You know, where I found the pretty rocks that wouldn't tumble," he added.

"You said your MeMaw won't let you go, but you didn't tell me why."

"It ain't our property."

"Whose is it?"

"I don't know. It ain't ours. MeMaw told me never to trespass on anyone's property."

"You really think she'd know if you and I went there?"

"She'd know all right," Dusty said with absolute certainty. "Ain't nothin' keeping you from going if you want to," he said and then added, "but I'd watch out for snakes – especially copperheads."

C.J. had never been the outdoor type, even though her mother and father had tried to expose her to the fun, adventure, and freedom of outdoor camping. But C.J. was particularly averse to all things reptilian – especially the slithering kind. In C.J.'s mind, the only good snake was a dead snake.

"Snakes?" she asked, with a tone of discomfort.

"If it gets too hot, they'll probably go in the rocks where the cool air comes out of the cave," Dusty said. "Don't get bit. Even the baby snakes can kill you. Best to go in the morning, before it gets too hot."

If she had had any thought of venturing into the back country alone, C.J. put an end to those thoughts right there on the spot.

"What if I find out who owns the property and get their permission," she said hopefully.

"Well..." Dusty hesitated.

"Your MeMaw just said you couldn't trespass, right?" C.J. said. "It's not trespassing if you get someone's permission."

"I guess that'd be okay," Dusty said. He had wanted desperately to go back and explore the cave anyway. Now C.J. had just given him a loophole for doing so. "You'll want to bring a flashlight, if we do get to go," Dusty added.

"For what?"

"It's a cave. It's dark. You can't go very far without one."

"I have no intention of going in the cave. I just want to see why someone would be interested in taking samples there."

"Suit yourself," he said. "But if I get the chance, I'm going to take a look and see if I can find some better rocks further inside."

C.J. didn't argue. She'd have to talk some sense into Dusty when and if, they ever got as far as the cave.

*

"I'm afraid I have some bad news, Mrs. Davidek," Christine said.

"What is it? Is someone hurt?"

"Oh no," she said, "nothing like that, but it could affect your health and the health of your family."

"What do you mean?" Maggie asked.

"We were contracted to do some groundwater testing – by a company that is interested in locating in the area – and it looks as though the water has unusually high levels of nitrates."

"Meaning?"

"Meaning, your groundwater may not be fit for consumption."

"We've been drinking this water for years. It tastes fine."

"Mrs. Davidek, at the risk of prying, did your husband happen to die of cancer?"

"Yes. But you don't think that had anything to do with the water do you?"

"It's impossible to tell. Let's just say there is a strong correlation between the long-term consumption of nitrates, and various forms of lymphoma."

"Oh my Lord," Maggie said. "What about the neighbors? Will they be affected, too?"

"I won't know until the tests are back, but it's quite likely. I don't think I mentioned it, but I'm a hydrogeologist. I study the underground movement of water based on a number of factors."

"But how did the... what did you call it?"

"Nitrates."

"Yes. Nitrates. How did they get in the water?"

"Could be a number of sources – including some natural – but I'd most likely say fertilizers from farming operations over the years. Probably from adjacent parcels of land."

"Can't they just stop applying the fertilizers?"

"Maybe. But even if they did, it takes years, probably decades for nitrates to leach through the geologic strata and make their way into the groundwater. Even if they stopped fertilizing today –

assuming you could get a court order to make them stop – it would take years for the existing subsoil nitrates to leach out. The nitrates we detected could have been from surface applied fertilizers 20 or 30 years ago."

"So what should we do?"

"For one thing, stop drinking the water immediately. Soon, you'll want to have an uncontaminated source of bathing water, too."

"Where can I get that?"

"I guess you'll have to build a storage system and have the water hauled in."

"That could cost thousands of dollars."

"I'm sorry, Mrs. Davidek." Christine stood.

"Thank you for alerting us," Maggie said sincerely.

"Best of luck," Christine said without really meaning it. She ambled to her truck.

In the distance, C.J. had seen the white truck pull from the driveway and head down the road. She rode through the lingering dust to the house.

When she bounded into the living room C.J. saw Maggie sitting on the sofa – the same sofa that her mother and father had been sitting on just a few days before. But this time her great aunt was crying.

C.J.'s sudden appearance startled Maggie. She tried in vain to collect herself, but there was no hiding her swollen eyes and her running nose.

"Aunt Maggie, what's wrong?"

"Oh nothing dear. I'm just missing Henry."

Instinctively, C.J. sat next to her great aunt and put her arm around her in an effort to bring some comfort.

"Are you sure? You've been crying. Who was in the truck?"

"Oh just someone who's been doing some water testing."

"What did she want?"

"To let us know the results of some of the tests," Maggie said. "We're going to start drinking bottled water, dear. Just to be safe."

"What?" C.J. asked with a palpable tone of skepticism. "What's wrong with the water? It tastes okay to me."

"It tastes okay to me, too, dear. But you can't always taste harmful chemicals."

C.J. put her head on her aunt's shoulder and intuitively knew that her gesture was helpful.

"Honey," Maggie said, "I haven't told you everything I probably should have told you about my... ah... situation." While Maggie dabbed the corners of her eyes with the tear-soaked remnants of a wadded tissue, C.J. sat in stunned silence. Her great aunt had seemed so together – so happy – in spite of her recent loss.

C.J. was sitting beside a woman who seemed to be coming apart at the seams. How ironic, C.J. thought, that she had an apparently miraculous gift of communicating with dogs, but her ability to see the obvious in her aunt had been woefully deficient.

"I really did not want you or your parents to know," Maggie began. "But the investments Henry and I had hoped would sustain us in retirement just didn't come through the way we wanted them to."

"What investments, Aunt Maggie?"

"Henry was certain his mining company holdings were as good as gold – the company he had once worked for in South Africa. It seems as though he was wrong. I really didn't know how bad it was until I met with our accountant in Little Rock a couple of weeks ago – that's why I was so late getting back."

C.J. thought she knew what Maggie meant, but she had to seek clarification. "So does that mean you don't have any money to live on?"

"Oh I have a little, honey," Maggie said, "but the only real asset I have now, is this place. And Charlie said I should consider selling it, and putting the money in some mutual fund or something that could generate funds to help me through retirement."

"You can always live with us Aunt Maggie," C.J. said sincerely.

Maggie smiled, though the tears continued to cascade down her wrinkled cheeks.

"Really you can. You'd like it where we live," C.J. continued. "There's lots to see and do, and we could go shopping, and to the library..."

Maggie took C.J.'s hands. "You are such a sweet dear, C.J. You really are," she said. "But I cannot – will not – be a burden on anyone."

"But you would never be a ..."

Maggie cut her off mid-sentence. "No honey, I'll be fine. I've lived a life of independence and I intend to continue doing so. It's just that now with the problems with the water and all... so if I really have to sell, I may get even less for the place than I was hoping."

"You don't really think you'll have to sell this, do you Aunt Maggie?" C.J. asked.

"I don't think I'm going to have much of choice, sweetheart. Sometimes you just have to do what you have to do."

Chapter Twenty

"Brilliant, Christine. Brilliant," Hugh Gunther repeated as he rocked back in his black leather executive chair. "And you think she'll sell?"

"Not only will she sell, Mr. Gunther," Christine said confidently, "she'll sell at whatever we decide to give her for the place." Christine realized with some satisfaction, that Mr. Gunther had not corrected her when she used the pronoun "we," as if Christine was already part of the Cornerstone executive management team.

"This is quite an impressive feat. You're certain no one at GeoTherm knows about your... shall we say 'extracurricular' activities?" Mr. Gunther queried.

"Quite certain," Christine said confidently.

"You've done an extraordinary job for us," Mr. Gunther said. "I like the way you get things done. So, tell me," he continued, "why aren't you running GeoTherm instead of Frank?" From the coy smile on Mr. Gunther's face, Christine could see that it was a rhetorical question, so she just returned the smile.

"Ever consider joining a company that would more fully appreciate your scientific and strategic skills?" Gunther asked directly.

It was precisely what Christine had planned all along. She took great pleasure in realizing that her keen mind and her tenacious will was leading her closer to her ultimate reward.

"I certainly have, Mr. Gunther," Christine said.

"Better get used to calling me, Hugh then," Gunther said. "Members of the executive management team at Conerstone, address each other causally," he said as he reached across he desk to shake Christine's hand. "We'll just need to clean up a few items before we can proceed," he said. "In the interim, I think you know what to do."

"I certainly do, Mr. Gun...," Christine corrected herself, "Hugh." She stood and walked out Mr. Gunther's office door.

*

C.J. had nearly forgotten about the two folded up pieces of paper in her hip pocket. Her idle curiosity about finding the location of samples had been preempted by the far more serious situation of her aunt's financial situation. The two spent the evening, as they had since C.J. first arrived, reading quietly on the porch and letting the sounds of the evening serenade them. As C.J. sat at the breakfast table the next morning, she remembered that she had been on a mission when she had entered the house yesterday afternoon – a mission to find the spot of the apparent water sample. With the news about the apparent problems with her great aunt's drinking water, getting to the bottom of the water sample mystery was taking on greater meaning.

She pulled the papers from her pocket and unfolded them, using her index finger to remove the creases so the papers would lay flat on the table. As she scooped spoonfuls of floating Cheerios and milk into her mouth, C.J. studied the aerial photos before her.

"What do you have there, sweetheart," Maggie asked as she walked casually by en route to re-fill her cup from the coffeepot on the counter.

"An aerial photo of some place near here I think," C.J. said. "Dusty said he knows where it is."

With her back to C.J., Maggie held her cup over the kitchen sink and poured some of the black liquid into her cup. "He probably does," Maggie said, "he stays pretty busy hunting and fishing. Need some coffee?"

"Yes, please. Just a splash," C.J. said.

Maggie walked over to the table and added some coffee to C.J.'s mug.

"Mind if I see that? Maggie asked.

"Not at all," C.J. said and slid the papers in Maggie's direction.

"Is this what you were looking for at the library?" Maggie asked.

"Uh-huh. Dusty found a bottle that had these GPS coordinates written on it. I thought it would be fun to find out where they're from," C.J. said.

Maggie continued to study to papers.

"Do you know where that is?"

"I think so," Maggie said as she slid the papers back in C.J.'s direction.

"Where?"

"Back at the end of our property – back where the old spring is," Maggie said. "Haven't been back to that old spring since Henry took me there after we bought the place."

"Can I go see it?" C.J. asked enthusiastically.

"I don't know, sweetheart. I wouldn't feel very comfortable with you going. There are just too many snakes around here," Maggie said.

C.J. did not relish the thought of running across any snakes, but with Dusty as a guide, she figured she'd be safe.

"If Dusty goes with me, would it be okay?"

"Well, I don't know."

"He knows what to look for. We'll be okay."

Maggie thought for a moment. If, or rather when, she had to sell the place, C.J. wouldn't have another chance to see the one investment that she and Henry had managed to hang onto together.

"I suppose so, but you tell me when you're going, and when you'll be back. Take a snake whopping stick with you in case you run across any."

"What's a snake whopping stick?" C.J. asked.

"Just what it sounds like. A stick that you can whop a snake with – ah, if you see any."

C.J. did not plan on "whopping" any snakes, but a long stick might come in handy if she needed to keep one away from her.

"Thanks, Aunt Maggie. We'll be careful." C.J. reflexively kissed her great aunt on the cheek and walked over to rinse her breakfast dishes before adding them to the dishwasher.

"Remember what I said about being careful," Maggie repeated.

"Oh I will. I promise," C.J. said.

"It's not you I'm worried about," Maggie said with a smile.

C.J. understood what was being left unsaid. "I'll make sure he doesn't get into any mischief," she said as she headed back to her room.

*

"It won't be trespassing," C.J. said. "Aunt Maggie said I could go, if you'd go with me. I don't know anything about finding my way around these back woods and sure don't know anything about looking out for snakes. I've had to keep an eye out for creepy things at the mall, but not the slithering type," C.J. said with a smile.

"I don't know," Dusty said. "I don't think that'll matter to MeMaw."

"But Maggie said it was okay. Would it help if she called her?"

"No. Don't do that," Dusty said emphatically. He turned to walk back toward his rock tumbler. Outside, Cleotis lay in shade alongside the building. He was still tethered to the stake in the ground. He hadn't barked when C.J. rode her bike to Dusty's house this time and when she and Dusty walked by on their way to Dusty's rock tumbler, the dog didn't even lift his head. Cleotis no longer seemed hostile or even interested in her presence. For that, C.J. was grateful.

Dusty looked around cautiously. "Maybe it'd just be better if I went with you and we didn't mention it at all to MeMaw."

"I thought you said she'd know," C.J. said. The two stopped outside the outbuilding's door.

"She'd know if I was lying, but I ain't lying. Maggie said we could go, right? So I guess we should go," Dusty said now with more confidence. In just a few moments, Dusty had weighed the pros and cons and the pros came out on top. "We'll need to bring a flashlight and a couple of buckets," he said. "We'll have to go early before the snakes get too hot and make their way toward the cave."

"I'm not going in," C.J. said. "And neither are you. I just want to find the place and see the spring."

"That's the whole point," Dusty said as he opened the door and walked out. When the door closed, C.J. found herself standing alone inside with just the humming of the tumbler motor and slow grinding of the rocks to keep her company. She thought she heard a chuckle and looked over to see Cleotis panting – seemingly with a smile upon his face.

C.J. opened the door and followed Dusty out into the daylight. "Okay. Bring your buckets. I don't care," she said. C.J. didn't see any need in arguing now. She concluded that she would put her foot down and insist on Dusty obeying her orders not to enter the cave AFTER he had delivered her to her destination.

"Let's go about six tomorrow morning. I'll bring the bucket," C.J. said with a bright smile, and tramped down the pathway toward her bike.

*

159

"Why'd you bring that stuff," C.J. asked incredulously. "We're not going fishing."

"No kidding," Dusty said with sarcasm.

C.J. crossed her arms and awaited an explanation.

After a long pause, Dusty said "Of course, I'm not going fishing, but if I don't take my fishing stuff, MeMaw will ask where I've been – leaving the house so early and all. Hopefully, this way, she won't ask."

"Did you bring some water?" C.J. asked.

"Don't need it. It's a spring, remember?"

"The water's probably no good," C.J. said. "I bet that's why they were testing it."

"Are you kidding? That water's fine. I drink it all the time. I have since I was old enough to walk over here – and there's nothing wrong with me."

C.J. lifted her eyebrows to suggest "I rest my case."

Dusty said, "Get your water then."

C.J. ran into the house, fetched two plastic bottles of water from the refrigerator, tossed them in a plastic grocery bag and started out the door. On her way past the pantry, she gave in to a sudden impulse to grab a couple of granola bars and some pre-packaged peanut butter and crackers. It wasn't likely she'd be hungry in the short time they would be gone, but the bag of goodies didn't weigh much, and it might be nice to have a little mid-morning snack by the spring.

As C.J. reached for one more granola bar, she inadvertently snagged a book of matches, too. Rather than wasting the time to put them back, C.J. just tied off the plastic bag and tossed it into her backpack. At Maggie's suggestion, C.J. had rolled an extra pair of shorts, panties, and socks up in a clean T-shirt and put it in the bottom of her backpack. It seemed like overkill to C.J., but Maggie said in all of the time she had traversed the world with Henry, she had never regretted always keeping a change of clothes nearby.

"Little accidents can happen," Maggie said with a wink. "A woman should always be prepared." C.J. understood the implications of the statement. Besides, the set of clothes wouldn't weigh much and helped keep the backpack's form.

"You finally ready?" Dusty asked as C.J. closed the screen door quietly behind her. "I thought you got lost in there."

"Relax," C.J. said dismissively. "Come mid-morning, you'll be thanking me," she said. With that, the two bounded off into the gray morning light.

*

As Trent Martin passed her cubicle, he couldn't help but notice that Christine had been in an unusually good mood for the last few days. Not only had she been relatively civil to her colleagues, she hadn't flown off at Becky or anyone else in the marketing department. Moreover, she hadn't had one of the patented temper tantrums she was notorious for throwing.

"How's the analysis coming for Cornerstone?" he asked, being careful not to sound too demanding.

"We're almost there," she said. "Lab work looks good."

"When your report is done, be sure to cc the team, so they can incorporate your findings into the final report," he said.

"Sure," Christine said, looking up just in time to see Trent walk on down the hallway. She returned to studying her printout. Now that she had what she wanted, and knew that Hugh Gunther would get what he wanted, she could play nice. Or at least act like she was playing nice. GeoTherm was a little pond with little fish. By the time "the team" had figured out what happened, it would already be too late. Christine would be on her way to a lucrative career at Cornerstone.

*

It had taken much longer to get to the spring than C.J. had estimated. She was not nearly as sure-footed as Dusty, and the pace he had set exhausted her. She had nearly consumed the first of two water bottles by the time they made it to the confluence of

161

the clear flowing spring water and Simmons's Creek. Now all they had to do, Dusty said matter-of-factly, was follow the meandering clear creek up to its source.

"It's not too much further," Dusty said, looking behind him, trying to encourage and speed along the struggling C.J.

"My God," C.J. said, "it's all uphill."

"Yeah," Dusty said, "but there's not many briars or tall weeds, so it'll be easy. Come on," he barked.

The fact that there were few weeds or briars was of little consolation to C.J. Nonetheless, she followed the nimble-footed Dusty along the creek as it meandered and cascaded down, through and along the rocks. She was grateful she had brought along the "snake whopping stick." Not because they had come upon any snakes – mercifully, they had not – but because it helped her keep her balance as she ascended the rocky outcropping of the hill.

By the time they found the gaping mouth from which the little spring gurgled, C.J. was sweating profusely and breathing heavily. She tossed her stick aside and plopped herself onto a moss-covered rock in the shade. The scene around her was tranquil, and the water bubbled and flowed out of the mouth and then over the smooth black rocks that surrounded the entrance.

"Why I'm compelled to find the exact location of the water sample is beyond me," she said to Dusty who had already pulled a flashlight from his pocket.

"Pretty cool isn't it?" he said.

C.J. had to admit that it was indeed a beautiful spot. Had it not been so difficult to get to, C.J. would love to come here more often.

"So this is the spot," C.J. said looking around.

"Yep," Dusty said absently.

"Well, for what it's worth, we got to the bottom of the mystery. We found it," C.J. said with satisfaction.

"Uh-huh," Dusty said. He was carefully examining the cave's entrance.

"I bet the woman you saw was the one taking the water samples," C.J. said. "She took the sample you found, right here. Right here," C.J. repeated.

"You coming?" Dusty asked. He knew it was a rhetorical question.

"What?" C.J. said, looking toward Dusty. "Ah, no. I told you that. Besides, I have this thing about tight places."

"What kind of thing?" Dusty asked.

"I don't like cramped spaces," C.J. said. "I get anxious sometimes."

"You mean you're scared?"

"I just don't like close spaces, that's all," C.J. said.

"Well, they don't bother me," Dusty said as he headed into the opening.

"No," C.J. said firmly. "You're not going in there."

"You're not the boss of me," Dusty replied.

"I am now," C.J. said. "And besides, if you go in there, I'll tell your MeMaw what you did."

"And I'll tell her you made me come with you. And that you told me Maggie said I could go."

C.J. realized she wasn't going to be able to rationalize with a rock-hound with an unquenchable thirst for finding sparkling rocks. So she opted to make a minor concession.

"I'll let you go, if you promise not to go in there very far," C.J. said. "Promise me that. Because if you fall or something, I'm not going in there to pull you out," she said.

"I'm not going to fall," Dusty said confidently,

"Well, I told Aunt Maggie we'd be home by noon," C.J. said.

"We will. Don't worry. You just sit here with that stick. You see any snakes," Dusty said, "give 'em a whack with it."

She had no intention of "whacking" anything. "How long will you be in there?" C.J. asked, suddenly conflicted with staying outside alone or going with her guide into the darkness.

"Not long."

"Don't do anything stupid... I mean crazy," C.J. said.

Dusty didn't reply. The last thing C.J. saw was a duck-walking Dusty as he made his way into the darkness – flashlight in one hand, an empty gallon bucket in the other.

Chapter Twenty-One

He must have grown much more than he had imagined. The last time Dusty was in the cave, he could duck walk all the way in. Now, about half way down the entrance chute, he had to abandon the duck walk and crawl on his hands and knees along the rock floor and through the cool flowing water.

After trying in vain to find a convenient way to handle the flashlight in his right hand and drag the bucket along in his left, he decided to just toss the plastic bucket ahead several yards then crawl to it; he repeated this process, until he got deeper into the cave. Each time he did, the hollow bucket drummed against the floor. It solved the problem of not having enough hands for the task, but the bucket toss also had the added benefit of snake patrol. It wasn't likely that there would be any snakes this far into the cool, dark cave, but if there were, the concussion of the bucket would surely send any snake scattering.

Dusty did not yet know how he would manage to come out of the cave with a bucket full of rocks, but he would address that problem when faced with it. As for now, he had a solution to his most immediate problem. The cavern's floor ran just slightly uphill – but not enough for the bucket to roll back down as he tossed it ahead. Dusty looked over his left shoulder and saw that the light source at the entrance to the cave was nearly gone now. His heart was racing in anticipation of what he might find ahead. He envisioned great stalactites and stalagmites with beautiful glimmering stones lying about in huge piles on the cave floor. Equipped with a flashlight this time, he could explore all of the cavern's wonders and harvest its bounty.

"You okay in there?" The familiar voice reverberated off the walls.

Dusty recognized C.J.'s voice, turned, cupped his hands around his mouth and shouted, "No. I'm being eaten by dragons!"

"Bon appetit!" C.J. said, returning the sarcasm.

Dusty caught up to the plastic bucket and flung it once more into the darkness. This time he heard a discernable splash and deep echo.

As he crawled the last few feet of the cave's entrance chute, his flashlight's beam seemed to lose its intensity. Dusty looked down to see that the bulb was still glowing brightly. He pointed the flashlight to his immediate left and saw the beam reflect off the dark gray wall. He traced the beam along the wall to the left and then back up. The cavern was much larger than he had imagined, and the dark gray walls seemed to absorb any light he sent their way. Entering the open cavern, he could now stand fully erect.

As he stood, he pointed the beam downward. The light reflected brightly off his now wet tennis shoes. Dusty could see what he had only been able to feel since he began crawling along the cave's entrance chute – the water soaked knees of his blue jeans.

As he stood alone in the great abyss, Dusty could almost feel the darkness sapping his sense of adventure. He wasn't necessarily afraid to be alone, but having someone alongside right now, would have been welcomed.

He picked up the bucket and pointed the flashlight along the cave's smooth, rock floor. The water formed pools of varying widths and lengths as far as Dusty could see. To his great disappointment, there were no beautiful stalactites hanging like great mineral icicles from the rock ceiling, or magnificent stalagmites pushing up from the floor to meet their ceiling-clinging counterparts. Also to his utter frustration, Dusty could see no colorful rocks or brilliant crystals. A single, monotonous, layer of gray smooth rock seemed to cover everything.

Surely, he thought, there had to be more. He pointed the flashlight at his left wrist and glanced at his watch. It was after 9 a.m. He calculated that he could spend no more than 30 minutes exploring further, before he'd have to begin his egress from the cave.

He looked ahead to the pools of water that stretched across the cavern's floor and surmised that by following the water, he could safely explore further into the cave. If, for any reason, he got disoriented, Dusty figured he could always follow the water back and easily find his way out.

His sneakers were saturated with the cool water as he waded ankle deep through the black pools. The flashlight's beam reflected off the black glass of water and reflected onto the cave's wall – the slight movement of the water caused the flashlight's beam to cast ghost-like, shimmering reflections. Dusty pressed ahead.

After about 25 feet, the smaller pools of water merged into one wide pool that Dusty estimated to be 30 feet wide. He stopped. Glanced at his watch again, then shuffled ahead. He still had 15 minutes.

The depth of the water increased only slightly as he made his way further into the darkness and across the seemingly endless pond. Dusty stopped, and pointed his flashlight ahead. The darkness seemed to absorb the beam, and despite straining his eyes, Dusty could see only a few feet ahead.

For no other reason than to break the pervasive silence, Dusty yelled, "Hello!" into the darkness. The echo replied once, twice, three times before it faded. The sound of his own voice made Dusty feel better.

A mild but noticeable feeling of anxiety began to well up in Dusty's stomach. The darkness began to close in around him. Just 20 feet more, he said to himself, and then he would turn around and head back toward daylight. He continued to shuffle his feet through the water, the sound of the sloshing was amplified by the cave's echo.

His beam pointed ahead and down, each step forward revealed the same monotonous featureless scene as the last. Then a small but dazzling sparkle pierced the darkness.

Instantly his anxiety was replaced with an overwhelming sense of excitement and wonder. Just 15 feet across the pool, where the cavern narrowed dramatically, Dusty could see rich, green shards of rock. The green shards were interspersed with points of intense red, pink, yellow and white points of light that seemed to blink off-and-on as the flashlight's beam panned to and fro. It was only then that Dusty realized he wished he had brought his mineral hammer. If he were to retrieve any of the specimens, he could only hope that some of the stones were broken and lying about the cave's floor. Otherwise, he'd be out of luck.

Tossing caution aside, Dusty dashed through the shallow pool of water and toward the awaiting geologic the prize. As he moved, the sparkling points of color seemed to intensify and shimmer as the flashlight beam painted the area with haphazard stokes of light. Without a doubt, it was the most beautiful display of color Dusty had ever seen. His eyes were transfixed upon the stunning splendor. Unable to contain his excitement, he dashed the last few yards toward the awaiting prize.

It was the last thing he saw before he was swallowed into a liquid world of total darkness.

Chapter Twenty-Two

Had it not been for her very real claustrophobia, C.J. would most certainly have accompanied Dusty into the cave. Unquestionably, it would have been more exciting than simply sitting there, watching the water flow over the rocks, while scanning the surrounding terrain for any snakes that might seek the cool refuge of the spring's shaded oasis. She had peered into the cave once to check on Dusty shortly after he began his voyage. C.J. debated whether she should yell into the darkness again, but opted not to – she didn't want to sound like a nervous or frightened girl. But the boredom was taking its toll on her patience. C.J. looked at her watch. It was nearing 11 a.m.

She took her snake whopping stick and poked it into the cascading water where it had formed shallow pools amid the rocks at the top of the hill. C.J. looked around for smaller rocks and tossed them down the side of hill. Then she stood and walked around and over the rocky outcrop – always keeping an eye out for snakes. She glanced at her watch again, and then looked expectantly at the opening of the cave. If he didn't come out in other 10 minutes, C.J. thought to herself, she would yell again into the darkness to remind Dusty about their deadline. She walked back toward the cave's opening, being careful to stay on the rocks and not in the surrounding brush where a snake might be resting.

When she hoisted herself up to the summit, she glanced at a small pile of dead leaves to the left of the cave's open mouth. She hadn't remembered seeing them there before – and she had had plenty of time to look around and study the area waiting for Dusty. Then the leaves began to re-arrange themselves and move toward the opening.

C.J.'s heart began beating harder and faster. What had appeared to be a small clump of leaves was in reality a snake. And it was headed toward the cave's opening. Every instinct in her body compelled her to move in the opposite direction of the snake, yet she knew that she would have to yell into the cave, to warn Dusty of the menacing serpent or he could easily be bitten when he crawled back out of the darkness.

C.J. gripped the whopping stick with both hands and held it in front of her like a divining rod. Slowly and cautiously she crept toward it.

Then she heard a rustle in the bushes to her left. A large, brown, speckled dog came bounding toward her. C.J. quickly raised the whopping stick and prepared to unleash its devastation upon the charging animal, but the dog raced right by her. When it stopped, C.J. realized it was Cleotis – Dusty's dog.

"Dusty scared. Dusty hurt."

"What?" C.J. said.

"Help Dusty. Help Dusty." The dog paced quickly toward the opening then back toward C.J.

"How do you know?" C.J. asked, not aware that she was conversing, again, with a dog.

"Dusty. Hurry. Dusty." The dog went toward the mouth of the cave.

"There's a snake in there, don't," C.J. yelled. But the dog splashed through the water into the darkness.

"Wait!" C.J. yelled, then ran to follow the dog. When she got to the opening she heard a vicious growl and the sound of a scuffle, followed by more splashing in the water and more growls. The commotion suddenly abated. To her simultaneous horror and relief, C.J. watched a lifeless snake float by in the stream's current. For a brief moment she thought it was swimming directly at her. She raised her stick to strike it. Then it suddenly rolled over, exposing its light beige underside. In another moment the current pushed the snake over again revealing its chestnut and copper camouflage pattern. The snake, she realized, was dead.

"Go," Cleotis said. "Dusty."

"I... I... I can't. I can't go," C.J. stuttered. She wondered how she could explain that she was too frightened to go.

"Friend," the dog said. "Dusty." The dog peered at her intently, then whimpered, turned, and padded impatiently back into the cave.

"But I can't. It's cramped. I can't," C.J. said pleading with the dog. Then C.J. realized she was crying.

She squatted down and poked her head into the cave's opening. "Dusty," she yelled tentatively. "Dusty!" There was no reply. She yelled again – and again, there was no reply.

C.J. looked hesitantly into the mouth of the spring.

Cleotis paced quickly back to C.J..

"Dusty. Help. Help..." the dog whined. "Help." The dog was panting heavily. "Please."

C.J. looked at the knotted end of the of the dog's long rope. Then she wrapped it around her hand, inhaled deeply – as though she were about to dive into a pool – and took her first steps into the darkness and toward her greatest fear.

RON NICHOLS

Chapter Twenty-Three

Christine was seething in anger. Had she acted on her immediate impulse she would have strangled the old woman to death. Christine did not know why the obtuse biddy had suddenly – inexplicably – changed her mind. But now that she had, Christine forced her intellect to supersede her lust for vengeance. Retribution could wait. Christine's plan could not, she thought. Unless she could bring the whole deal to Cornerstone, Christine would continue to be just another cog in the wheel of the GeoTherm team. Cogs did not become corporate V.P.'s. She simply had to deliver the deal, and she vowed that she would – no matter what it took.

In retrospect, Christine realized she had overplayed her hand when Maggie Davidek would not sell her home and her land. Christine believed she had her quarry cornered. When Maggie simply handed the sales contract back to Christine – unsigned – she could not believe her eyes.

"Are you nuts?" Christine had said to Maggie. "If you don't take this offer, there will NOT be another one. Do you understand me?" Christine said raising her voice.

To her surprise, Maggie did not capitulate to Christine's demands. Instead, Christine's confrontational attitude seemed to fortify Maggie with a renewed sense of resolve.

"I understand you perfectly," Maggie had replied. "Now get out of my house and off my land. Do you understand me?"

As she drove the company truck back down the dusty road, Christine thought about the geography of the area, and wondered why God, in all of His infinite wisdom, had chosen to place the perfect water supply on the land of that incorrigible old woman. Why, Christine wondered, couldn't the spring be in one of at least a dozen other eruption points around the area? Why? The answer, she knew was simple luck – pure geologic happenstance. The source water was simply following a path of least resistance.

What if happenstance could be altered, Christine suddenly wondered. "If the exit point for the spring water was suddenly shut off, wouldn't the water seek another geologic exit point?" she asked quietly to herself. A natural geologic shift had occurred years ago. It was the reason the spring flowed from its current exit point. Still, Christine thought it was geologically possible to change nature. All she had to do was give it a little help. But how?

As she continued her drive along the road, Christine knew that what was really needed was an earthquake. But that wasn't likely, and anyway, the resulting geologic shift could send the water anywhere. She would need a more controlled earthquake, Christine concluded.

Then she had an epiphany. She could create the perfect, controlled earthquake with dynamite.

The more she considered that option, the more she realized it just might work. The force of the explosion would cause a shift – or possibly a crack in the geologic vein that could allow the water to spring to the surface where she wanted it to. At worst, given the volume and pressure of the water, the spring would surely re-emerge somewhere, Christine knew. The major question, of course, was where.

No matter where the spring might re-emerge, it was likely that the water would cause a significant inconvenience to the landowner upon whose land the spring would suddenly appear. Depending on the total water flow, a spring could flood pastures, erode cropland, and even threaten a home or two. Wherever the spring emerged, however, Christine was confident that the landowner would be more than happy to find someone to rid him or her of the problem. She would be ready to purchase that problem, and enough of the surrounding land to locate the factory for Cornerstone.

Λ controlled explosion was a perfect solution. A solution that not only satisfied the rational side of Christine the scientist, but one that also satisfied her thirst to make Maggie Davidek regret her decision. When the old woman finally had to declare bankruptcy, Christine thought, she would make certain that the rumors about the unsuitable drinking water would keep the sales price down to an absolute minimum.

Christine stepped down harder on the truck's accelerator. The tires spun on the loose gravel, spewing rocks and dust behind it. She wanted to get to Geo-Therm's storage facility before sunset. By sunrise she would be in possession of enough dynamite and blasting caps to undo Mother Nature's unfortunate placement of *her* source of water.

RON NICHOLS

Chapter Twenty-Four

"We'll be making our presentation to Cornerstone a week from tomorrow," Frank Rahe said to the GeoTherm team. "I want to thank all of you for a job well done. I especially want to thank Christine for her leadership and her hydrogeologic groundwater models, without which, we would not be able to deliver such great news to our client." He smiled and looked in Christine's direction. She was seated equidistant from her other team members around the oval conference room table. Her colleagues applauded politely following Frank's introductory remarks.

Christine feigned a smile and nodded her head to acknowledge the recognition. This was the type of respect that she deserved, she thought to herself. It was, however, too little, too late. All the trite expressions of gratitude from the mediocre engineers, soil scientists and technicians who made up the so-called "team," were meaningless anyway. Those expressions would be made all the more meaningless when Christine announced that she would be leaving the firm. As far as she was concerned, that day couldn't come soon enough.

She glanced at the clock. It was almost noon. She wanted to be out the door in a few minutes so she could implement her plan.

Mercifully, Frank Rahe dismissed the gathering with an upbeat note. "This is the type of watershed event that will put GeoTherm on the map. I don't want to raise any unrealistic expectations, but if things continue to go well, it could be a very good year for all of us." He raised his eyebrows. Everyone knew what Frank had meant. This year, for the first time in a very long time, the team was on track to land significant performance bonuses. Frank smiled. "Great work everyone."

The team rose from their chairs nearly simultaneously. A few milled around the conference table briefly, others headed back to their offices and cubicles. Christine was not among either group. On her way out the door, she stopped by the white, dry-erase scheduling board. She slid the dime-sized, orange magnetic puck across the row and into the column that indicated "OUT." On the memo section of the slick white board she scrawled the word "Field." No one would ask where in the field she might be. And better yet, as long as her time was billable to some client somewhere, no one would care.

She hadn't set a charge since graduate school. It was the summer she had worked for a mining company, when she had been conscripted to go afield with a group of technicians whose only purpose in life, or so it seemed, was setting charges and then blowing things up. She had never really shared in the thrill of the explosion. For one thing it was painfully loud, and the prospect of being pummeled by large stones that had been sent rocketing into the air before falling back to Earth was not something she enjoyed either. Christine figured the "joy of explosion" must have something to do with just being a guy. But during her summer in the field, she had learned how to set charges, how to properly handle and bundle the sticks, and how to set the fuse. But most of all she had learned the single most important lesson about dynamite: It must be respected.

There was no way to predict with absolute certainty, where or even if the spring might re-emerge. Thanks to Maggie Davidek's regrettable decision not to sell, there was no time to model all of the potential outcomes. Christine's back was against the wall. She had to operate on instinct, and her instinct told her that by diverting the spring's outlet channel deeply enough underground, the spring would find another outlet nearby. All Christine had to do was make certain she created a blast of sufficient magnitude to "force the issue." Twelve sticks, she had concluded would be more than enough to "bring the spring's geologic house down."

Christine had hoped that she could put the charge deeper into the spring's opening, but the rock opening quickly narrowed, and given her size, age, and lack of agility, she realized she would have to set the charge just a few yards deep. Nonetheless, given the amount of explosives she would have on hand for the project, the resulting explosion would more than do the trick. She hoped, however, to put the charge deep enough into the cave's opening that anyone within a mile or so of the blast would likely hear nothing, or feel perhaps, only a brief rumbling – like that of a passing tractor-trailer truck.

An electrical charge would have been safer, but Christine wanted to buy as much time to exit the property as possible and to leave no evidence of her geologic manipulation in the process, so she opted for a few hundred feet of pyro-fuse. It was an old style fuse that would burn slowly until it burned into the charge of the bundled dynamite. It wasn't as clean or as precise as an electric detonation, but under the circumstances, it was the perfect solution to her dilemma.

When she arrived at the gaping mouth of the spring's opening Christine scanned the interior of the cavern. She estimated that even with her large frame she could crawl a few yards into the cavern, just far enough to plant the charge that would bring the house down. She patted the upper chest pocket of her vest, making certain that the flap over the pocket that contained the pyro-fuse was secured by the Velcro tab.

She eyed the pathway that she would have to navigate – mostly on her hands and knees because of the low cavern ceiling. By crawling along the smooth rock floor on either side of the water channel, Christine concluded she could stay dry. Unfortunately, it would still be an uncomfortable distance to travel. She would likely have few aching muscles in the morning as a result of the maneuver. Still, she thought, the inconvenience would be a small price to pay for success.

It took her a little over an hour to get to the site; prepare the charge; place it as deeply as she could; and return to her vehicle. As she left the area, Christine looked back at the trailing pyro-fuse that snaked its way haphazardly along the cavern floor, and then out the mouth of the spring. After she ignited the fuse, she watched it spark, fizzle and smoke along and through the green vegetation about 25 yards below the spring's mouth. The fuse would burn at a rate of about two-feet a minute. Based on the length of the fuse, Christine knew she had at least an hour to get back to the truck and drive to the office. When the blast was felt by the locals – if it was felt at all – Christine would be hard at work in her cubicle. If anyone cared, or wondered about the rumble, Christine would be well beyond suspicion, especially because she planned to be seen by the guy with the knotty hands who ran that dumpy little gas station down the road. What was more likely, Christine thought, was that no one would hear, feel, or care about the explosion. The visit to the gas station would be "alibi insurance," however, should she need it.

She took one more glance over her shoulder and saw small, intense bright flashes in the underbrush. As she watched the sparks of the fuse chew their way toward the charge, Christine wondered to herself how long it would take for the water to push its way to the surface, once the explosion was complete. More importantly, she wondered from where the water would ultimately flow. Without more sophisticated models, she could only guess – maybe a few days – maybe a few weeks. There was no way to really know.

Either way, the water would eventually find a new exit point and Christine was certain it wouldn't be on the Davidek property. Now, she thought, it was just a matter of letting Alfred Nobel's genius nudge Mother Nature in the right direction.

RON NICHOLS

Chapter Twenty-Five

Something was trying to swallow him – to kill him. Completely disoriented Dusty found himself sinking into a pool of infinite darkness that seemed intent on pulling him into the abyss.

Dusty refused to comply, kicking fervently against his foe.

When he finally broke the water's surface, he made a desperate, flailing attempt to reach for something – anything – that might help him overcome the force that seemed intent on consuming him. In that brief moment above the water's surface, he gasped for air, but took in more water than air. His nostrils and throat burned with pain, and he once again sank below the surface, all Dusty could see was the dim yellow glow of his own flashlight dance about him as he fought his way toward the life-giving surface.

He continued kicking his legs and splashing wildly with his left hand, all in an effort to keep his head above the water –to capture a precious breath of air. Kicking harder than he would have needed to without being encumbered by his soaked blue jeans and tennis shoes, Dusty was soon able to keep his head above the water's surface.

One, two, three good breaths of air. Dusty's panic began to subside, and his instinct to survive remained strong.

183

With rhythmic kicking, Dusty was able to keep his face from dipping into the inky liquid, and he began to weigh his escape options. He thought about dropping his flashlight in favor of another free hand to help him tread water, but chose, for now, to hang onto it. He was a good swimmer – another one of MeMaw's life-saving lessons that she had insisted upon giving to him as a small child. Dusty continued to tread water. With brief flashes of light from his flashlight, he managed to illuminate enough of his surroundings to find the point at which he had taken his last fateful step. Despite his strong swimming ability, Dusty knew that he would have to get himself and his flashlight to high ground, or the light from both would both soon be extinguished.

After kicking over to the edge from which he had apparently stepped, he grasped for the rock face above his imprisoning pool of death. Unfortunately, he could not get a grip on the smooth, featureless rock ledge. Several times he thought he had his fingers gripped into the rocks, but the moment he tried to pull himself and his water-logged clothes above the water's surface, his fingers slipped away. It was as though some cruel tormentor was offering, then snatching Dusty's lifeline away right at the very moment it seemed to be within reach.

Despite his best effort to remain calm, the darkness, the silence and the solitude began to take their toll. Not only were his legs and his arms beginning to ache from the exertion and the cold water, but now Dusty wondered – truly wondered – if he would be able to make it out of his predicament alive. For the first time since he was five, Dusty wanted to cry. Perhaps MeMaw had known all along – perhaps that's why she had been so insistent that Dusty not explore the spring cavern. His curiosity had taken him into the great mouth – and it appeared he might soon pay the ultimate price for that curiosity.

*

She was being pulled so hard that C.J. felt that her arm would be pulled out of its socket as Cleotis clawed his way intently though the darkness.

With just an LED flashlight as her only other companion, C.J. could catch only glimpses of her surroundings while making her way through the pools of darkness in the spring cavern. "This is complete madness," C.J. said to herself. "I'm not only talking to dogs, now I'm actually listening to them. I must be completely insane."

Regardless of the apparent insanity of her decision, she had little time to be reminded of her most intimate fear – tight spaces. Tethered to a giant brown beast that seemed hell-bent on getting to his master, C.J. could only try to slow its progress as the dog moved without hesitation into the impenetrable darkness. In a vain attempt to keep up with the dog, C.J. had battered her head against the ceiling of the cavern and now had so many scrapes and contusions on her knees that she wasn't sure she would be able to stand up again.

"Slow down," C.J. shouted, breathlessly to the dog.

"Dusty. Dusty," the dog repeated.

"I know. I know. Is that all you can say?" C.J. said in frustration, not realizing the absurdity of conversing with a dog.

The beam from C.J.'s flashlight reflected nothing. The little light it produced seemed to be swallowed by the vacuum of the cave's infinite darkness. It was then C.J. realized with relief that she could finally stand. With some discomfort, she righted herself and took a deep breath. As soon as she did, she felt the hands of fear clasp around her throat and her heart began to pound deep in her chest.

But just as she felt herself submitting to her fear, C.J. was catapulted further into the darkness by the crazed dog. Fighting to stay upright, fearful that she might run face first into a low hanging slab of rock, C.J.'s claustrophobia was compounded by an uncontrollable fear of death as the two splashed their way further into the abyss.

*

Perhaps it was the cold or perhaps it was simply exhaustion. Maybe it was the realization that his life was really coming to an end, but Dusty began thinking back to the woman who had raised him; the wonderful woman who had done everything in her power to keep him away from the dangers of the streets; to keep him safe from harm. He wished that he had hugged her and told her how much he had loved her, but in his attempt to deceive her, Dusty had also deprived her of one last goodbye. He had done her wrong, and her sorrow would be his goodbye gift to his wonderful MeMaw.

Unable to hold the flashlight any longer, Dusty felt his only source of light slip from his fingers. He glanced down and watched the bright beam dim quickly as it plummeted into the shadowy depths below him. His only companion now plunged to its final resting spot, somewhere in the terrifying darkness below.

Dusty wondered when it would be his turn.

He felt his will slipping away – just as the flashlight had slipped from his fingers a few moments before.

He had to rest – he couldn't go on like this forever. He allowed himself to stop kicking for a brief moment. The respite from the constant exertion to stay above water was glorious. To Dusty's surprise his head stayed above the water – but only for a moment. Then the cool water enveloped his face. Dusty found himself submitting to its will. He was so tired. So very tired. At this very moment, he thought how wonderful it would be to just float, to sleep. Just sleep.

"Don't you quit!"

The voice was full of anger. It startled Dusty and he instinctively kicked and stroked upwards, gulping air and water as he broke the surface.

"Help!" he yelled to the voice.

"Help!"

But there was no reply.

*

"Dusty!" Cleotis said. The dog's ears were perked and pointed.

"What?" C.J. asked, still trying to keep pace with the dog.

"Dusty. Help. Dusty."

C.J. yelled. "I know. Dusty. Help Dusty," she screamed – mocking the dog.

Cleotis moved resolutely into the darkness. C.J. could only follow, knowing full well that she was being led deeper and deeper into the darkness.

*

The only sound Dusty could hear was his own labored breathing and the rippling of the water as it splashed against the walls of his liquid internment.

"Don't you quit, Dusty! I mean it."

It was MeMaw's voice.

"MeMaw."

"Dusty!" He heard the voice clearer now.

"MeMaw I'm here! Here!" Dusty said as he treaded harder, gulping mouthfuls of water as he yelled into the darkness.

"Dusty! I'm coming."

He saw an intense flash of white-blue light, and was blinded by its intensity. "Is this the light everyone said they saw in those near-death recollections?" Dusty wondered to himself. "I'm moving into the light," he thought. "Is this what it's like to die?"

Suddenly he felt a rude whack across his face. The impact stung his cheek and thumped his head. Dusty wanted to shout out an expletive, but had all he could do to keep his head above water.

"Grab it, Dusty. Grab the rope."

He groped in vain for the object that had hit him in the face. With the menacingly bright light still in his eyes, he could not see the rope, nor anything else around him.

Whack! The object hit him on his shoulder this time and the water splashed into his face. Still kicking his legs, Dusty turned and lunged for the object that had just assaulted him. This time he felt the line brush up against his body as it descended into the water. He latched onto the coarse twine with his right hand, and reached immediately with his left hand to secure his grip. He had never been more relieved in his life and Dusty tenaciously clung to the lifeline.

"Hold on, Dusty," the familiar voice said. The light was extinguished and Dusty was once again in the darkness – but this time he knew he was not alone.

"Come on Cleotis. Come on boy. Pull!"

Dusty felt himself being pulled through the water. When his body hit the side of the rock pool, he felt the rope slip through his hands. Had it not been for the knot at its end, Dusty would not have been able to stop it.

With his hands aching, fingers cramping, he felt himself slowly being tugged up and along the cold dark sloping prison walls. The slick, angled walls that had once impaired his escape, now acted to facilitate it. With each tug, Dusty slid higher along the slippery rock until; at last, he felt the rope go slack. A moment of panic ensued, as Dusty thought he might slide back into the ink-black prison from which he had just escaped. To Dusty's relief, he did not.

Utterly exhausted, he laid sprawled on the rock, his hands still clutching the rope. He coughed, and continued to breathe rapidly, still unaware – or unconcerned – about the identity of his savior or saviors.

The menacing light darted into his eyes yet again. For a brief moment, Dusty felt as though, perhaps, he had died after all. Then he felt the warm and familiar texture of something lapping up the water droplets on his face. Maybe he was in heaven after all.

Then Dusty recognized the memorable stench of Cleotis' breath. Normally, it would have been enough to make him gag.

But under the circumstances, Dusty believed it was the most wonderful aroma that had ever assaulted his nostrils.

"Dusty," he heard a familiar voice echo throughout the cavern. "Are you okay? Can you move? Is anything broken?" The questions came at him in rapid fire succession. He was soaked and tired, and embarrassed. But he managed to answer. "Yes, yes and no," he said as he rolled over onto his side. The blinding light was in his eyes again.

"Turn that darn thing away," Dusty said, annoyed.

"Dusty okay."

"Yes. I can see that," C.J. said.

"Happy."

"Good."

"What's good? Who are you talking to?" Dusty asked, trying in vain to peer into the darkness.

"No one," C.J. replied, then added, "I… I mean, just to myself," she said. She quickly changed the subject. "What happened to you?"

"I fell in that pond or hole or whatever it was, what do you think happened," Dusty said.

"I mean what were you..." her words trailed off. "Oh never mind. Let's get out of here, or we're both going to be in trouble. Do you know what time it is?" C.J. asked.

"No," Dusty said.

Then C.J. realized that during the last few minutes while Dusty was nearly drowned, time probably wasn't exactly a big concern.

"I knew this was a bad idea. I don't know why I let you talk me into letting you come in here," C.J. said.

"You're not my boss," Dusty said defensively. "What time is it anyway?"

"It's nearly noon. We're supposed to be home right now. Let's get going and maybe if we hurry we'll only be an hour late," C.J. said, calculating how much time it would take to make their way back out of the cave and then to the house.

She swept the flashlight beam across the cave walls. Simultaneously C.J. felt the anxiety enveloping her like a crashing wave.

Dusty stood.

C.J. willed herself to repress the growing angst that was simmering within. "Here," C.J. said. "You take the flashlight. I'll hold on to Cleotis and follow."

Dusty began sloshing through – but now mostly around the shallow, glossy pools of water. "You should have seen the color in those rocks," Dusty said, suddenly remembering what had captivated him before his fateful fall into the deep pool.

"Well you can forget about ever coming back here," C.J. said assuredly.

"I just have to be more careful next time."

"You were almost killed. Don't be stu..." C.J. stopped in mid-word. "Don't be foolish. You are NOT coming back here," she said.

"Well, I'm coming back. I can tell you..."

WHAOOMP! An immense concussion and air blast swept over the trio, cutting Dusty's words off mid-sentence. The gust of air was so strong that it nearly knocked C.J. off her feet. Dusty lost his grip on the flashlight, its light extinguished the instant the flashlight hit the hard rock cavern floor.

"Oh my God," C.J. said. "What was that?" Now her claustrophobia was returning in earnest. She struggled to breathe.

"Where are you?"

"Here. I'm here," C.J. replied. "Where's the flashlight?" Her heart raced and her fears began to choke her like a snake constricting a helpless victim.

On his hands and knees, Dusty began to feel around the cavern floor for the flashlight. "I'll find the light. Just stay where you are," he said. The soft sobs from behind him increased his sense of urgency. "I'll find it. Don't worry."

"Dusty find."

C.J. patted the dog – trying to assure herself as much as her canine companion. The presence of the dog was the one thing that kept her from completely falling apart. C.J. stooped to embrace the dog.

"Found it!" Dusty shouted.

"Turn it on. Turn it on," C.J. said. More than as a navigational aid, C.J. needed the light to re-kindle her fortitude.

Dusty shook the flashlight and it flickered. The light briefly illuminated his face before it lapsed into darkness.

"Turn it on!" the panic in C.J.'s voice was palpable.

"I'm trying," Dusty said. "It doesn't..." he felt for the battery compartment's end cap. He loosened it and screwed it tight again. The light shone brightly. He turned its beam toward C.J.'s voice.

A long cone of light, tapering outward through the dust, found its target. C.J. had her arms around the dog's neck as she kneeled next to Cleotis. His eyes shown like two huge emeralds reflected in the light. Dusty carefully walked toward his two friends.

"We've got to get out of here," C.J. said, stating the obvious.

"Do you want the flashlight?" Dusty asked, sensing C.J.'s growing anxiety.

She continued patting the dog. "No I'll stay with Cleotis. Just don't drop it again."

"I didn't mean to drop it the first time," Dusty said defensively. He pushed his hand through the flashlight's wrist strap to ensure that even if he lost his grip, he wouldn't drop it again.

"Let's go," C.J. said

"Stay close," Dusty said still dripping water.

The three began making their way through the dust and the smoke – following the shallow chain of pools and the gently flowing stream that had led them to the inner cavern.

"How much farther?" C.J. asked. She vowed that when she gazed upon the sunlight she would never ever go into another cave for the rest of her life.

"I'm not sure," Dusty said. "It shouldn't be..." he stopped in his tracks.

"It shouldn't be what?" C.J. said as she and Cleotis closed the gap and stood beside him.

C.J. held her hand over her mouth to keep herself from screaming.

The flashlight beam scanned the horrific scene before them. A mountain of gray rocks that once formed the ceiling of the narrow stream corridor was now a wall of gray boulders that reached from the floor to the ceiling.

"Oh my God," was all C.J. could think to say.

*

Christine looked down at the dashboard. A red light on the enunciator panel read "Low Fuel." She cursed. "Idiots," she said blaming the unknown team member at GeoTherm who had failed to re-fuel the truck before returning from the field. It had not occurred to Christine to check the fuel gauge before she had embarked upon her mission. Fortunately, she was only a half-mile away, so if the engine were to quit, at least she could coast down the hill to the gas station. Besides, she had wanted to establish an alibi if she needed one. Having Otto see her before any explosion noise should do that perfectly.

She pulled alongside the island of gas pumps.

"Howdy!" Otto's friendly voice greeted her as she stepped out of the truck.

"Yeah. Howdy." she said without sincerity.

"Fill 'er up?"

"Yeah, sure," Christine said not even trying to feign congeniality.

Otto lifted the nozzle from the pump and turned the handle on the side of the pump clockwise a quarter turn. The numbers on the rotary dials rolled to zeros.

"Sounds like we might get some rain," he said.

"Is that so?"

"Yep. Thought I heard a rumble a few minutes ago," Otto said, as he scanned the sky. Darkening cumulus clouds moved like silent ships across the sky. In the distance, a few massive clouds boiled up from their flat purple bases like immense scoops of cottage cheese.

Christine looked at her watch.

"We could sure use the rain," Otto said, turning his attention back the numbers on the gas pump dials. The wind was picking up and the temperature was dropping.

"Don't count on it," Christine said dismissively.

"You folks ever find what you're looking for?" Otto asked more out of an attempt to jump start a conversation than to probe for information.

"Maybe," Christine said. "Won't know for some time."

"What are ya'll lookin' for anyway?"

"I think I'll grab a Coke," Christine said, clearly trying to avoid the topic. She walked around the front of the truck and made her way through the open glass door. She looked down to see the big blonde dog.

Duke wagged his tail and lifted his head, but did not attempt to get up off his comfortable blanket pallet.

Christine walked to the soft drink cooler, extracted a can of Diet Coke and carried it to the counter. Duke finally stood, stretched and then sauntered over to Christine as she sat her soft drink can near the cash register. Duke stood next to the large woman wagging his tail. She looked down, and stepped away from him.

Duke moved closer again.

"Go on. Get," Christine said not trying to disguise her agitation.

Otto suddenly appeared through the doorway. "It's $45.50," he said. "Must have been near empty."

Christine did not reply, but instead sidestepped the big dog and met Otto near the cash register. She pushed the company credit card at him. "Here," she said, pointing at the soda can, "and put this on there, too."

"Otto swiped the card through the credit card processing unit. While he waited for the receipt to print, Otto watched Duke walk back to the crumpled pile of blankets that constituted his bed. The big dog seemed disappointed.

"You know you shouldn't have a dog in here," she said. "It's unsanitary around the food you have stocked, plus you never know what they're going to do."

"Duke? I know what he's going to do. Sleep," Otto said, chuckling at his own joke.

Christine's sour expression did not change.

"Don't like dogs, huh?" Otto asked as he waited for Christine to sign the credit card receipt.

"How'd you guess?" Christine asked and smirked.

"Well, have a nice day," Otto said, ignoring Christine's expression and sarcasm. He handed her the unsigned copy of the receipt and tried to look her squarely in her eyes, but she would have none of it. Otto watched the woman walk steadfastly toward her truck. Christine fired up the engine, threw the truck into gear and sped away from the island. The spinning tires spat rocks back onto the concrete slabs around the gas pumps. Two or three errant projectiles pinged off the door frame and bounced inside the station.

Otto walked over to Duke and knelt beside him. Duke's inch-thick tail whapped the blanket repeatedly.

"Can't imagine anyone not liking you big fellow. Don't take it personally. I'm darn sure she doesn't care for me either." Otto rubbed the dog's silky ear.

"Not nice person."

Otto looked out the open glass door. "Not a nice person," Otto said. "I can't say I'd ever miss her if she didn't come by again."

In the distance a low, muffled rumble of thunder made its way across the countryside and rattled the large pane of glass on the front of building. Duke looked worried. He whimpered.

Otto stood and walked past the cash register, tilting his head slightly to look beyond the island's awning at the threatening sky. The phone on the counter clanged abruptly. Otto turned his eyes to the beige plastic phone and reached for it.

"Otto's," he said a little too loudly into the mouthpiece.

"Otto, it's Maggie," the nervous voice said.

"Hi Maggie, looks like we might get some rain…"

"Otto, MeMaw just called," the voice said abruptly. "She's worried about Dusty. She has one of those feelings."

Otto listened intently. He, like many others, knew about MeMaw's uncanny ability to "see" things before they happened, and therefore understood the gravity of Maggie's words.

"I think C.J.'s with him," Maggie said.

"Do you know where they are?" Otto asked.

"They were heading to the old spring cave," Maggie said. "They must still be there. MeMaw said Dusty was someplace cold and damp, surrounded by complete darkness," she said. "That's got to be it."

"Let me close up, Maggie. Duke and I will be right there," Otto said. "We'd better go take a look. Can you get us a couple of flashlights, some rope, and anything else you think we'll need?"

"Sure," Maggie said. "Henry kept his field pack in the shed. It'll have everything we could possibly need."

"Duke and I are on our way," Otto said, and hung up the phone. He looked at the big dog. "Let's go big fella. We've got work to do."

Duke sat upright on the bench seat of Otto's old pickup as it bounced along the dusty road. Under normal circumstances, it was Duke's favorite place in the world to be, especially in the summertime with the window rolled down. As he sat on his perch, the world came to him on the breeze – amazing scents of places and animals and some things he did not know. Memories and emotions and sensations rushing past him as the truck made its way through this marvelous world. For Duke, every trip in the truck was a trip through a fantastic world of the experienced and the yet-to-be-experienced.

Through the windshield Duke could see the menacing clouds as they boiled in the truck's direction. He looked at Otto who looked intently ahead. There was a familiar aroma in the breeze – it was one of rain and of life. But there was another scent that Duke could not discern. The scent wafted to him, then burrowed into his gut. He did not like it.

"Almost there, boy," Otto said, continuing to look ahead.

"Duke worried."

"I hope those kids are okay," Otto said as he applied the brakes and then turned into the drive that led to Maggie's house.

As they approached the house, Duke saw Maggie's diminutive figure on the stairs that led to the porch. She was bent over going through a duffle bag. Duke wagged his tail as Otto opened the driver's side door. "Come…" Otto said to Duke, holding the door open and gesturing with his head for Duke to get out.

With an energy that defied his age, Duke leapt from the seat of the truck and ran to Maggie, his big yellow tail swishing as he approached.

"Hi there, Duke," Maggie said as she threw her arms around his massive neck. Duke slurped his tongue along the side of Maggie's face.

"Happy."

"I'm happy to see you, too," Maggie whispered. "But we need to get a move on."

"Got here as quick as we could, Maggie," Otto said following quickly behind. "You test those batteries?" he asked as she placed the flashlights back into the pack.

"Good to go," she said. "Otto, I'm worried. Even Henry didn't venture far into that cave. What if those kids…" her words trailed off.

"Worried." Duke nuzzled up against Maggie.

"We'll find them, Maggie." Otto said reassuringly. "They probably just lost track of time. You know how Dusty is when he's rock hounding."

A jagged streak of silver ripped suddenly across the sky before disappearing. All three looked heavenward in response. Within a couple of seconds, a thundering boom rattled the glass windowpanes of Maggie's house. Duke whined and tried his best to wedge his body between Maggie and the stairs leading up to the porch.

"Scared."

Maggie stood, and then slung the backpack over her shoulders. "We're gonna get wet guys," she said.

Duke bounded ahead and onto the pathway that cut through the field behind the house as Maggie and Otto followed. "We won't melt, will we Duke?" Otto said, putting an arm around Maggie as the three began their trek to the spring cave.

RON NICHOLS

Chapter Twenty-Six

"What happened?" Dusty asked.

"I don't know," C.J. said. "Give me the flashlight." She swept its beam back and forth across the seemingly impenetrable wall of rocks in front of her. The dust from the crumbled rocks lingered in the air, giving the flashlight beam a Star Wars saber-light appearance. With the beam from the light, she searched frantically for an opening. But rather than giving into panic that had moments ago enveloped her, C.J. decided that she had to, as her parents had instructed so often, "solve the problem." And she knew that panic would not solve anything.

"What's that smell?" Dusty asked.

"I'm not sure," C.J. said, sniffing the air.

"Smells like when MeMaw shoots her shotgun," he said. "I wonder if someone shot at something in here that caused the cave-in?" He shivered as much from the thought that someone might be under the rocks as he did from the cold, wet clothes he was wearing.

"It doesn't matter, Dusty," C.J. said with some exasperation. "We have to find a way out of here." She walked a couple of feet over to Dusty and placed her hand on his shoulder, then turned the light out.

"Hey, what happened?" Dusty asked.

"We'd better save the batteries," she said. "I just hope the flashlight didn't get wet on the inside – because if it did..." C.J. didn't finish the statement.

"It's a Maglite," Dusty said assuredly. "It has O-ring seals."

"Meaning?"

"Meaning the water won't bother it."

"I hope you're right," C.J. said.

They stood in the darkness hearing nothing but Dusty's occasional sniffling. The silence seemed odd. Even before, as they made their way through the cave, it never seemed so still. Now it seemed as though they were completely removed from every living thing on the planet. Worse, it seemed they were the only inhabitants of a cold dark planet of their own. She shivered. The cold rose up from her feet and began to slowly possess her. C.J. turned on the light to illuminate her cold feet, which she could see were completely submerged in the water. C.J. painted the floor of the cave around them with the light. She could see that the water no longer flowed just within the confines of its rocky channel. It was beginning to rise higher on the floor.

"We can't stay here, Dusty." She said. "We have to go."

"Go where?"

"We have to go back. We have to find another way out."

"But we don't know if there is another way out," Dusty said.

"Do you see what's happening, Dusty?" C.J. asked. She swept the pool of rising water with the light. Dusty did not reply. "The water's rising and we obviously can't get out this way."

"What if there isn't another way out?" Dusty said. "I didn't see any other way out before I dropped into the pool."

"You weren't exactly looking for another way out were you? You were probably more interested in those pretty rocks," C.J. said in a way that she hoped sounded optimistic.

"I… I… don't want to go back there," he said. "I don't want to go near that deep pool again."

"We have to, Dusty," C.J. said. "There's no point in staying here. Even if the water wasn't rising there's no way we could get through that wall of rocks. Here," she said, "take the flashlight. Shine it on your belt." As he did, C.J. tied Cleotis' rope leash through Dusty's belt loop and across his belt. "Cleotis is a strong dog. If you slip, you won't go far. We'll make sure of that."

C.J. didn't know if this added measure of safety was sufficient to keep Dusty from peril, but it accomplished one important task already – it gave him a much-needed boost of confidence.

"Guess we'd better go," Dusty said.

"Go slow, and don't take any chances," C.J. said. For once, her instructions were completely unnecessary; Dusty had absolutely no inclination to take any more chances.

*

The first few drops of rain spat through the canopy of tree leaves just as Maggie and Otto made it to the mouth of the spring. Thunder continued to rumble in the distance as an uncharacteristically cool breeze swirled through the underbrush that surrounded the rock outcropping.

Duke, his nose to the ground zigzagged along the trail and into the brush that led to the spring cave. "C.J. Dusty. C.J. Dusty."

When they arrived at the cave entrance, Maggie put her hands to her mouth. "Oh my God," Maggie said as she fought back her tears and gazed with disbelief at the pile of rocks where the cave had once formed the gaping mouth of a frog. It no longer resembled anything in particular – just a haphazard pile of rubble.

"You don't think…" Otto's words trailed off. He did not say what he thought – what they both feared – that C.J. and Dusty might be entombed behind the wall of stone they were gazing upon.

Otto and Duke scurried to the pile of rocks to look for any gaps that might suggest a route in.

"Bring the backpack, Maggie," Otto said. "We're going to need a flashlight."

"Are there any other entrances to the cave?" Otto asked.

"None that I'm aware of," Maggie said with growing panic in her voice. She looked around the side of the hill. Suddenly Maggie's eyes brightened. "Henry thought the spring cave might be an ancient Kimberlite pipe, so there might be other fissures around."

"Kimberlite pipe?" Otto asked.

"It's sort of a volcanic shaft that originates deep in the earth. In a very few of these pipes, diamonds are found. That's why Henry bought this place," Maggie said. "It was going to be his full-time hobby when he retired. To explore this old cave and see if it might be a Kimberlite pipe."

"That's fascinating, Maggie," Otto said, "but does that mean there are other entrances?"

"From what Henry taught me about other Kimberlite pipes, there could be, but they could be anywhere. Or," she said with dejection, "nowhere."

"We'll have to try to get in there one way or another," Otto said, nodding in the direction of the wall of debris. We'll need some help if we're going to have any chance of getting through this," Otto said. "We need to call the sheriff."

Maggie had said with some pride for years that cell phones were the bane of modern society, causing constant interruptions and leading to an erosion of common courtesy. Plus, she knew they had also caused countless car wrecks. At this moment, however, she would have given her soul for one.

The rain began falling harder. Thunder rumbled across the hills and marched menacingly toward them.

"Can you make it back to your house okay, Maggie?" Otto asked.

"Of course," she replied.

"Duke and I will look around and see if we can find any other openings. Anything in particular we should look for?" Otto asked.

"I wish therewere," Maggie said. "But these Kimberlite features are ancient – even by geologic terms. It's not likely you'd see anything through the undergrowth, but Kimberlite is a soft green rock, so if you see that kind of rock around the hillside, it may lead to the same pipe that formed the cave here."

"You go call the sheriff," Otto said. "One way or another, we'll find them."

Maggie looked briefly at the sky then scurried down the rocky slope of the hill.

"Duke," Otto shouted, summoning the big dog. He put his thumb in the corner of his mouth and his forefinger in the other corner, pursed his lips and whistled a high pitched shrill. Otto stood still and waited. Across the nearby hill he watched the leaves from the underbrush jostle. The dog was panting heavily but with energy that belied his age, he bounded enthusiastically and directly toward his master.

"Come with me boy," he said when the dog approached. "We're gonna need that nose of yours."

RON NICHOLS

Chapter Twenty-Seven

Dusty could feel an intermittent tug on his belt from the big dog behind him. On the one hand, he was reassured to be tethered to Cleotis. On the other hand, the erratic tugging caused some uncertainty in his footing and he had to concentrate more diligently to maintain his balance as he sloshed through the deepening pools of black water. As the trio made their way into the bowels of their subterranean world and toward the deep pool that had nearly cost Dusty his life, the walls and the ceiling narrowed. The effect gave C.J. the feeling of moving through the stomach of a snake – of slowly being constricted. Walking through the darkness, it was fear that was beginning to constrict her now. She fought back the same fear that had nearly consumed her before, when Cleotis had first led her into the darkness.

This time, however, C.J. knew they would not be coming out a familiar exit. Their one sure exit was now gone.

"A little longer through here," Dusty said, grunting as he squatted and worked his way along the narrow passage. "Then we'll be in the big cavern." His observation broke the silence and C.J.'s anxiety lessened, albeit slightly.

Based on the eagerness in his voice, C.J. wondered if Dusty understood the gravity of their predicament. If they were unable to find another way out of the cave, which was a very real possibility, the few snacks C.J. had brought with her would not last long. If the rising water didn't kill them first, they would eventually starve or perhaps even die from hypothermia. The coolness of the cave had been a welcomed relief from the oppressive Arkansas heat and humidity. Unfortunately, without proper clothing or heat, warm-blooded creatures would find it impossible to maintain their body temperatures in the chilly cave. It was true that they wouldn't freeze to death as if they were in the Arctic, she knew, but their bodies could cool to a point where they'd simply shut down. She worried mostly about Dusty. His clothes were still soaked, and he was starting to shiver. Unless they could make their way out soon, C.J. knew they could "cool" to death and dead was dead.

C.J. fought back her tears. She couldn't let Dusty see her fear or feel her sense of hopelessness. If he did, it would only make matters worse.

"Scared," she heard the voice. "Scared."

"Shush," C.J. said in a whisper to the dog.

"What?" Dusty asked.

"Nothing. I was…," C.J. stopped. "I was talking to myself."

The three had made their way through the narrow, rock enclosed shaft, which then gave way to an expansive chamber. Dusty shone his flashlight around the cavern, just as he had when he'd first discovered it. However, the beam of light – which earlier seemed to slice through the darkness now only weakly bumped up against it. The flashlight batteries were deteriorating. He recognized that the light which had guided them into the ink-black darkness was slowly losing its power. Once those batteries were drained, the trio would be in darkness.

"Let's stop for a while," C.J. said. "How 'bout we split one of the granola bars I brought, and give the flashlight a break."

"Okay," Dusty said. "I am getting hungry. What time is it?"

"Shine the flashlight toward me," C.J. said as she peered down at her watch. "It's almost three," she said. "The good news is someone's probably coming to look for us," C.J. said. "The bad news is we're gonna be in big trouble when we get out of here."

"Can I have one of those?" Dusty asked, apparently unaffected by C.J.'s assessment of their impending disciplinary dilemma. He aimed his flashlight at the foil-covered bar as C.J. fished one out of the plastic bag.

"Okay," C.J. replied, "but we'd better not eat any more for a few hours. We could be in hereawhile. We have to make this last" C.J. peered into the bag that held the few snacks she had brought along. "We don't know how long it might be before we can get out of here." Then she thought to herself, *God, I hope we can get out of here.*

She handed the bar to him, took his flashlight and shone the light on the packet so he could unwrap it. Once he did, he reciprocated – holding the flashlight for C.J. When she finished unwrapping her bar, Dusty doused the light. The three were immersed in utter darkness.

"What the?" C.J. said loudly.

"We'd better save the batteries," Dusty said, noticing the anxiety in C.J.'s voice.

"I just thought…"

"Sorry 'bout that. I should have told you I was gonna turn it off."

"Hungry." C.J. heard the voice.

"Okay," she said. "I almost forgot." She broke off a piece of her bar.

"Are you talking to Cleotis again?" Dusty asked, snickering.

"No," C.J. said defensively. "I was talking to myself."

"Sure," Dusty said. He had lived with MeMaw long enough to know that there were forces and gifts that could not be explained. MeMaw seemed to be able to communicate with dogs and see things before they happened. A girl who thought she could hear dogs talking did not surprise him.

C.J. broke off a piece of the bar, holding it in the open palm of her hand. "Here you go boy," she said. Instantly, she felt Cleotis' warm, moist tongue wipe the bar cleanly off of her hand. The dog's open-mouthed crunching echoed in the cave.

"I… I'm getting cold," Dusty said as he chewed his portion of the granola bar.

"We've got to get you some dry clothes," C.J. said.

Dusty said nothing, realizing that he had no way of drying his.

Then C.J. realized Maggie had suggested she pack an extra set of clothes for herself. "Oh, wait," she said to Dusty, "I have an extra pair of shorts and a T-shirt."

"No way," Dusty protested immediately. "I'm not wearing a girl's clothes." His words quivered as he spoke them.

C.J. wondered if the quivering voice was a result of the cold or of the prospect that Dusty might have to wear girl's clothing. "That's stupid," she said. "You need dry clothes or you'll freeze to death. Besides, no one's going to see you in them."

C.J. dug all of the items from the backpack. "Here." C.J. held them out for Dusty. "Nobody's going to know."

"Okay," Dusty said reluctantly. "But not those." He was pointing to the pair of cotton panties that made up the ensemble.

"Fine," she said. "But get into these."

Dusty took the shorts and T-shirt. "Okay, but turn the flashlight off and leave it off."

"Fine," C.J. said. "I don't want to ruin my appetite anyway."

After a few moments, Dusty had changed clothing.

"These feel funny," he said. "But they are warmer," he added.

"Well don't get used to them," C.J. quipped. "I'll want them back."

"Don't worry, you can have them back," Dusty said defensively.

They were inching their way toward the deep black pool that had tried, but fortunately failed to swallow Dusty just a short time earlier. In the beam of light, C.J. could see the green rocks, speckled with bright red and orange glints of glitter as she looked over Dusty's shoulders beyond the pool. Aware of the danger ahead, Dusty did not move with the same carefree enthusiasm he had felt when he was spellbound by the geologic treasure earlier in the day. This time, he stayed as far away from the deepening channel of water as he could, hugging the side of the cave wall as he led the trio closer to the pool. He genuinely feared the deep pool and respected it as if it were a rattlesnake – giving it as wide a berth as was physically possible.

He flicked the flashlight beam along the edge of the pool where the glass surface of the water met the wall. "It's going to be tight," he said. "I don't know if we can make it around."

"What about the other side?" C.J. asked.

The beam of light illuminated the wall on the right side of the cavern and answered the question for Dusty. Where the left side of the cavern offered a challenging, but possibly passable slope, the slope on the right side of the cavern was almost vertical.

"We'll have to make it around here," Dusty said. "The other side's just too steep."

"Go slow and be careful," C.J. said. Her warning was not necessary.

The group crept along the wall until the slope of the wall became too extreme to navigate safely by walking upright. The wall ahead of them formed a crescent shape – which restricted their ability to stand.

"We'd better crawl or scoot from here," Dusty said.

"Is the rope still tight?" C.J. asked.

Dusty gave it a tug. It was.

Dusty sat on his bottom, his back along the cold gray wall. With the flashlight in his left hand, he crab-walked slowly along the wall – his feet within inches of the black water. C.J. assumed the same position. A few inches taller than Dusty, C.J. had to pull her legs closer to her chest as she inched along the wall. Her muscles ached from the exertion, but she concentrated intently to keep her footing.

Surefooted, Cleotis walked slowly behind Dusty, his head slightly above his seated master. Ahead, the cavern walls yielded their slope making it easier to walk upright again.

"We're almost there," Dusty said. His flashlight scrapped along the rock wall as he continued his slow advance.

"Don't get in a hurry, Dusty," C.J. said.

"I'm the one who fell in the last time, remember?" he said, grunting as he did.

C.J., who had managed to keep pace with her two companions, felt her left shoulder bump up against the hindquarter of Cleotis. The dog stumbled, causing its back end to slide down the side of the wall slope. Cleotis instantly extended his claws in a desperate attempt to keep from being swallowed into the pool. He scrambled desperately to sink his claws into the rocks, but Cleotis could not grip the impenetrable rock.

The dog flailed helplessly into the pool.

As he did, the tether that was supposed to have been his lifeline jerked violently at Dusty's waist and wrenched him backwards toward the abyss. Instinctively Dusty flattened his body and hugged the rock flooring beneath him, simultaneously attempting to maintain his toehold on the rock to avoid being pulled into the pool.

The beam from Dusty's flashlight jerked wildly in every direction, making it impossible for C.J. to see enough of the scene to know precisely how to respond to the commotion.

"Help," Dusty said breathlessly.

C.J. scooted as close to Dusty as she could. She could hear, but could not see, the panicked dog in the water below her as it tried without success to traverse the wall from which it had fallen.

"I… can't… hold..." There was desperation in Dusty's voice.

C.J. groped in the darkness until her hands felt the taut rope that was tied to Dusty's belt. She wrenched it toward her but felt her own foothold weakening as she did. Every time Cleotis grappled his claws into the rocks to pull himself to safety, he came closer to pulling C.J. and Dusty into the pool with him.

C.J. blurted, "Don't pull Cleotis. Swim! Swim! Don't pull. We've got you. Swim alongside."

Miraculously, the rope slackened.

"Come on alongside, boy. That's it, boy," C.J. said encouragingly. "Scoot Dusty, scoot." The two scooted in tandem alongside the wall. "Keep swimming Cleotis. Don't pull. Come along. We're almost there."

C.J. and Dusty continued scooting until the slope of the wall tapered, providing a wider footing. When it was sufficiently wide to stand, Dusty did so, followed by C.J.

"Shine the light on Cleotis," C.J. said, as she held onto the rope with both hands. "Come on boy. You can make it."

It was all but impossible to see the black dog in the dim abyss. Only the emerald-green reflection of the dog's eyes could be seen as he made his way along the pool's tapered edge and toward safety. C.J. felt slack in the rope as the dog came closer to the shoreline. Then they watched as Cleotis walked casually out of the water beside them.

Exhausted, the two collapsed on the fine sand that lined the shore. A feeling of relief washed over C.J. and Dusty. That relief was followed quickly by a shower of water droplets from Cleotis as he violently shook his body to rid his fur of the pool's water. It was an unwelcome shower, but the two laughed uncontrollably in response to the spray.

"Happy," C.J. heard. Then she felt a warm moist tongue lap at the rivulets of water that were streaming down her face.

"I'm happy, too, boy," she said softly.

"While you're talking to the dog, tell him not to try to drown me next time," Dusty said, rubbing his rope-burned hands.

"What's that boy? Okay, I'll tell him that." C.J. turned toward Dusty. "He told me to tell you that now you're even," she said with a laugh.

"Did he really say that?" Dusty asked sincerely.

"Yeah, and he also told me to tell you that he's smarter and better looking than you, too."

Dusty knew that was a lie. "Very funny," he said. He stuck out his tongue for good measure.

Now that they were safe, C.J. pointed the light to the soft green sand dune that glistened with the red and orange sparkles. The three made their way to the sand bar.

Dusty couldn't resist picking up some samples. "Point your light here," he said. "These are pretty." C.J. complied. Dusty shoved a few of the shiny stones in his pockets – the pockets he had already filled with the soft green stones.

"We need to get moving," C.J. said.

"Can I use the snack bag to put some more in?" Dusty asked. He was mesmerized by the glistening sight before him.

"No, Dusty," C.J. snapped. "You cannot use the bag to put some more of your stupid rocks in. This isn't some kind of a game you know. We're in real trouble here. You almost drowned. Cleotis almost drowned. We don't know if we're going to get out of here. Don't you understand?" She was screaming. "And all because of your stupid infatuation with these stupid rocks." C.J. was seething. "Now let's go."

Dusty wanted to say something in return, but didn't dare. C.J. had gone from laughing heartily a few moments before, to nearly biting his head off. Girls, he thought, were beyond predictable.

He walked in silence behind C.J. As the minutespassed, he realized that C.J. was probably right. They were in this mess because of him. Still, C.J. didn't need to speak to him like he was some kind of child, he thought, trying to recover some of his pride. As the three made their way deeper into an unknown darkness Dusty remained uncharacteristically quiet. It would take a while for his wounded pride to heal. He was still none-too-happy that he was unable to harvest the sparkling rocks that had brought him here in the first place.

RON NICHOLS

Chapter Twenty-Eight

"You're certain your groundwater models are right?" Dave Gunther said, peering at the topographical map on his desk.

"Positive," Christine said confidently.

"How soon can we expect the water to flow?'

"A week at the outside," she said.

"And you're equally certain the water will re-emerge somewhere in here?" he asked, tapping the tip of his cap-covered fountain pen on the yellow-shaded area of the map.

"Certain enough to have purchased the property," Christine said. It was the bombshell she had waited all of her life to drop.

Dave Gunther looked into the eyes of the cunning woman seated across from his desk. "You mean, 'on behalf of Cornerstone,'" he said, waiting to see if this important correction to her statement would elicit affirmation or confrontation.

"Of course," Christine said showing just a hint of a smile.

Mr. Gunther smiled broadly as he rocked back in his chair. "I presume GeoTherm doesn't know anything about this little 'property acquisition,'" he asked.

"It's a personal investment," she said. "My plans are to hand the property over to Cornerstone at my cost, just as soon as the water starts flowing."

"Which," Gunther added, "will be about the time the champagne starts flowing in celebration of your addition to the Cornerstone executive management team." He reached his hand across the desk. Christine shook it heartily. "I'll have the papers drawn up this week," he said. "By this time next week, you'll be the newest – and if I might be so bold – brightest of Cornerstone's vice presidents."

"Should we talk compensation now?" Christine asked. For the first time in her life, she was in the driver's seat and she intended to extract every perk she could from her brilliant coup.

Mr. Gunther chuckled. "I think you'll be pleased with the executive package I'm recommending," he said. "Plus, considering your extraordinary service to the company before your employment – and your tremendous potential to become one of our top executives, I'm recommending to the board of directors that you receive our top executive's stock option and bonus package. No one in the company – except me, of course, has a better package. It's sweet," he said with a smile, "Very sweet."

Christine had to work to suppress her elation. "Well then," she said as she stood, "I guess I'd better get back to work."

She pushed her seat backwards and turned to walk toward the door. "You might want to peek in on your soon-to-be office," Gunther added. "For the record, it's the biggest office on the second floor."

Christine nodded, and then discretely admired Mr. Gunther's palatial office and exquisite furnishings as she made her way out the door. Soon she'd get the respect she'd deserved from the day she began her career. Thanks to her efforts assisting Mother Nature in its re-direction of spring water off of the Davidek place and onto the adjacent property she'd purchased for a song, she'd also have the power and prestige that goes to someone who's not afraid to create her own opportunities.

Now she couldn't wait to tender her resignation at GeoTherm. They'd be shocked and, of course, disappointed, Christine believed. But not half as shocked and disappointed as they would be when she eventually acquired the fledgling little company in one of her first moves as Vice President of Cornerstone. The only thing she didn't know yet was who on the GeoTherm management team, she would fire first.

*

While the big cavern offered some relief for C.J.'s growing claustrophobia, it did little to relieve her growing anxiety over their predicament. As far as she knew, there was no other route out of the cave, making each step the trio took, a step deeper into potential hopelessness.

To amplify her anxiety, as the three made their way out of the cavern, the route along the waterway began to funnel into a smaller and smaller passageway. The cold damp walls began to close in around them. C.J. was finding it more difficult to breathe as the walls constricted the route.

"Hold on," she told Dusty, with just enough volume to be heard over the trickling water through which they were wading.

"You okay?" Dusty asked, turning and shinning the flashlight's beam into her face. Then he saw the terror on her face.

"C.J?"

She was gasping.

He took a few steps toward her. "Are you okay?" he asked.

C.J. didn't respond. Her eyes had a distant, desperate look that frightened Dusty to his soul.

Not knowing what reaction such a move might bring, Dusty placed a tentative hand on her shoulder.

"C.J?" He looked for some response, but could see only detachment. In an attempt to retrieve her from that other place where she had slipped, he began to gently stroke her arm.

That simple, genuine gesture of care appeared to break the trance.

"Hey. Cleotis wants to talk to you," he said to her, smiling. He trusted that his good-natured teasing would return to him the C.J. he knew. It seemed to have no effect. "You want to rest again?" He asked with sincerity.

"No. I'm okay. I just, I just freaked out there for a minute," she said.

She looked directly into Dusty's eyes. Her apparent re-awakening settled his nerves. "We can wait if you want to," Dusty said. He held her hand gently.

"No, let's get out of here. I, I, just hope this doesn't get too much tighter," she said. She squeezed his hand in return, and then released it.

"Yeah, me too," Dusty said. He added, "Don't worry. We'll be out soon." He could only hope his words would come true.

C.J. smiled at Dusty. His heart felt instantly better, his mind reassured – at least for the moment.

C.J. felt the warm, rubbery appendage of Cleotis' tongue caress her dangling hand.

"Okay. Okay." Cleotis' tail swung enthusiastically.

"Yeah, buddy. I'm okay. Let's get moving." C.J. patted the big dog on its broad head.

Guided only by a noticeably weakening beam of light, they turned and continued their slow, cramped ascension into the unknown.

*

"Come on, Duke. Work it, buddy. Find me a scent," Otto said, encouraging the yellow dog to find an opening that might lead into the cave. Duke did not need additional encouragement. Like some kind of four-legged robot, he jabbed his muzzle into the vegetation, snorted, then scampered to another location. In a zigzag pattern along the hillside, Duke repeated his reconnaissance until he reached the crest of the hill.

The rain, which had begun with an occasional heavy droplet, had now worked itself into a downpour. Through the torrent, Otto spotted a tree limb on the ground, which he snatched up then stripped of extraneous branches. With a few quick slashes from his pocket knife, he fashioned it into a walking stick. Trailing along behind the big dog, Otto probed between the rocks and underbrush with quick thrusts of his walking stick, hoping to get lucky and find another opening into the cave. He realized it was a long shot, but until the sheriff arrived and assessed the possibility of removing the debris from the cave's previous opening, searching for another opening was the best use of his time.

Sheets of rain blew in successive waves across the hillside, soaking everything and everyone – including Otto and Duke – in their wake. Had it not been for the brim of his baseball cap, Otto would have been unable to see his own hand in front of him. The lightning flashed bright against the gray sky, momentarily turning the world an eerie phosphorous white – then, just as quickly, turning it back to gray again. Standing outside in a thunderstorm was risky, if not completely foolish, Otto knew, but every moment counted. Getting to C.J. and Dusty preempted all of his personal safety concerns.

Otto continued poking and prodding the ground until he heard a muffled "woof" in the distance. He stopped, trying to hear through the wind and the incessant spattering of raindrops that were pummeling his baseball cap.

"Woof." It was louder now, and Otto began to home in on the sound. It was coming from over a spine of rocks that ran nearly directly up the hillside. The irregular, pointed rocks looked like rows of jagged shark's teeth through the rain, and Otto headed directly for them.

"Good Duke. What'd you find, boy? What'd you find?" Otto shouted ahead to the dog.

"Woof, woof, woof."

It took Otto five or six minutes to ascend the crest of the hill. He was gasping for breath as he scanned the ravine below. About 30 feet below he saw the unmistakable backside of his yellow dog – its tail whip-sawing intently in the air.

"Duke," Otto yelled. The dog turned its head toward the voice of its master, and plunged its entire head back into the ground. Mercifully, the wind and rain had dissipated considerably, and the thunder was quickly dissolving into a low, distant grumble. Such was the manic nature of thunderstorms in the south: Instantaneous fire and fury – followed almost as quickly by peace and tranquility.

As Otto reached the dog, Duke retracted his head from the ground in time to see his master approach. Otto patted the old dog's muscular frame.

"Good boy, Duke. What'd you find, buddy? Let me take a look." Duke backed off just enough to allow Otto to drop to the ground and peer into the opening in the ground. It could be just a fissure in the ancient hill, Otto thought. But as he pulled one of the overgrown rocks to the side, a cool, damp breeze rushed up to meet him. The air from the ground smelled musty and wet. But the breeze was constant and strong – as though created by an electric fan. Otto pulled another rock from the narrow opening. The top of the rock looked like all of the others, with moss and mud obscuring its natural features. Otto tossed it quickly aside, where it rolled down the slope a few feet before coming to rest. Something in his peripheral vision made Otto take a second glance. The bottom of the rock – free from vegetation – was decidedly a green mineral color. Was this the Kimberlite green coloration Maggie had mentioned? Otto reached for another bowling ball sized rock, turned it over, and smiled. It, too, was green. This might just be an indicator of a Kimberlite pipe, or as Maggie had said, an indicator of another route into the cave. Excitedly, he began moving rock after rock until he had created an opening just large enough for a person or a dog to fit through.

He yelled into the cave. "C.J! Dusty! Can you hear me?" He waited quietly for a response. The sound of his heart pounding in his chest and the breeze blowing across his ear made it difficult to hear subtle sounds. He bellowed into the opening again. "C.J! Dusty!"

Still, he heard no reply. Otto decided that he would have to wait for Maggie and the sheriff to return, with the ropes, the tools and the lights necessary for a descent into the unknown opening. He turned to Duke who sat patiently at his side, panting rhythmically. Duke's fur was wet and gathered in small darkened spikes over his body.

"We'll just have to wait for Maggie," Otto said to the dog. Otto stood to stretch his cramping legs. His muscles ached from the stress of the hike. His cold, rain-soaked trousers only served to exacerbate the dull muscle pain. "We'll find 'em though, boy. Thanks to you, we'll find 'em," he said, and patted Duke on the top of his head.

As he did, a bright, nearly blinding ray of sun sliced through a break in the clouds. Otto shielded his eyes from the sudden illumination. The thunder cell that had delivered the wind and rain, had passed to the east, its black curtain of rain swept across another hill in the distance. The warmth of the sun blessed Otto's face and he turned again to watch the parting shroud in the distance. This time, however, he gazed upon the most beautiful double rainbow he had ever seen. He prayed that the rainbow was a harbinger of good things to come.

*

"I'm hungry," Dusty said as he crept along in the darkness. His words echoed as his stomach growled in agreement.

They were now only using the flashlight when they absolutely had as they made their way slowly through a seemingly endless corridor.

C.J. did not know how much time had passed since they each had eaten one of the granola bars she had had the good fortune to bring along. It was difficult for her to imagine why anyone would think of eating at a time like this. Ignorance was clearly bliss, she supposed, and perhaps it was better to be consumed with hunger than it was to be consumed with the panic that had nearly paralyzed her earlier. At least she had a temporary antidote for Dusty's hunger pains. She could do nothing to quell her own growing pain of despondency.

For a brief moment, she thought about those movies where the leader of a group that was stranded on an island or adrift on the ocean would insist on rationing the remaining food. To do so in this situation, made perfectly good sense, still C.J. didn't have the heart to deny Dusty a respite from their peril.

"Okay. Stop," C.J. said. "Let me see – or rather feel – what I have left in my pack. By pure tactile sensation, C.J. slid the backpack from her shoulders, and felt for the zipper along the side of the canvas bag. She pulled the metal zipper upward and reached her free hand into the pack, as she groped through the various items for any remaining goodies.

"Fried chicken or steak?" C.J.asked, then almost immediately regretted her attempted humor. Until she had uttered those words, she had not felt any prangs of hunger herself. Just the recitation of those words conjured warm, delicious sights and smells that nearly overwhelmed her.

"What?" Dusty said. "You have chick-,"

C.J. cut him off mid-sentence. "No, I'm kidding," she said quickly. "Granola or peanut butter crackers."

"I'll take the peanut butter."

C.J. felt for the familiar shape and touch of the cellophane wrapper that contained six pairs of disk-shaped, salted crackers that sandwiched six pats of brown, peanut butter paste between each pair. But as she did, she felt something at the bottom of the backpack that she hadn't remembered putting there herself. To her amazement, she felt a small, square box and a cylindrical metallic object. Overcome with excitement, she nearly dropped the whole backpack as she extracted her find. She let the pack strap slide along her arm until it rested at the "V" created by her elbow.

She fumbled for a switch but could find none.

"Hand the crackers this way," Dusty said in the darkness, not knowing that C.J. was no longer interested in dispensing food.

Finally, C.J. twisted the flanged end of the cylinder and a bright beam of light pierced the darkness. C.J. felt her spirit lift immediately and was nearly giddy with excitement. As she twisted the flanged end, the beam narrowed, penetrating deeply down the dark corridor. It was another small, but powerful Maglight – a gift of extraordinary value given their circumstances. The narrow beam offered more than eyes into the darkness. It offered hope. And hope was something she hadn't felt for some time.

"Hey where'd you get that?" Dusty asked, forgetting, for the moment, his hunger. Reflexively, C.J. turned the beam toward Dusty's voice. Having seen only the faintest of light for more than an hour, the pupils of Dusty's eyes were complete dilated. The light hit him with an intensity that caught C.J. by surprise. He recoiled, turning immediately away from the source of the pain and said, "Shit!"

"Sorry," C.J. said quickly, realizing her error. "You okay?"

"Yeah. Don't do that."

"I didn't mean to. I forgot," she said apologetically.

"Where'd you get it?"

"It was in the bottom of the backpack I borrowed from Aunt Maggie. I had no idea it was there," C.J. said, excitedly directing the beam toward the cave walls – away from her unintended victim. The light from Dusty's flashlight seemed anemic in contrast. "I guess she forgot to take it out the last time she used the pack."

"Anything else in there?" Dusty asked. He paused, then added, "Like a map out of here?"

In her excitement of finding the flashlight, C.J. had almost forgotten the small box she had also fondled in the darkness.

"Hold this." C.J. handed the small Maglight to Dusty. He dutifully pointed the bright light into the gaping mouth of the open backpack. The beam reflected off the cellophane and illuminated the shiny foil wrappers of their meager provisions, as well as the white, cotton panties C.J. had packed.

Reaching deep into the pack, C.J. seized the box with her right hand and retrieved the item – holding it to her side. The light from the flashlight revealed white lettering on a red box. A narrow strip of black ran lengthways along the side. It was a friction strip.

"Matches," C.J. said. She shook the box gently, and then applied pressure with her left index finger to nudge the box's inner drawer to slide open. Inside were a dozen or more wooden sticks, each coated with a small red, tulip-bulb shaped head, and topped with a dab of white.

"Great," Dusty said. "Now if we can just find some dry wood, we can start a fire and have a weenie roast."

"You never know," C.J. said ignoring Dusty's sarcasm. The truth was C.J. couldn't fathom a possible use for the little match sticks, either. But they were in survival mode now, and from watching various shows on the Discovery Channel, she had learned that even the most inauspicious item could be helpful when your life depended on it. She dropped the box back into the sack. "You want those peanut butter and crackers now?" she asked.

"Sure," Dusty said. "Can I have a drink from your water bottle?"

"I thought you said the water from the cave was safe to drink?" C.J. asked.

"It is. I just thought we could share yours, is all," Dusty said.

C.J. handed him the bottle.

"We can refill it when it's empty," he said. "At least there's lots of water around."

They each opened a six pack of the disks. Conserving their precious new gift, C.J. tightened the flanged end of the Maglight and doused the light. The two sat on the cave floor, crunching their meal in total darkness. The darkness didn't seem as foreboding as it had just a few moments earlier.

RON NICHOLS

Chapter Twenty-Nine

Duke, as always, had been the first to notice the approaching figures. It was his guttural "woof," that alerted Otto to the people who were advancing up the hill. Otto turned to the dog. He could see that Duke's eyes and ears were locked onto his targets. His ears stiffened and turned slightly to collect the sound riding in the wind. His wet nose twitched, sniffed and probed for additional clues that might reveal a familiar smell.

A few moments later, Otto himself saw four people working their way up the hill. As they drew closer Otto recognized the smaller figure as Maggie, who was leading the pack. Behind Maggie was a stout man in a tan uniform, followed by two taller, but identically uniform-clad men. Otto was relieved. It was Sheriff Dirk Mueller and his deputies. All were burdened with ropes and equipment.

"Up here," Otto shouted while waving his arm from side to side. Duke barked twice. Otto could see two of the three figures pointing in his direction. Otto continued to wave although he knew he had been spotted.

"Let's go down and help them with the equipment," Otto said to Duke.

"Good. Good." Duke's tail wagged enthusiastically.

"Glad to see 'em, too, buddy," Otto said as the two bounded down the slope.

*

"Are you serious?" Frank Rahe asked.

"Very," Christine said, attempting with some difficulty to mask her pleasure. She stood decisively with hands on her hips, in front of the mustachioed man behind the modest, wooden desk.

"May I ask why?"

"Opportunity," Christine said confidently. She had rehearsed the answer to this very question and had vowed not to reveal anything more about her intentions until that future day when she would walk into the offices at GeoTherm with the termination papers of the dozen employees in her hands. It would be the day she announced Cornerstone's buyout. Until that day, she would be as trite and evasive as possible, to avoid tipping her hand.

"Perhaps," Mr. Rahe said, "we could match your offer? Depending on our expected growth here, I can't see any reason why you couldn't move up to our Executive Management Team, and you know that would make you eligible for the executive bonus package," he said.

"Bonus package, my ass," Christine thought, but she did not say it. She knew GeoTherm's management team hadn't qualified for the profit-based bonuses for years, and probably never would, given the fact that their parent company set its profit goals impossibly high. Plus, she thought, "why should I wait for a possible offer, when I'll be a senior vice president at Cornerstone the day I walk back through their doors?"

"Thank you, but no," Christine said emphatically. She wanted to embarrass the man behind the desk by laying out the details of Cornerstone's generous and appropriate offer, but opted to let the word spread throughout the company by mentioning those details to one or two of the company's clerks. By the end of the day, everyone at GeoTherm (and many at GeoTherm's parent company) would be in awe of Christine's new executive position and compensation package thanks to an informal, yet effective, communication process. Nothing spreads faster than news on the grapevine.

Christine stood in silence for a moment, studying the stunned expression on her previous boss' face, then added abruptly, "My resignation is effective in two weeks." She placed a plain white envelope that contained the concise wording of her resignation on Mr. Rahe's desk.

She turned on her heels, and exited the office, leaving in her wake a speechless and confused Mr. Rahe – a man whom Christine believed had never deserved to be her boss. Soon he would be a man whose fate she would hold in her hands.

Had she not been so out of shape, Christine would have leapt into the air as she sauntered down the hallway to hercubicle. Her new job meant that she was moving out of cubicle city, permanently. This was the beginning of a new career, a new life for her. Finally, she would get what she deserved. All that was left was for nature to run its course and send the spring's water onto her newly acquired property – a course she had re-directed thanks to a few, well-placed sticks of dynamite.

*

He swept the beam from the old Maglight back and forth across what appeared to be an impenetrable petrified forest. Then the dull beam simply gave out. Dusty twisted the lens on the flashlight in a vain effort to bring it back to life as he had done before. But this time, he could not.

"Darn," Dusty said. "It's gone."

C.J. pulled her flashlight from the backpack and switched it on. The light was bright and steady. She was grateful they had had the good judgment to use one flashlight at a time. As she shone the beam around, Dusty and C.J. could see that the narrow granite corridor they had been in had opened into a broad room where stalagmites rose from the cavern's floor. Stalactites hung from the low ceiling and met the rising stalagmites to form hundreds of narrow columns so closely aligned that getting between them might prove to be difficult, if not impossible.

It was a beautiful, yet frightening sight.

"Now which way?" Dusty asked.

"I, I, don't know," C.J. said.

Having no immediate solution to their dilemma, C.J. asked Dusty to shine the light onto her wrist. She looked at her watch in disbelief. They were now way overdue. C.J. couldn't imagine the trouble she'd be in with her parents when Aunt Maggie filled them in on the details of this debacle. Perhaps time would dull the sharp edge of the situation's seriousness. And perhaps by the end of the summer, when her parents finally returned from Brazil, all would be forgiven. Then again, she thought to herself it might be possible that they would eventually be given up for dead in the bowels of this granite beast.

"What time is it?" Dusty asked.

"About eight."

"In the morning or night?"

"Evening," C.J. said. "I think."

"You think they're looking for us?" Dusty asked.

"I know they are," C.J. answered, satisfied in her mind that, Aunt Maggie would try to find a way into the cave, assuming she deduced that they were there and not somewhere in the woods or along the creek.

"MeMaw's gonna kill me," Dusty said. "But I don't care. As long as I get out of here, she can blister my bottom. I won't care."

"We've got to find a way though this," C.J. said. "Let's see if we can work our way as close around the side as we can. Maybe there's another corridor that leads into here."

"How will we know if it'll lead us out?" Dusty asked.

It was a good question. One that C.J. did not have an answer for.

"We'll cross that bridge when we get to it," she said dismissively.

The salmon-colored columns were smooth, wet and cold to the touch. They were formed, C.J. remembered from some nature show she had seen on television, from thousands of years of water dripping slowly from above, transporting with it the minerals that collected on the ceiling and on the floor, eventually building the cone-shaped stalactites and stalagmites. When the two met, they formed elongated hour-glass shaped columns.

Dusty led the pack through the maze, trying to stay as close to the left cavern wall as possible. Fortunately, the space between the columns was sufficient to move between them so the three made good progress as they negotiated the rock column forest. In less than five minutes, they were confronted with that metaphorical bridge to which C.J. had referred to moments earlier. Ahead of them were three, nearly identical openings each three or four feet in width and height, separated by several feet of granite. It reminded C.J. of that game show she once saw where contestants had to pick between door number one, door number two and door number three. In that game, only one door had a good prize. It was likely, she thought, that only one of these openings held the prize that could spare their lives – the prize of freedom.

"Now what?" Dusty said. He beamed his light into each of the openings. Both C.J. and Dusty peered into them with keen interest. Each opening appeared to be an identical corridor that led into infinite darkness.

"Which one?" Dusty asked. There was a distinct note of desperation in his voice.

"I don't know. I need to think," C.J. said. She looked at Cleotis. The dog had been quiet. "Which way Cleotis?" C.J. asked. She waited in the darkness for the words. But none were forthcoming.

"Shine the light on Cleotis." Dusty did.

"Which way, boy?" C.J. asked, confident the dog would lead them into one of the openings. Cleotis did not move, but simply looked at her, cocking his head in what C.J. interpreted as genuine confusion.

"What's he saying," Dusty asked. This time, he wasn't making fun of C.J.

"He's not saying anything," C.J. said with disappointment. "He's not saying a darn thing."

It was time for another snack break. When all else fails, grab a snack, C.J. thought. She plunged her hand into the backpack and felt around for one of the remaining packs of snacks. The corner of the matchbox stabbed the back of her hand. "Ouch."

"What happened?" Dusty asked.

"Oh, I stabbed my hand on the…," her words fell away.

"On the what?" Dusty asked.

"Matches," C.J. said softly. "Matches!"

"What about the matches?"

"It's worth a shot," C.J. said.

"What's worth a shot?" Dusty asked, growing more confused by the moment.

"You'll see," C.J. said. "Shine your flashlight over here."

*

Sheriff Mueller and Otto leveraged their railroad picks between the rocks to ply them away from their silt-based, earthen adhesive, the two younger and leaner deputies added the final measure of muscle to extricate them from the opening. During this painfully slow process, Maggie busied herself with examining the rocks from the opening as well as those surrounding it. The sky was brightening now and Maggie could make out additional details about the rocks' characteristics.

"I'm certain this is another Kimberlite pipe," Maggie said, as she studied, then tossed one of the smaller rocks aside. "I just hope it's an off-shoot of the one C.J. and Dusty are in, and not a separate one."

"We'll find out soon, I guess," Sheriff Mueller said. "We should be able to go take a look in just a couple of minutes."

"Hand me the flashlight and backpack, Maggie," Otto said, walking in her direction.

"You better let us handle this, Otto," Sheriff Mueller said, placing himself between Maggie's outstretched arm and Otto. "That's why I brought these young bucks along," he said, intercepting the backpack. "Matt and Cory here live for this kind of adventure, don't you boys?"

"Yes sir," the two said in unison.

"I want to secure a line to the lead searcher," Sheriff Mueller said. Cory, the smaller of the two deputies stepped forward.

"I'll take the lead, boss," he said. He tugged at the belt around his trousers, "I believe I had a few less biscuits for breakfast than Matt did." Everyone smiled. Before the two deputies began decending into the darkness, Sheriff Mueller took both aside and gave them some last minute instructions.

"One hour, boys. One hour," Sheriff Mueller said. "If you're not back to me within an hour with your assessment of the situation, you'll both be on permanent guard duty at the county fair. Understand?" The two nodded. Then Sheriff Mueller added, "Let's be safe, and bring us back those two youngins.'"

With those final words, the deputies squeezed through the small opening in the side of the hill. In an instant, they were gone – as though they had been swallowed by the earth itself.

"Good luck," Otto shouted into the opening. Duke stood by his master's side, his yellow, water hose of a tail whipping from side to side.

"Find C.J?"

"Yeah, they'll find her boy. Then you'll get that hug you've been waiting for C.J. to give you."

*

C.J. fished around in the bottom of the backpack before finding and retrieving the box of matches.

"What exactly do you plan to do?" Dusty asked. "Start a signal fire?"

"You might say that," she said, feeling as hopeful as she had insince becoming trapped beneath the surface.

"Who's it a signal for?"

"Us," C.J. said.

"Us?"

"Yep. Point the light right here."

Dusty complied. C.J. slid the package drawer open and pulled one of the red-tipped sticks from the box, then closed it again. Then she placed the stick between her thumb and forefinger and placed its white-tipped red head atop the black friction strip. With a quick stroke, C.J. slid the match along the side of the box. Dusty could see a white spark as it leapt briefly into the air before dying, like countless shooting stars he had seen on moonless summer nights. But there was no flame. C.J. rotated the stick's head and repeated the stroke. Another spark. But this time, it was followed by a small inferno that flashed with intense light before settling into a yellow glowing flame. It danced atop the little stick C.J. held in her hand.

"Now what?" Dusty asked.

"Just keep your flashlight pointed in this direction."

Mesmerized, the two watched the flame slowly work its way down the length of the stick. C.J. held the stick vertically. In a few moments the flame gave up its intensity melting from hot white, to yellow, to a small cool blue flame. Then it was gone, leaving behind a glowing red ember at the tip of the remaining wooden stick. Light gray smoke poured from the ash covered stick toward C.J., then dissipated in the darkness.

C.J. followed the trail of smoke to the left side of the cavern.

"Put the light here," she said, before striking another flame. The two watched the flame glow and then burn out again. And again, C.J. followed the smoke that the flame had left behind. This time it moved with greater certainty, before dissipating again in front of the smallest of the openings. Dusty needed no prompting for the light. He held the flashlight's beam dead on C.J.'s hand as she struck the third stick. When the flame died, the gray smoke was swept directly toward and then into the small opening.

"That's our signal?" Dusty said.

"That's our signal," C.J. repeated. "Remember the cool breeze we felt when we walked into the cave? It's headed in a new direction, and I'm betting that it's still headed toward daylight."

"How do you know it's heading toward daylight, and not deeper into the cave?" Dusty asked.

It was a good question. "Have you ever walked by this cave and not felt a cool breeze hit you?"

"I guess that's right," Dusty said "I never thought about that before. You're pretty smart," he said, "for a girl." Without hesitation, he took Cleotis' leash and tucked his head through the small opening, then turned his flashlight so C.J. could navigate safely through. "Let's go." Dusty was now convinced this small opening held the key to their freedom.

C.J. followed her friend into the small entrance where the trailing line of gray smoke had preceded them. As she squatted to fit through the opening, she said a silent prayer that Dusty's apparent confidence was not misplaced.

Chapter Thirty

"What's all this about a Kimberlite pipe, Maggie?" Sheriff Mueller asked after the two deputies vanished from sight.

Rather than explaining the diamond-bearing aspects of the pipe, Maggie cut to the part relevant to the two kids' possible escape route.

"Kimberlite pipes are off-shoots from ancient volcanoes, Dirk. Millions of years ago they allowed magma and other minerals from deep inside the earth to flow to the surface," she said pointing to the green rocks. After the pipe spewed its cargo, and the formation cooled, it created these tubes, or pipes. That's why they're called Kimberlite pipes."

"And you think those kids may be in there?"

"The major pipe is probably the one they entered, but I'm hoping there are other pipes that may also lead to the surface," she said. "We'll never be able to clear all of that debris from the old spring, and judging from the debris field, it's possible the entire bedrock roof above the cave floor collapsed," Maggie said. Then she gasped realizing what she had said. "Oh my, God, what if the kids were..." her words trailed off. She did not want to say what she knew was a very real possibility – that the two could be lying under tons of rock. She turned her head and began to sob.

Duke loped immediately to her side and plopped his hip on her foot.

Otto was close behind and put his arm around Maggie. She turned her head into his shoulder and softly cried.

"We'll find 'em, Maggie."

The big dog whined and leaned further into his friend. She reached down and patted his head.

Duke looked up with chocolate brown eyes. "C.J. okay."

True to their words, and cognizant of Sheriff Mueller's warning, the two young deputies emerged from the opening on the side of the hill a full five minutes before the deadline. Though the evening light was fading fast, they squinted their eyes like moles who had poked their heads through the soil after a long, subterraneanhiatus. Each deputy shed the loops of ropes draped over his shoulder. The coils plopped unceremoniously to the ground.

"How's it look?" Sheriff Mueller asked, standing beside the two men.

"There are a few tight spots," Matt said, "and we had little trouble getting down there very far. But the shoot looks like it could go on for a long time."

"How far'd you make it?"

Matt turned to Corey. "What would you say, two-hundred yards, maybe?"

"Seems about right," Corey said. "I believe we could have gone farther, but we had to get back, per the boss' orders."

"Good thing you did," Sheriff Mueller said with a firm pat between Corey's shoulder blades. He meant what he'd said about patrol duty at the county fairgrounds, and the two deputies knew it. Then Sheriff Mueller added with a nod of approval, "Nice work."

"What's next, Dirk?" Otto asked as he and Maggie walked toward the uniformed men.

"Well, we'll start by setting up a small command center down near the road. Then we'll get some more help from the volunteer fire department, and get some more equipment and people in that hole," he pointed in the direction of the opening. "We'll work round the clock to get those young'ns, Maggie. I'll get the National Guard out here if I need to – and you know I'm not kidding." The stout, slightly balding man used his intensely blue eyes to peer directly into Maggie's and said, "You need to get back home before it gets too dark and get hold of MeMaw. I'm sure she's worried sick," he said. "You let her know we'll do whatever we have to do to get those kids."

Maggie nodded and forced a smile.

Then Sheriff Mueller put his arm around her. "You know, Maggie, I don't know who I feel more sorry for, MeMaw for not knowing where Dusty is, or Dusty for when MeMaw lays into him." They all smiled. "Now get some rest. We've got work to do here."

"Let's go," Otto said. "Duke and I'll get you home. We'll come back first thing tomorrow morning." The yellow dog fell in line behind Maggie and Otto – his tail still swinging from side to side – his tongue flopped from the side of his perpetually grinning mouth.

The uniformed law enforcement officials watched Otto, Maggie and Duke make their way back toward the main road. "Let's get things rolling gentlemen," Sheriff Mueller said. "We'd better start by calling our own families to let them know we'll all be working late tonight."

*

The passageway was tight. And after nearly an hour of duck-walking, crawling and climbing up and over rock formations, C.J. and Dusty were exhausted.

"I've got to stop," C.J. yelled ahead to Dusty. Her heart was pounding so hard she thought it was going to explode in her chest. Even in the cool, wet atmosphere of the cave, beads of perspiration formed on her forehead.

"Me too," Dusty said, breathlessly. "What time is it?" he asked as he pointed his flashlight beam in C.J.'s direction.

"You got somewhere you need to be?" C.J. asked. "Hey, wise cracks are my department," Dusty said with a smile.

The casual banter lightened the mood for a few moments, and helped distract C.J. from her continuous thoughts of doom. Though they seemed to be on an upward track, C.J. had seen nothing that would lead her to believe that the route the smoke had taken was the escape exit she had hoped and perhaps even bet their lives on.

"It's almost 10 – at night, I think," C.J. said.

"Yeah, it looks pretty dark," Dusty said. It was another attempt at humor.

Without really thinking, C.J. replaced her thoughts of doubt with the prospect of a snack. She reached into the backpack – her hand located the remaining provisions. They were down to their last six-pack of peanut butter crackers, and there was but one granola bar for the three to share. Now that their trek was taking them higher, neither had had a drink of water for more than an hour. Water was the one thing that previously had been in abundant supply. Fortunately, the two had refilled C.J.'s water bottle after draining it as they ate their last snack.

"I'm thirsty," Dusty said. It was the first time he hadn't mentioned food at a rest break.

"Me too," C.J. said. "The good news is we're apparently moving upwards, closer to the surface and away from the water."

"I guess that's good news," Dusty said. "What snacks do you have left?"

C.J. held the two packs in front of her in the darkness. Dusty painted her hands with his light. "This is it," she said matter-of-factly.

"That's it? For the two of us?" Dusty asked.

"Hungry."

C.J. looked down at Cleotis.

"No. That's it for the three of us," she corrected. "Guess we should split everything up three ways, then try to get some sleep."

"Okay by me," Dusty said. "But I get to sleep next to Cleotis' head. He farts sometimes and I don't want to be near the back end."

C.J. smiled and handed the remaining provisions to Dusty, and then tossed Cleotis his two peanut butter crackers. With one gulp followed by a second, the ravenous dog appeared to swallow them whole. As though to savor the last bite of food he might see for some time, Cleotis slowly chewed his portion of the granola bar, then licked up the few crumbs that had fallen to the cave floor. For extra measure, he licked his lips to extract any remaining morsels that might be lodged between his cheek and gums.

"Hungry. Thirsty."

"Me, too, Cleotis. We'll get something more to eat and drink first thing tomorrow," C.J. said to the dog.

She opened the water bottle and poured some of the liquid into her cupped hand. The dog lapped it up quickly. C.J. repeated the task and said, "That's your share for now, Cleotis."

"You know they're going to put you in a loony bin if you keep talking to dogs," Dusty said.

"They ought to put me in a loony bin for following you in here," C.J. countered. Dusty didn't respond.

"How's this for a place to curl up?" Dusty asked pointing his flashlight beam on a flat area of the cave floor.

"Looks as soft as a feather bed," C.J. said sarcastically.

C.J. was the first to lie down. The cold from the floor soaked through her clothes and into her body. She wadded the cloth backpack into a small pillow and laid her head on it. She was completely exhausted. She felt the big, warm dog lie down next to her and then she was out like a light.

Dusty doused the light, and curled up next to the huddled mass on the floor, laying his head on the shoulder of the big dog. Dusty felt the dog's warmth through his ear and his head rose and fell with each of Cleotis' breaths. The gentle rocking reminded Dusty of the time Otto had taken him fishing in a small boat on a lake, when they had spent the entire day, baking in the sun, not catching a single fish. Still the rhythmic undulations had an almost immediate sleep-inducing effect. As he fell asleep, Dusty wondered for the first time, if he would ever see that glorious sun again.

*

C.J. was awakened by a growl. Not the deep guttural growl, similar to the one she had heard when she had first come face-to-face with the suspicious Cleotis, but a higher pitched, curious sort of growl. Groggy and unable to see anything in the absolute darkness, C.J. gently patted the dog as her heart began beating faster, not knowing what danger the dog sensed.

"What is it boy?" she whispered.

The dog sat up, unceremoniously removing Dusty's soft pillow from beneath his head.

"What, what's going on?" Dusty asked, yawning, not yet fully joining the ranks of the awakened.

Cleotis "woofed" softly.

"Turn on your flashlight," C.J. barked to Dusty.

He fumbled to find it. Then, he quickly rotated the flange and the beam appeared. He moved the light in the direction of the shaft.

Cleotis' nose twitched with intensity, as he attempted to catch some clue on the breeze. But the breeze was blowing from behind them. Whatever was ahead of them was downwind not upwind. His ears, perked and he concentrated to catch a sound, but there was none forthcoming.

"What do we do?" Dusty asked. "What if there's some kind of bear or monster up there?" he asked.

"There's no such thing as monsters," C.J. said, feigning confidence. "We have to keep going," she said, "it's our only," she paused, "hope. Let's go."

"Let Cleotis lead," C.J. said. Dusty stepped aside, dropping the rope leash. The dog leapt by, climbing further up into the rock shaft. If there was truly danger ahead, C.J. thought, Cleotis was willing to meet it head on. She, on the other hand, was not quite so willing.

On his hands and knees, Dusty followed the dog, holding the flashlight, butt end down, in his right hand. C.J. groped behind in the darkness, keeping her head low in case Dusty failed to alert her to any overhead obstacles. Having whacked her head before, she had become quite adept at mastering the art of "blind navigation," constantly feeling the space in front of her by moving her outstretched arm, side-to-side like an awkward insect antenna.

"Woooof." "Wooof, woof, woof!" Cleotis' bark echoed through the shaft of rock.

"He's found something," Dusty said, grunting to get through the narrow passageway. C.J. was right behind Dusty, who inadvertently placed a shoe atop her forehead as he attempted to vault through the opening.

"Hey, watch it," C.J. yelled ahead.

"Hello...." Dusty's excited greeting echoed off the chamber walls.

"Did you hear that?" Dusty asked, but didn't wait for a reply from C.J. "Hey. We're here!" Cleotis barked repeatedly as if to reiterate Dusty's words.

"Did you hear that?" Dusty said.

"What?"

"A voice ahead."

"There. Did you hear it?" Dusty said.

"Shush. No. I can't hear anything. Be quiet," C.J. said.

Somewhere ahead in the darkness she finally heard the most magnificent sound she had ever heard. The sound of man's voice.

"C.J? Dusty? I'm Deputy Corey. Are you okay?"

"Yes," Dusty yelled into the darkness above him. He couldn't see a thing. The beam from his Maglight seemed to be swallowed by the dark earthen walls of the larger cavern.

"Where are you?" Dusty yelled into the darkness. Then he saw a glimmer of light about 20 feet above and to his right. His heart fluttered with excitement.

"We're working our way down to you. Looks like we're going to need to lower some rope. It could take a little while, but don't worry. We'll have you out soon."

"We made it, C.J! Did you hear? They've come for us!" Dusty turned the beam of light toward the narrow opening from which he had just come and found a red-faced C.J., pushing in vain with her arms and elbows.

"What's wrong?"

"I can't, get, through," C.J. said with a tone of pure exasperation. She could get her head, shoulders and arms through the opening, but her slightly broader hips were apparently just wide enough to keep her from getting through the rock opening.

"Give me your hand," Dusty said. He pulled as hard as he could, but C.J. didn't budge. He sat the flashlight down. Give me your other hand. Pull," he said.

"I, am, pulling!" C.J. said in successive grunts. Still she couldn't get through.

"Your butt's too big to get through," Dusty said.

C.J. slid her head and shoulders back and began to sob. Nearly two days of darkness and uncertainty were taking their toll. Now after finally making it within the grasp of the rescuers, she was being denied because of her wide hips. Or because as Dusty had said "her butt was too big." She had never thought her hips were too wide or her butt was too big. But now, apparently, destiny did. The tears flowed and she wept uncontrollably.

"That's not what I meant. I mean," Dusty said looking for the right words, " I didn't mean your butt's too big, I mean we'll get you out. Don't worry."

Cleotis walked over. "Happy."

"I'm glad you are," C.J. said to the dog through her sobs. The dog licked her directly on the lips. "Oh yuck," C.J. said wiping the dog's saliva from her mouth.

"Happy."

"Yeah. Happy," C.J. said.

"Happy."

RON NICHOLS

Chapter Thirty-One

It wasn't the first time the fire rescue squad had to de-wedge someone from a tight squeeze. Usually, the victims were either intoxicated adults or panicked toddlers whose sense of space was still in the developmental and experimental phase. To C.J.'s immense relief, the calm, confident voices of her rescuers made the whole embarrassing situation, nearly tolerable.

The solution to C.J.'s dilemma, while embarrassing, was remarkably simple. As the rescuers applied some vegetable oil around the narrow opening, C.J. removed her blue jeans. A harness was passed down through the opening, and C.J. buckled in. With some discomfort to her hips, the men pulled C.J. through the opening. Like a cork slowly being pulled out of a wine bottle, the squeeze was tight, but C.J. – hips and all – glided through the opening. After all of their tribulations, after all of their fateful decisions along the way, C.J. thought, the width of the blue jean fabric was nearly the difference between her life and her death. What a story she'd have to tell her friends back in Missouri.

The rescuers were mindful and courteous enough to allow C.J. the dignity of putting her blue jeans on in private – turning away until she gave the "all clear" signal.

"You ready to get out of here and join your friends topside?" Deputy Corey asked C.J. rhetorically.

"Am I ever," C.J. said with a bright smile. She glanced at her watch. It was almost noon.

The handsome young deputy keyed the transmit button on his walkie-talkie. "We're coming up."

*

"Those danged ole rocks almost got him killed," MeMaw said to Maggie. "And if it hadn't been for C.J., he probably would be dead. I could feel it the second that boy went in there." She took a sip of coffee. Dusty was confined to his room, and would likely be grounded through high school unless Maggie and C.J. could convince MeMaw to show some leniency. The three sat at MeMaw's kitchen table. A week had passed since "the incident" but the passage of time had done nothing to diminish the realization that both C.J. and Dusty could have been entombed forever, and MeMaw was still seething with anxiety-fed anger.

"You know, MeMaw, Henry would have done the same thing. You know, heading off down in that cave. Once you get rock-hounding in your blood, you just can't get rid of it. That's why he bought the land, cave and all. He said it was going to be our ticket to wealth. I think to this day, he'd be looking for diamonds." Maggie smiled, thinking of her husband of more than 40 years. "He was an old, wishful-thinking fool, I guess," she said. "He was sure right about it being a Kimberlite pipe though, even if it wasn't a diamond-bearing one."

"There'll be no more rock-hounding for Dusty, I'll tell you that," MeMaw said determinedly. "That boy almost put me in my grave, I was so worried."

Maggie let the words settle in the silence of the kitchen before she replied.

"He's a piece of work, for sure, MeMaw, but Dusty's a good boy. It's true that he shouldn't have gone in alone, but it really wasn't Dusty's fault that the cave roof collapsed."

"Sheriff Mueller thinks someone used dynamite to collapse the opening," C.J. chimed in.

"Who'd want to do that?" MeMaw asked. "And why?"

"He's not really sure," Maggie said. "But Dirk thinks it may have something to do with spring water. Hopefully," she added, "He will find out."

"Spring water. That's just crazy," MeMaw said.

The three sat quietly sipping their iced teas for several minutes. "Come on in, Dusty," MeMaw said without turning her head. Again, she seemed to have eyes in the back of her head.

Dusty sheepishly shuffled into the kitchen. He looked at C.J. and could not restrain a smile.

"I've been meaning to ask you, if I could take a look at a few of those rocks you found in the cave," Maggie asked. She sensed he needed some positive attention.

Dusty's face lit up. "Sure," he said enthusiastically. "I only have a couple of handfuls though. Too bad I couldn't get to the pretty ones. They were the ones I found last year. They're in my rock bucket in the shed where I do the tumbling. Can I go get them, MeMaw?" he asked.

"Okay, but you come right back here," she said.

In a blur he was gone.

"That's nice of you to ask about those old rocks," MeMaw said. "If they have any value, or if you want them, Dusty knows they belong to you. They came from your property."

"Oh, I doubt they'll have any value," Maggie said. "But I am interested in seeing what kinds of minerals might be associated with the pipe," she said.

The screen door banged with a "whap," announcing Dusty's return. The ladies turned their heads in unison as he came through the doorway and into the kitchen toting the rusted pail. He plopped the container on the table.

Reaching in, he extracted a handful of what he believed were the most colorful and potentially valuable gemstones. "Look at these," he said, thrusting his open hand toward Maggie and C.J.

Maggie used her thumb and forefinger to tweeze one of the blood-red stones from Dusty's palm. She examined it carefully.

"I haven't had time to tumble any of these yet," he said. "I think they'll be a lot prettier when I do."

"You have a magnifying glass, MeMaw?" Maggie asked.

"Sure do," she said. "It's the only way I can see anything anymore," she said. "Dusty. Go fetch my spyglass next to my rocker."

"I can't say for sure, but this might be a pyrope garnet," she said holding the stone toward the light.

"Really?" C.J. asked. "Is it valuable?"

"It might be, but more than likely, it's probably not a high enough quality stone to be commercially valuable. But," she said, "it is one more piece of evidence that Henry may have been onto something when he bought our land."

"What do you mean, Aunt Maggie?" C.J. asked.

"Pyrope garnets are sort of cousins to diamonds. From a chemical and mineral composition standpoint, there's not that much that separates diamonds from some of these indicatorstones," Maggie said, "so where you find one type, you'll often find the others. That's why they're called 'indicator' stones."

Dusty re-appeared with the magnifying glass and handed it to her. Maggie peered intently through the glass at the stone, rotating the deep red gem between her fingers. She examined a few of the other, smaller stones Dusty had placed on the table. They varied in shades from light pink to deep purple.

"Yep, my guess is that the old cave is – or rather – was an open Kimberlite pipe."

"So did it have diamonds?" C.J. asked. Her love for diamonds nearly equaled Rusty's love of pretty rocks he could tumble.

"Maybe I should give you a little short course on diamonds and the Kimberlite pipes," Maggie said. "Have a seat Dusty."

Maggie recounted all Henry had taught her, and what she had learned herself about diamonds. She said that though the Earth itself is home to great rivers of diamond-bearing rock, the stones are remarkably hard to find. Many diamonds are found in rivers, she explained but they did not originate there. "They were created deep within the Earth and transported, you might even say regurgitated, to the surface by volcanic eruptions," she said. "The ultimate diamond source, is a kind of extinct volcano called a pipe that is filled with a soft, green rock called Kimberlite," Maggie said.

Dusty sat at the table, intently looking at Maggie, hanging on every word.

"The Earth has a liquid metallic core and a thin crust. We're walking on that thin crust," she said. "In between the crust and the liquid metallic core is a zone of rock approximately 2,000 miles deep that's called the mantle. There temperatures reach as high as 1,000 degrees Centigrade. It's a place of enormous pressure. That's where carbon exists as diamond."

C.J. listened intently. She was amazed by her great aunt's knowledge of geology.

"In the Kimberlitic eruption, a stream of gaseous rock plasma drills its way upward, finding cracks in the rock above," Maggie said. "If," Maggie paused, "and that's a big 'if,' the rising Kimberlite happens to force a passage through a zone of diamond-bearing rocks it can break some away, sweeping some rock and diamonds up along the way. The Kimberlite rock is the transportation chute for the diamonds. Without that, the diamonds would stay miles below us. But, if the Kimberlite pushes the diamonds up too slow, the diamonds are transformed into graphite from the lower temperatures and pressure," she said. "And obviously, graphite is much less valuable than diamonds."

"Wow," Dusty said. "So there really are diamonds down there."

"You're not going anywhere close to find out," MeMaw said, squelching Dusty's rising enthusiasm.

"That's the point, Dusty," Maggie added. "It's highly unlikely there'd be diamonds in there, even with the indicator stones you found – it's a one in a million shot. Now that the entrance has collapsed there's no way we'll ever know."

"Couldn't there be diamonds deeper in the cave, or in the pipe C.J. and I came through?" Dusty asked, not wanting to give up his hope.

"It's just not likely," Maggie said, "and now that the spring is no longer flowing, it's likely that the entire Kimberlite pipe, the whole cave, is now underwater."

The disappointment on Dusty's face was obvious.

"Do you have any other interesting rocks?" Maggie asked in an attempt to divert Dusty's attention away from his disappointment.

"Sure. But these are no good," he said placing a second rusty pail on the table.

"What do you mean?" Maggie asked.

"They don't tumble very good," he said. "I bet I tumbled these four or five times, and they just won't get smooth and pretty. Some of the white rock along the side came off okay, but these clear ones just won't get smooth. I got 'em about a year ago just inside the cave where the spring used to come out. I bet I wasted two pounds of course grit trying to get them to polish up."

"May I see one?" asked Maggie.

"Sure." He fished one from the pail. It made a grating sound as the stone scraped along the rusty bottom. He handed the specimen to Maggie.

Maggie's eyes widened noticeably. She took the magnifying glass and looked intently at the small translucent stone.

"Oh my," she said. Then repeated, "Oh my."

"What's wrong?" C.J.asked, concerned.

Maggie did not answer, her eyes transfixed on the stone in her hand. "Dusty, how many rocks like these do you have?" she slowly asked.

"Just a couple of handfuls. They're all right here in the bucket, where I kept all of the rocks I got from the cave the first time. I was going to toss them, but never got around to it, I guess," he said.

"And it's a good thing you didn't," Maggie said, holding the small stone in the palm of her hand. She smiled. "This is a diamond."

RON NICHOLS

Chapter Thirty-Two

After more than a week, Christine was surprised to find that the water from the spring, had failed to appear within the area she had predicted. This was also the property she had recently pulled all of her retirement savings to purchase so she was beginning to feel anxious. Christine had made several trips to her recently acquired property and had checked and re-checked her underground water models, but the water had yet to surface. Still, as she sat back in the leather chair in her new office, Christine felt confident that the water would be forthcoming. When it appeared, she would sell her property to Cornerstone at a modest profit, and receive a generous finder's fee to-boot.

In the space of seven days, she had already accomplished one of her goals – becoming senior vice president. Convincing her new boss, the president of Cornerstone, to acquire GeoTherm and then dismantle it had been much easier than she had expected. While GeoTherm posed no real competitive threat to Cornerstone, their expertise in water quality could prove to be an asset for Christine's expanding division. Cornerstone's attorneys had wasted no time finalizing the deal. Soon, GeoTherm and a few of the remaining employees would be reporting to Christine.

Anytime now, she presumed, the GeoTherm employees would be receiving the news. Some employees would be laid-off, while a lucky few would be offered jobs working in Christine's new division. It pleased her to know that some of her new subordinates would be faced with a dilemma: Work for someone they did not care to work for, or face the prospect of long-term unemployment. Either decision would cause her former colleagues great dismay. That, Christine thought, was almost as rewarding as her new executive salary.

As a new division director, her goal was to ruthlessly and mercilessly, squeeze every drop of blood from her new employees. For those GeoTherm employees who weren't up to the task, Christine would revel in the prospect of personally dismissing each one. This was her world now. After nearly three decades of feeding at the bottom of the professional ranks, finally she would receive career justice.

She glanced at the clock on the wall. It was now almost four in the afternoon. It was time to personally deliver the news to her former colleagues at GeoTherm as to the specifics of who would be laid off and who would be retained. Christine couldn't help but covet the thought that in a few moments she would be delivering the paperwork that would, for most of GeoTherm's employees, transform a weekend of pleasure into one of consternation and painful decision-making.

Christine reached for the one-inch-thick cream-colored manila folder the human resources department had delivered to her earlier in the day. About half of the papers contained therein were simple termination notices. The remainder consisted of new contracts, written to Christine's specifications, with just a few perks – only those required by Cornerstone's corporate human resources policy. She had carefully reviewed each offer to make certain that no contract offered any sign-on or performance bonus opportunities. Those who agreed to stay would be hourly-billing factories – none of this "team and family" crap Christine had detested when she worked at GeoTherm. Sooner or later, Christine knew she would drive the GeoTherm employees away. In the interim, she intended to make those who did stay, very uncomfortable.

Christine opened her leather satchel and placed the folder amid her hydro-geologic model printouts. They were the models that had made all of this possible. Christine congratulated herself on her work and her ruthless execution of her plan, and then made a quick mental note to buy a more appropriate briefcase this weekend – something that was more representative of a corporate vice president.

Her car was parked in one of only six "reserved" parking places near the front of Cornerstone's brick and glass corporate headquarters, which was located in a trendy business park on the outskirts of Little Rock. The convenient and prized parking places reinforced the well-established corporate hierarchy. By virtue of the fact that she parked in one of the few reserved spots, it was clear to everyone that Christine was one of the top dogs now.

After starting her car, she glanced briefly in her rearview mirror before shifting into reverse. A figure suddenly appeared in her peripheral vision and she shoved her foot on the brake quickly to avoid backing over the form, muttering an expletive as she did. Rrather than moving quickly out of the way, the figure held out a hand, as if to convey a command to halt. This gesture enraged Christine. Anyone who kept her from her long-awaited task would be on the receiving end of her wrath, especially since it was likely to be some mindless Cornerstone subordinate who had slowed her down. She threw the gear shift into park and opened the door angrily.

"Move out of the way…" her words trailed off when she saw the uniformed officers approach.

"Christine Larson?" the older officer asked.

"Yes," Christine said, still standing by her car door. "What's this about?" she asked, her tone morphing from restrained anger to overt indignation.

"We'd like to talk with you about an incident near Ricksville last week," he said.

Christine was momentarily taken off guard, then thought that the inquiry might be related to the re-emergence of the spring water somewhereoff-site. She had assumed the water might be flowing over a county road or perhaps through an adjacent landowner's property. But she had prepared for that eventuality. The good news was the water had finally re-emerged on her property as she had predicted.

"Does this have something to do with my property? The property I just purchased?" she asked. "If it's about the water, I'm prepared to make,"

"No ma'am," the officer said, cutting Christine off in mid-sentence. "This is about an incident on the Davidek property."

"I'm not aware of any incident on the Davidek property," Christine said.

"One of your former employer's pick-up trucks was seen in the area, the morning of the incident we're investigating. We checked the vehicle log book at GeoTherm. The vehicle was checked out to you," he said.

"What incident are you talking about?" Christine asked impatiently.

"I think it would be better if you just come with us," the officer said.

"Are you arresting me?" she asked incredulously.

"No ma'am, we just want to ask you a few questions. You see, there was an explosion in a cave on the Davidek property the day your vehicle was spotted," he said. "Not only did it destroy the old spring cave, but it darn near killed a couple of kids. That makes this a rather serious matter," he said. "We also know that GeoTherm is missing some dynamite from its inventory."

"I don't know what you're talking about," Christine lied. Then understanding the magnitude of the situation said defiantly, "I want a lawyer before I say another word."

The officer smiled. "I think that would be a good idea," he said. "You can make that call down at the station," he said, leading Christine by the arm to the backseat of the awaiting patrol car.

*

Barely a moment had passed before the phone rang again. Since the news of the diamond find, it had scarcely stopped ringing in her great aunt's house. C.J. had initially enjoyed her moment in the spotlight. Being interviewed by the talking heads on the network morning shows had been the highlight of her life, but now even she was growing tired of answering the same questions from inquisitive reporters. Dusty had grown tired of the attention much more quickly, primarily because the attention took time away from his youthful pursuits around the farm. Every time he appeared on TV, his grandmother had insisted that he wash up and put on clean clothing.

Still, the requests for interviews had been unrelenting. Dusty's matter-of-fact attitude and round cherub face proved to be perfect cuisine for the television producers' palate. Before each interview, the news outlets would show a picture that was taken by a Little Rock newspaper photographer of him wearing C.J.'s shorts and T-shirt just after the two had emerged from the cave. While few others noticed, the photo proved to be a constant source of embarrassment to Dusty. MeMaw had called it poetic justice.

C.J. turned slowly to pick up the headset.

"Let the answering machine get it," Maggie said letting out a sigh of exhaustion. She had had her fill of the questions, microphones, cameras and glaring lights long before her great niece had grown weary. "I'm ready to get on with my simple country life," Maggie said.

"Yeah," C.J. said, plopping down beside Maggie in the kitchen. "I'm tired too." The volume on the answering machine was turned down and after the ringing ceased a flashing red light indicated that there was another likely request for an interview awaiting them.

Maggie glanced at the now silent machine. "I bet you thought your time here in Ricksville would be a real bore, compared to a summer in St. Louis," Maggie said and then added, "And you haven't even been here two weeks."

C.J. realized that her aunt was right. Now C.J. regretted thinking and saying some of the things she had said to her parents. Her thoughts turned quickly to her parents. While she was having a good time getting to know her great aunt, she was still missing them. "I'll certainly have a story or two to tell mom and dad," she said. "You think they've seen any of the coverage?"

"I doubt it," Maggie said. "I don't think they have cable television in the middle of the Brazilian rain forest. We should be getting a call from them soon, though, I would think. Then you can fill them in on your celebrity status."

C.J.'s smile lit up the room.

"I'm glad I've been able to spend some time with you," C.J. said. "I know you really miss Uncle Henry," she said, placing her hand atop Maggie's. "I guess in the end, his nose for diamonds paid off."

"Yeah," Maggie said. "Looks like he took care of all of us, including Dusty and MeMaw."

The total weight of all of the "rocks that wouldn't tumble" as Dusty had said, had come to a little more than 124 carats, including one extremely rare seven-carat yellow diamond, and six white diamonds that weighed six carats each. It was a remarkable find that had resulted in an outbreak of "diamond fever" in the area. Nearby Diamond Crater State Park recorded record-levels of visitors in the weeks and months that followed the discovery of what the media had come to call the "Dusty Diamond," as gem hunters sifted through bucketfuls of dirt in search of buried treasure.

"It was good of you to set up a trust fund for Dusty's college expenses," C.J. said.

"I know MeMaw didn't think Dusty was entitled to any of the diamond money, but if it hadn't been for Dusty, there wouldn't have been any diamonds," Maggie said, placing her other hand atop C.J.'s. "And without that handful of diamonds, there wouldn't have been any money to pay off the mortgage on this place, either. It was the right thing to do." Maggie looked tenderly into C.J.'s hazel eyes and added, "But none of this would have been possible if you hadn't come to stay with me," She removed her hand from C.J.'s in time to dab a tear as it rolled down her cheek.

C.J. had to divert her thoughts to avoid tearing up, too. "Dusty is more excited than ever to become a geologist," she said.

"He sure is. I've never seen a fifth grader so eager to go to college," Maggie said.

"He's a piece of work, all right," C.J. said. "Deep down, I think I knew Dusty was a diamond in the rough."

The two smiled at each other.

"Oh. I almost forgot," Maggie said. She blinked her eyes suddenly as though awakened from a trance. She reached into her shirt pocket and pulled out a small, deep blue, felt bag and handed it to C.J.

"What is this?" C.J. asked

"Open it up."

Sheepishly C.J. began to tug at the fabric that pursed the bag's opening closed. She pulled at the fabric pucker until the bag's mouth was agape, then she slowly inverted it. Out tumbled three glittering stones. They danced haphazardly on the walnut table, sending flashes of light in every direction before coming to a rest. C.J. stared intently at the jewels that seemed to emanate, not merely reflect the light from the kitchen window. They were stunningly beautiful – almost hypnotic because of their brilliance.

"I had a few of them cut just for you, honey," Maggie said. "These two are the smaller ones – a little over a carat a piece. But they're rated among the most brilliant ever found, at least in this part of the world. I thought that after all you went through, you deserved to have a few mementos to remember your little adventure with Dusty." Then Maggie pushed the two smaller stones near one another. "These would make a beautiful set of earrings, don't you think? And this one..." she held the larger stone between her thumb and forefinger. It was nearly twice the size of the other two. "This one will make a beautiful solitaire necklace, I think."

C.J. had to resist the urge to cry. "I can't take these, Aunt Maggie," C.J. said. "You need the money to for you."

"Already taken care of," Maggie said, dismissing the comment with a wave of the hand. "The sale of the largest diamonds was more than enough to pay off the mortgage, set up the education trust for Dusty, and to set aside some money for a rainy-day fund." She looked into C.J.'s eyes. "I want you to have these, sweetheart. Henry would have wanted you to have these, too. None of this would have been possible if it weren't for you and Dusty." She paused and smiled again. "Think of Henry and me when you wear them, won't you, dear?" Maggie asked.

C.J. leapt toward her aunt, throwing her arms around her as she did. "Aunt Maggie, I'll always remember you, with or without the diamonds."

How could she ever forget what she had experienced this summer, C.J. wondered? A couple of months ago all she had cared about was hanging out with her friends at the nice, air-conditioned, predictable mall. In the course of a few weeks she had discovered she could communicate with dogs; had met some remarkable new friends; had been on every major network's morning news show; AND had been part of one of the single most prolific diamond discoveries the United States had ever experienced. But more importantly, she came to know and love a relative who, just a couple of weeks ago, had only been a name.

What a remarkable turn of events, she thought. It had been an amazing summer in Sticksville.

Little did she know, her amazing summer had just begun.

ABOUT THE AUTHOR

Ron Nichols is a former journalist-turned-marketing-communications professional. *C.J. Brown's Diamonds in the Rough* is his second novel for young adults. He and his family (wife, daughter and two dogs), reside in North Carolina.